SEAN

A LOVE TRIANGLE ROMANCE

GIULIA LAGOMARSINO

Cover Design courtesy of T.E. Black Designs

www.teblackdesigns.com

Photography courtesy of Paul Henry Serres

https://www.paulhenryserres.com/

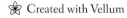 Created with Vellum

To all the ladies in my book reviewers club who were so excited for Sean's story. I hope I did it justice.

PROLOGUE

Vira's heavy breathing filled the room, reminding me once again how wild she was in bed. Her long, black hair lay spread over the bed and her olive toned skin glimmered with a fine sheen of sweat. Thick, black eyelashes fluttered as her breathing returned to normal. Her plump, full lips begged me to kiss her until I exhausted myself in her. I couldn't get enough of this woman. Ever since I met her, I needed her. She was everything I wanted in bed, but not so much out of bed. She refused to have any kind of intimate relationship with me, or anyone else.

Vira was one hundred percent against relationships. She'd had a boyfriend when I met her, but she insisted on it being an open relationship. The guy had been fine with it at first, but once he realized how amazing Vira was, he pushed for more, and that had been the point that she walked away.

I had been through a lot with this woman. Her best friend, Cece, had hatched a plan with her to get revenge on Cece's now husband and my friend, Logan. It had worked in the sense that she got her revenge, but somewhere in the middle, they'd fallen in love and were now married and had a little girl.

Part of me hoped that I could be the one that would change Vira's mind and have her commit to me. I kept thinking that if I showed up and made her see how great I was that she would finally open her eyes and commit to me. When Vira was shot at a nightclub, I took her home and did my best to care for her, but even then, she didn't want me helping her. So here I was, a year and a half later, still pining away for a woman that would never give me what I wanted.

"Thanks for stopping by, Sean. I needed that."

"Sure. What plans do you have for the weekend?"

"Well, now that Cece has a newborn at home, I guess I have to find some new friends to hang out with."

"Why don't you let me take you out? We can grab some dinner and go dancing at the club."

"Yeah, we can do that. As long as it's not a date."

Shit. She always added that in. It was like a knife to the heart every fucking time. I wasn't sure why I stuck around. Was it the great sex? We were explosive in bed and she knew what I liked. She was always up for trying anything.

Then again, it could be her personality. She was fun and didn't take shit from anyone. She didn't care that I was a cop. That didn't make her wary around me or make her feel like she had to be on guard at all times. In fact, when I first started seeing her, she had been doing some illegal shit to get Logan in trouble. She didn't even care when I found out. She told me that she would do anything for Cece and if I didn't like it, I could lock her up.

That was another thing about Vira. She was fiercely loyal to the people she cared about, which now included all of my friends. That was one of the things that made our relationship so difficult. If I decided to move on, I would still see her at get togethers. Then I would have to see the next man that became her fuck buddy and I really didn't want to lose my badge by shooting whoever the dumb fuck would be. Whoever he was, he wouldn't be good enough for Vira.

"You can leave now."

I was pulled out of my thoughts when she said that. She never let me stick around to hang out. Once we were done, I was expected to leave.

"Do you have something you need to do?"

"No. I'm going to watch some movies and veg out."

"I don't have to be at work until ten. I can hang out-"

"Sean, don't do this. You know the rules. If you keep pulling this shit, we can't sleep together anymore."

I rolled over and caged her thin frame with my large one. Despite my size, I never could intimidate her. I ran my nose along hers and then over her cheek to her ear.

"One of these days, you're not going to be able to push me away anymore."

Before she could say anything, I pressed my mouth to hers and slid my tongue inside. I kissed her breathless while I ground my growing erection into her cunt. When she started to wrap her legs around my waist, I pulled back.

"Where are you going?"

"I'm tired of just being your fuck buddy. You know I want more, so you're going to have to give me something if you want this to continue. I'm not asking for all of you, just give me something."

"I can't."

She didn't even hesitate. There was no change in her eyes telling me that she didn't mean what she was saying. Her heart rate didn't increase and her breathing didn't change. For the life of me, I couldn't figure out what this woman was holding back for. She never shared, but insisted that this was just the way she wanted her life to be.

With no sign that I could break through to her, I decided that I was going to have to move on. I just couldn't keep torturing myself anymore. I nodded and started gathering my clothes.

"So what time will I see you Saturday? We could go to the new steakhouse outside of town."

"I won't be here."

Her confused expression made me laugh humorlessly. She really didn't get it. She didn't understand that she was stomping on my heart and then asking me to just go on like we didn't mean anything to one another.

"I don't understand. You said you wanted to go out, so what changed?"

"What changed is that I'm not going to be the schmuck that waits around for you anymore. I can't. It's been a year and a half and I can't get any more from you than a quick lay and a night at the club. You don't even share normal details of your life with me."

"Like what? You want to know about my day?"

"Well, yeah. That would be nice. The most I know about your job is that you manage a club that you hate. You don't tell me why you hate it or even what your work day is normally like."

"And what would be the point of that? That stuff's all boring. Do you really want to come see me at the end of the day and have me tell you every minute detail of my day?"

"Yes!"

"Why?"

"Because I care about you and I want to know what drives you, what makes you happy, why you stay in a job you hate. The only reason I know your last name is because I checked you out. Would it really be so awful to share those details?"

"No. It's not, but it's just not who I am. I'm sorry, Sean, but that's not something I can offer."

I shook my head in frustration. I pulled on my jeans and let them hang on my hips as I searched for my socks and shoes. I was surprised she actually let me get completely undressed this time.

"So that's it? You're just going to stop seeing me because you don't get your way?"

"This isn't about me not getting my way. This is about me finally seeing that you are a selfish person that doesn't care about anyone but herself. You may think you care about others, and up until a few minutes ago, I thought you did too. But now I see that you just don't have it in you to truly care about how your actions affect others."

"Sean, don't be so dramatic."

I pulled on the last of my clothes and headed for the door. "Do me a favor, if you see me around town, go the other direction so I don't have to see you."

With that, I walked out of the room and slammed the door on the worst relationship I'd ever had. It was time to move on with my life.

CHAPTER 1

SEAN

It had been two months since I walked away from Vira and every day was harder and harder to stay away. My cock ached for her and not just any warm body would take her place. I tried. I found a few random women to take home from The Pub, but none of them did it for me. At one point, Vira was there with Cece and watched me walk out with another woman. If I had thought she would step up and do the whole jealous girlfriend bit, I was sorely mistaken. Vira gave me a thumbs up as I headed out the door.

I had yet to find a woman that liked the kinky shit that Vira and I did together. A few of the women got freaked out when I started talking dirty to them. It was like they wanted a boy instead of a real man. It wasn't that I couldn't do normal shit in bed, but I liked to tell women how much I appreciated their bodies and tell them all the dirty shit I wanted to do to them. Vira always gave as good as she got, but now that I had walked away, I couldn't face going back to the situation I had been in. I was ready for someone to be mine, and that was something I would never get with Vira. She slept with other men over the last year and half and I just couldn't take it anymore.

The lack of decent partners recently had left me painfully hard most days. Even if I was able to get off, it wasn't the release I needed, which was probably why I was standing in the middle of a school with a raging hard on as I stared at a teacher's ass. The woman was about average height with dark brown hair that was pulled up into a bun. She wore dark rimmed glasses that kept sliding down her nose, making her push them back up. The killer was her outfit. It was modest by any standard, but had my cock pressing painfully against my zipper. She wore a tight pencil skirt that fell just below her knees and a loose, cream blouse that didn't show an ounce of cleavage. She reminded me of my naughty librarian fantasies.

"Sir, is there something I can help you with? I'm in the middle of class."

My gaze snapped up to her stern expression that did nothing to calm my woody. In fact, I imagined her taking her ruler and spanking me with it.

"I'm here for a student, a Jim Smith."

Her gaze narrowed in on me as she stepped forward and motioned for the door. After we stepped through, she softly shut the door behind her. "Can I ask what you need to see him about? You haven't told me who you are."

The principal came rushing up to us, making his apologies. "I'm so sorry to have been delayed. I meant to be here when you came for the student, but unforeseen circumstances.."

I held up my hand to ward off any more of the principal's apologies and turned back to the hot teacher.

"I'm a detective with the police department. We were conducting a drug search and found a sizable amount of drugs in his locker. He needs to be taken in for questioning."

"I see."

"So, if you'll send him out, I would appreciate it."

She pursed her lips and nodded. I bit back a groan as I imagined those lips wrapped tight around my cock. Shit. This woman could be the death of me. I glanced down and saw there was no ring on her finger. Fair game. She turned and walked back into the room, asking the punk kid to step into the hallway. He gathered his stuff and walked toward the door, but my eyes were still trained on the teacher's delectable body.

When the kid stepped into the hall, I was forced to get back to work. I took the kid to the principal's office and we had a chat about where he got the stash of drugs. Of course, he clammed up and wouldn't say anything. I took him down to the station and waited for his parents to arrive before I could really question him.

We had been having a major drug problem in town now for the past year and I didn't have a single lead where the drugs were originating. Drugs went missing from several busts that I made and while I was suspected at first because they all happened on my watch, the department was looking at other cops that were working the crime scenes. What we needed was to catch someone red handed, but now that people were aware of what was going on, whoever it was, was being extra careful.

I suspected that Officers Calloway and Sawyer were behind the drugs going missing. They had been suspended when they were busted for police brutality and then been demoted to patrolmen. I had worried that they would go after Vira in some way because she originally put Sawyer up to helping her take down Logan. So far, he hadn't come near her and I was pretty sure that was because he knew I would take him down if he tried.

After grilling the kid about where the drugs came from, his parents had enough and told the kid he would lose his car if he didn't give up his dealer. His parents' lawyer struck a deal with the department that he give up his source in exchange for a slap on the wrist. Personally, I thought the kid needed a swift kick in the ass, but it wasn't up to me.

I dragged my tired ass to The Pub after work to meet up with the guys. We usually did poker night during the week, but the girls wanted to get together tonight also, so we were all meeting up in town. I walked in the door and immediately regretted coming out when I saw Vira hanging out with Cece and Logan. Shit. I didn't want to deal with her tonight.

I headed over to the bar where I saw a woman sitting at the counter with long, dark hair that hung in long waves down her back, just brushing her plump ass. She was talking with some preppy looking guy wearing a sweater vest over a collared shirt. I sidled up to her other side and leaned in to whisper in her ear.

"Why don't you ditch sweater vest and let a real man buy you a drink."

She turned to me and, fuck me, it was the woman from the school today. She raised an eyebrow at me and ran her tongue along her top lip.

"I suppose you think you're just the man I need."

"Honey, there are two things I do really good and one of them is fucking."

"Well."

"Excuse me?"

"You said there are two things you do really good. It's really well."

I looked at her in confusion. Was this her idea of flirting? Was she seriously correcting my grammar?

"Fine. I do it well. Anyway, what can I get you to drink?"

She lifted her glass of wine in the air. "As you can see, I already have a drink, but thank you for the offer." Then she turned back to sweater vest and started talking to him again. Well, fuck me. I had never been turned down by a woman so fast in my life. Nor had I ever had my grammar corrected while trying to pick up a woman. I walked away, not wanting to make an ass out of myself.

I headed over to the table with all my friends and clenched my fists when Vira wrapped her arms around the neck of some shithead that had just walked over to her.

"Long day?" Sebastian asked, his arm wrapped around his girl-friend, Maggie.

"Just another day at the office."

"Any leads on the drug ring?"

Sebastian knew about the drug ring from when his girlfriend accused me outside the police station of being involved somehow in the missing drugs. He chewed her ass out and she was now living with him after they worked out their issues.

"None yet. I had to pull a kid out of school today after we sent the dogs in on a drug search. The kid gave up his dealer, but I'm not sure it'll lead to much."

"So, who's the broad at the bar?"

I glanced over to see the sexy teacher leaning in and placing a hand on sweater vest's arm. "She's a teacher that I met at the school today."

"And she turned you down for the sweater?" He huffed out a laugh and took a swig of his beer.

"She also corrected my grammar. I got lucky on that one. I wasn't sure I'd be able to make a polite escape, but luckily she turned me down."

Sebastian glanced over at Vira who was now making out with the prick from a few minutes ago. My fists clenched at the sight of her kissing another guy. I couldn't believe she was doing that shit if front of me.

"So, things are really over with Vira?"

"Yep." My gaze bore into her as I answered Sebastian.

"And you're okay with her dry humping a guy right in front of you."

"She can do whatever the fuck she wants."

I didn't have a drink yet, so I reached over and chugged the beer Sebastian had been drinking.

"Help yourself."

Sebastian asked a passing waitress for a few more beers.

"So, when are you going to take me paintballing with you guys?" Maggie asked.

"I'm not," Sebastian replied.

"What? Why not? All the other girls have gone."

"Not all of them. Alex and Sarah haven't gone yet."

"But I could show off my mad shooting skills. Or are you afraid that a bunch of girls will kick your ass?" Maggie teased Sebastian, knowing that he wouldn't back down from a challenge.

"Freckles, you may be a good shot, but there is no way you would beat us."

"From what I hear, Harper took you all out by herself and Vira and Cece did a strip tease to distract you all while Anna took out the guys by her. It seems to me that you wouldn't stand a chance against us."

"Fine. You name the time and place and we'll be there."

I stopped paying attention to their banter after that because the prick with Vira now had his hands on her ass and was lifting her against his very visible erection. Fuck. There was no way I was allowing her to go home with this dickhead. I got up so fast that my chair flew backwards, landing with a thud on the floor. I stalked around the table and wrenched Vira out of the arms of her would be lover. Now that I could see him, he was just a scrawny little shit. There was no way this kid could please her. What was she thinking?

I pulled Vira behind me, not giving her a chance to tell me if she wanted this or not. She had ruled our relationship for too long and now I was taking charge. We were just about to the door when I heard Sebastian yell out, "I thought you didn't give a shit who she fucked?"

When we got to my truck, I shoved Vira in the passenger seat and walked around to the driver's side. I was pissed. Partly because I didn't have enough restraint to hold out from Vira and partly because she thought some pissant would give her what she needed in bed.

"You know, if you wanted me, you could have just asked."

"And why the fuck would I ask? You've ruled this long enough, Vira. Now I'm just going to take what I want and you're going to like it."

I slid across the bench seat and pulled her into me, laying a scorching kiss on those beautiful lips. My hands roamed her body, searching out her heat. Her moans caused my cock to harden painfully behind my zipper.

"Goddamn, woman. I don't know why you have such a hold on me, but I just can't seem to let you go yet. Every pussy I used to replace you was just an empty hole to fuck. None of them could satisfy me."

"Then take me home and fuck me, Sean."

I ran my hand over her pussy, feeling the fabric of her pants was already damp. She was soaked for me.

"Were you going to fuck that scrawny, little shithead?"

"Maybe."

I kissed her neck and nipped down to her collarbone. My hands slid under her shirt to pinch her nipples through the thin fabric of her bra.

"Do you really think he could give you what you need?"

"You left. I needed someone to take your place."

"And you thought that fucker was a good choice?"

I slid my hands down to her pussy once again and rubbed circles around her pussy.

"Sean, please. Take me home."

I pulled back and adjusted my cock before throwing the truck into drive and speeding off to her apartment. I knew better than to take her to my place. She never stayed there and this time wouldn't be any different. We pulled up to her apartment minutes later and I hauled her out of the truck and up to her apartment. She was practically running in her heels to keep up with me.

"Keys," I demanded as we got to her floor. She didn't hesitate to hand them over to me and I quickly let us into her apartment, looking around quickly to make sure it was secure. After I cleared the second bedroom, I stalked back into the kitchen where she was leaning against the front door. My hands wrapped under her ass and hauled her up off the floor. Her cunt rubbed against my cock as I slammed her into the door. My tongue dueled with hers as I ground myself against her.

"Enough of this shit," I said as I tore my mouth from her lips. I carried her to the bedroom where I threw her down on the bed. "Tonight, you're mine to do with as I choose. You will keep your mouth shut and do as I say."

"If my mouth is shut, how am I supposed to suck your cock?"

"Sassy. I'm definitely going to show you tonight how useful that mouth can be."

"Shut up and fuck me, Sean."

I shot forward and grabbed a fist full of her hair, not enough to hurt her, but to show her I was in control. "I'll fuck you when I'm good and ready. Now scoot back against the headboard."

She moved backwards until her back was flat against it.

"Spread your arms up and out."

She complied and I climbed over her, pulling her down slightly so her mouth would line up with my cock. Reaching into her nightstand, I pulled out some cuffs that were lined with velvet so they didn't hurt her. I cuffed each wrist to the headboard before climbing off and shucking my clothes. I stood naked in front of her fully clothed body. I fisted my cock and stroked myself as I imagined how I would unwrap her and take her. Her eyes widened as she stared at me stroking myself. When she licked her lips, I walked toward her and pulled out my pocket knife.

Flicking the knife open, I pulled her shirt away from her body and sliced the material open so that her breasts were exposed to me. Then I grabbed her bra and did the same. Her breasts hung heavy in front of me, begging for my mouth to take those pretty nipples and suck them. I caressed her breast and rolled her nipple between my thumb and finger. Her moans grew louder when I leaned forward and took her other nipple in my mouth, biting slightly.

"Are you wet for me?"

"You know I am."

"Do you want me to fuck your pretty cunt?"

"Yes. I want your fat cock inside me, fucking me hard."

Vira knew I wanted to hear how much she wanted me and she never let me down.

"Spread your legs."

She complied and I slid down her body until my mouth was lined up with her pussy. I slowly licked her, tasting her sweet nectar and greedily went back for more.

"Oh, God. Sean, eat my pussy. Yes!"

My mouth ravaged her, my tongue darting in and out of her warm, sweet center. I flattened my tongue and lapped her juices up to her clit then sucked her little button hard. Her hips jerked up, pushing her mound into my mouth. She came moments later sending her cream down my face. I licked her clean before sitting up and kissing her hard. I wanted her to taste what I got to taste, to know how fucking incredible she was. When I broke away, I sat back on my haunches and stroked my dick as I thought about what I wanted from her next.

"Are you gonna stroke it all night or are you gonna let me suck your cock?"

"Is that what you want? My cock stuffed in your throat? Choking you until my cum is running down your throat?"

"You know that's what I want, so stop making me wait."

I got on my knees in front of her and held my dick to her lips.

"Open."

She did as I said and opened wide for me. Soon my dick was rocking in and out of her mouth, her lips expertly sucking me. I couldn't hold back for long, though. I never could. Within a few minutes, I was shoving my dick all the way to the back of her throat and fucking her hard. I braced myself by holding onto the headboard and I pummeled by cock in and out. Saliva poured from her mouth as she deepthroated me, moaning for more. I reached down and felt her pussy completely soaked again. She loved this as much as I did.

"That's right. Take my cock. Suck it and make me come."

A few more moans sent vibrations straight through my cock to my balls. I felt my orgasm burn through me, spurting in long streams down her throat. She continued to suck me as the last of my cum spilled into her mouth. She released my softening cock with a pop and then licked her lips.

"Thanks. I needed that. You can let me go now."

"I don't think so, honey. You're mine for the rest of the night."

She bristled in irritation. "Sean, that's not how we do things. We had a good time and now you need to leave."

"Honey, I'm not leaving until I've fucked your cunt and your ass, so you'd better get real comfortable."

I stood and went to her nightstand and started shoving crap aside, looking for her vibrator.

"Where's Mr. Big Cock?"

She smirked at my nickname for her vibrator. "He died. I wore him out after you left."

"Well, I guess we'll have to improvise." I walked into the kitchen and started rooting around in her fridge. When I found what I was looking for, I walked back into the room and sheathed a condom over the large head. Vira's eyes widened as she looked at the long, fat cucumber I had pulled from her fridge.

"What the fuck do you think you're gonna do with that?"

"I'm gonna fuck your pussy with it. Then, I'm gonna take you from behind while this is still in you. You're gonna know what it's like to have two large cocks in you at once."

"Sean, I-"

"Methinks the lady doth protest too much."

She pretended like she didn't want this, but I didn't miss how her legs widened and her breathing increased. Fire burned in her eyes as she watched me walk toward her with the cucumber. I ran the tip of it over her soaked pussy up to her clit and then down to her ass.

She shuddered and opened her legs as wide as she could, her pussy wide and juicy for me. I slid the cucumber into her slick entrance and slowly pushed it in. It was a very large cucumber, so I took my time so I didn't hurt her. Her eyes closed as she exhaled and then moaned. I took that as my sign to start fucking her with it. I thrust it in over and over, my cock getting harder every time she moaned in ecstasy. Finally, I'd had enough and shoved it in as far as she could take it.

Unhooking one cuff, I pulled her hand over to the other side of the bed, rolling her to her knees. She pulled up so her ass was perfectly lined up with my cock. I made sure the cucumber was shoved in as far as it could before pulling the lube and coating my dick.

I rubbed a little lube around her tight hole and then slowly pushed my thumb inside past the tight ring of muscles.

"Oh, God. Yes, Sean. Fuck my ass."

"I seem to recall you being awfully willing to let me go. Now you want me to give you what you want?"

"Yes."

I pushed my thumb in and out of her ass as I spoke.

"I don't think so. If you want this, you're gonna have to beg me. You're gonna have to tell me how much you want me, how much you want my cock."

"I want your cock in my ass."

"Not good enough."

I started to pull my thumb out.

"No! Don't stop. I need to feel your cock deep in my ass. I need you to pound into me until I can feel you deep in my throat. I need you to make me come. Please, Sean. Please give me your cock."

I chuckled lightly. "All you had to do was ask, darlin'."

"You arrogant ass-"

She didn't get a chance to finish that statement as I rammed my cock inside her tight ass. My chest tightened at the feel of her so tight around me, strangling me until I thought I would come. I stopped when I was fully seated inside her for fear that I would explode if I moved.

"Shit. That's tight."

"Move, Sean. Make me come. Fuck me hard."

When I had myself under control, I started ramming inside her, needing to find my release again. It only took a few minutes before we were both falling over the edge into oblivion.

I pulled out of her and lay back on the bed breathing hard. Damn, this woman was going to give me a heart attack.

"Sean, take off the cuffs now. My wrists are killing me."

I got up and uncuffed her from the bed, but kept one cuff attached to her right wrist. The other end of the cuff was now secure around my left wrist.

"What the fuck are you doing?"

"I told you that I was gonna fuck you all night. Now you can't escape me. Better get cleaned up. Round two is in a half hour."

I swatted her ass, laughing as she glared at me as we headed into the bathroom.

CHAPTER 2

LILLIAN

I had been thoroughly enjoying Andrew Worthington's company up until about five minutes ago. Even when the cop from school came and hit on me, I was able to avoid his advances and get back to my date with Andrew.

The cop was not someone I could get involved with. I knew this because he was extremely forward and that wasn't something I was interested in. I didn't want to be hit on and treated like some piece of tail. I wanted to be respected by a good man that would treat me with love.

I was raised in a religious house. It wasn't overly religious, but I went to church every Sunday and I still did. I was raised that you should give yourself to one person and that was your spouse, and I still believed that. No arrogant jerk was going to make me think differently. I'd waited twenty-eight years and I could wait a little longer until I found the man that was right for me.

The cop was easy enough to dissuade. Being an English teacher, I tended to correct people's grammar without thinking. Some people found it charming, but most found it irritating and didn't stick around to continue to talk. I couldn't help it. Hearing people say supossably, irregardless, happy belated birthday, and southmore, to name a few, irritated the living daylights out of me.

Which brings me back to my date with Andrew. He was a history professor at the local college and we both shared a fascination with English literature. He was well spoken and didn't use filthy language. He dressed nicely and was always a gentleman. In general, he was everything I'd been looking for in a boyfriend.

That was until about five minutes ago. A man came up to me and was making very crude remarks about my backside and remarking on the size of my breasts. Andrew just sat there. He didn't ask the man to leave or try to defend me. He sat there and listened for five minutes as the man rambled on and on. I was raised to be polite, especially in public, so I asked the man nicely several times to leave. When people started to listen in on the man's remarks, heat crept up my face and embarrassment set in. I hated extra attention, but I really hated that it was accompanied by a man thinking it was okay to speak to me this way.

I was just about to get up and walk out when a slender, blonde woman walked up to me.

"Is this guy bothering you?"

Unable to say anything, I simply nodded.

"Hey, jackass, you need to back the hell off. She's obviously not interested, so take your paunchy ass out of here."

"She's still sitting here talking to me, so I'm guessing she's interested. Why don't you go back to your table and mind your own business?"

"She's not interested. She's just too much of a lady to say anything to you. I'm not, however, so you need to leave before I have you removed." She turned and pointed to a table of men and women that were now facing us. The men were glaring at us and the women looked pissed. "You see those men? Not one of them will accept you harassing this woman, so leave while you still have your balls attached."

"If they won't stand for it, why are you over here?"

"I told them I would handle the situation."

"You're gonna handle me? Ha! I'd like to see you try."

"Listen, buddy. You're gonna walk out that door in two seconds or I'll grab your sack and twist until your balls are no longer attached."

"Pretty girl, please tell me you're not threatening to rip this guy's balls off."

A well muscled man walked out from the back hallway and over to the blonde woman, draping his arm around her shoulders.

"Sorry, man. She gets a little crazy when she's worked up, but I wouldn't take her threat lightly. She's a hellcat."

"Sounds like you need to put a leash on your woman," the first man sneered.

"A leash? Nah. I'm not into that kinky shit. Besides, if I tried, she'd have my balls and I like them where they are." He gave a heavy sigh. "Sometimes, you just have to let your woman have her way."

"Let me have my way? Since when do you let me do anything? You know that you don't have any control over me. You may have put a ring on my finger and knocked me up twice, but that doesn't mean-"

"Is that why you tried to poison me?"

"I never-"

The man turned to me, cutting off his wife.

"Yeah, I asked her to move in with me and she threatened to have me killed."

"I did not!"

"Something about a jack being pulled out at work and a car crushing me."

"That's not-"

"Of course, then she also threatened to cut off my balls in a fit of rage."

I stared at these two crazy people in stunned silence. I wondered what would make two seemingly insane people stay together when they argued this way, but then I realized there wasn't actually any heat behind their argument. It almost looked like..foreplay.

"Jack, you are taking everything that happened out of context and making me look really bad. You know you aren't completely innocent here."

"Hey, 'I'm just posing a scenario in which I may not be around anymore'." He used little quotes, so I was guessing this was something that had been said before. "Now someone outside of our group of friends will know who to look at if I ever go missing. We both know our friends are on your side. Hell, Logan offered to help you bury my body."

The man looked between the man and woman and then back to me. "You people are fucking crazy." He stormed out the front door and the blonde woman gave a big bow.

"See, Jack. I can handle myself."

"Pretty girl, I know you can, but the question is why did you have to? We have a whole table full of men that could have handled that in a few seconds, so why did you come over?"

"You know they would have started a fight and it wouldn't have been fair. That man would have been walking crooked for a month. Someone had to step in and be the voice of reason."

"And you thought that was you?"

"I'm sorry, but who are you?" I interrupted.

"I'm Harper and this is my husband, Jack."

I extended my hand and shook both of theirs. "I'm Lillian. It's nice to meet you. Thank you so much for taking care of that. He wasn't backing down and people were starting to stare."

"I'd like to know why your date didn't say something."

I looked back at Andrew, forgetting that we had been on a date. When I raised my eyebrow at him, he shrugged.

"He looked harmless. I didn't think it was a big deal. He had been drinking, but he wouldn't have done anything."

"Not the point, asshole. When you're with a woman, you protect her and stand up for her when she's being harassed."

"I have to say, I agree. I didn't need you to physically hurt him, but it would have been nice if you'd said something in my defense."

"Lillian, seriously, what would you want me to say to the man. He's obviously not worth dealing with," Andrew said in an uppity tone. How had I not seen this side of him over the past few weeks. I didn't think I needed a protector, but sheesh, a little help when someone wouldn't leave me alone wasn't too much to ask for.

"Yet my wife had to come over because he was making such a scene."

"Andrew, I think it would be best if we part ways here. I don't see this going any further. Thank you for the drink."

I grabbed my bag and drink and was about to find a different seat when Harper stopped me with a hand on my arm. "Why don't you come join us for a drink. You can meet everyone and hang out with us the rest of the night."

"Sure. That sounds great." We started to walk over to her table, but I stopped her with a hand on her arm. "All that stuff that you guys were saying..it wasn't, I mean, he was just making that up, right?"

Harper threw her head back in laughter. "Oh, honey. He was one hundred percent telling the truth, although it was taken out of context."

"So you didn't threaten to cut of his.." I waved my hand in the general direction of his crotch.

"Oh, no. I did that."

"And the poisoning?"

"That never happened, although I thought about it a time or two."

"What about the car and the jack?"

"He freaked me out when he asked me to move in with him. I told him that there were plenty of reasons it wouldn't work out."

"It wouldn't work out because someone would try to kill him?" I asked in confusion.

"I think it's best if we just skip over that one."

"Wait. What about his friend, the one that offered to help you bury a body?"

She pointed to a tall, muscular man at the table that had his arm wrapped around a gorgeous woman. "That's Logan, but I think he was joking." She moved her head side to side as she pursed her lips to one side of her mouth. "I think if the situation called for it, he'd be on my side."

I blinked several times, not sure what to make of this woman. In a way, she was kind of awesome, but I was worried I had just walked into some parallel universe. This wasn't how any of my friends behaved, not that I had many friends.

I followed Jack and Harper over to their table where I was introduced to Sebastian and his girlfriend, Maggie. Cole and his wife, Alex. Logan and his wife, Cece. Luke and his wife, Anna. Drew and his wife, Sarah, and Ryan.

"So, how did you all meet? I mean, you all seem like such good friends."

Logan took a drink of his beer before speaking. "Well, Cece and I know each other from when we were younger. I broke her heart and then met her again ten years later. She destroyed my house, got me arrested a few times, and tried to ruin my business. Now, we're married and have a kid."

I glanced around the table to see everyone else smiling. This had to be a joke. "Um. That's..interesting." I swallowed thickly.

"I met Harper on the side of the road," Jack said.

I was taking a sip of wine and choked when he said that. "Excuse me. You mean, like a.." I glanced around to make sure no one was eavesdropping on our conversation. "Like a hooker?"

Everyone at the table started laughing. "I like her. She's funny," Ryan said as he took another drink of beer.

"No, my car broke down and it was raining. Jack stopped to help me."

"Although, you were pretty scantily clad," Jack said. "And if you recall, we did have sex that day, so some might see it as me picking up a-"

"Don't you dare finish that sentence." Harper turned to me. "I was having a bad day."

"You have a lot of those," Jack said.

"I had to run out to a friend's apartment. I didn't think I'd be gone that long."

"Most people still wear clothes when they go out."

"No one was supposed to see me! Things just got out of control."

"That seems to happen a lot around her." The two of them were bickering again and my head was starting to spin, and I didn't think it was from the wine.

"What about you?" I asked Cole and Alex. "How did you two meet?"

"Alex was being chased by a serial killer. I took her in and helped her get better. The serial killer caught up to us and tried to kill us. Alex lost her memory. We eventually got back together. Another psycho tried to kill her. I killed him, and she was in recovery for about ten months. Now, things are pretty good."

He said everything so nonchalant that I wasn't sure if I believed him, but then Alex snuggled into him and I could see the pain on her face.

"I'm so sorry."

"Yeah, it's kind of a downer, but things are good now."

I gave a tremulous smile. I turned to Drew and Sarah. They looked normal. Surely someone in this group had a normal story.

"What about you two?"

"I met Drew when I moved in next door to him."

I gave a big smile. "That sounds like a promising story."

"I was pregnant with twins and he was a big jerk. He lost his wife years ago to cancer and he was still grieving for her. Eventually, we became friends and that turned to love. Although, I still have to compete with Harper, here. She'll always be his first love," Sarah said.

"Why does everyone always have to bring that up? She's like my sister," Drew said as he rolled his eyes.

"You have twins?"

"Yep. They're a year and a half old. Everyone here has kids except Maggie."

"And you're all here drinking in the middle of the week?" I said hesitantly.

"Honey, when you have kids, you'll understand," Cece said.

"Anna, how did you and Luke meet?"

"Sorry, sweetie. Our story is perfectly boring. We met through Harper, fell in love, and got married."

I smiled at the simplicity of it all. They all seemed to have such strange ways of meeting one another.

"And you and Sebastian are dating?" I asked Maggie.

"Yep. He was my bodyguard when I was a reporter."

"Oh, that must have been exciting. What kind of stories did you cover?"

"Did you hear about the mayor in Pittsburgh?"

"Yeah. Weren't there a lot of people that went to jail?" She nodded. "And didn't he have people killed?"

"Yep. That was me. I broke that story."

"And Sebastian was protecting you?"

"Yes. I had a few bumps and bruises in the end, but overall, we walked away unscathed."

"Right," Sebastian huffed out. "Gun shot wounds, pelvic fracture, concussion, and one dead team member."

Maggie bit her lip as tears formed in her eyes. She quickly blinked them away before turning back to me with a smile.

"A few things may have gone sideways. Anyway, I moved here to be with Sebastian. I work at his security company now."

"Aww. That's so sweet."

"Better for her to be here where I can keep an eye on her. She's like Harper, she steps outside and shit rains from the sky."

"Hey!" Harper said in indignation.

"Oh, come on, Harper. The turkey. The football game. The second turkey. The literal shit storm at Anna's house. The sprinklers."

"You know, I think we all know each other well enough now," Harper said with a growl.

"I saw you talking to Sean earlier. How do you know him?" Sebastian asked.

"Sean?"

"Tall guy, black henley, jeans, built like a MAC truck."

"Oh, I met him at school today. I'm a teacher there and he was doing a drug search. I don't really know him other than speaking a few words."

"So, what were you doing with that douchebag, Andrew?" Jack asked.

"He seemed like a nice man. He's alway been a gentleman and we have common interests. He dresses well and he's well spoken."

"So you like him because he looks good on paper." Jack deadpanned.

"Knock it off, Jack. Some women have standards and there's nothing wrong with that," Harper interjected.

I was beginning to feel a little awkward sitting here discussing my dating standards with complete strangers.

"Alright guys. Who's up for a game of darts?" Ryan asked.

"Harper, you sit your ass down. No one wants to play with you," Jack scolded. Harper stuck her tongue out at him and took another sip of her drink.

"Why doesn't anyone want to play with you?" I asked. "Are you really good?"

"I threw a dart in his shoulder once when I was pissed at him. He's never forgiven me."

I stared at her in disbelief. These two were married? "I..I don't know what to say."

She shrugged. "It's just the way we are. We fight a lot, but the making up is so much fun," she said grinning.

I blushed at her implications. "Well, I don't really..know anything about making up," I said as delicately as possible. I could feel my face flaming. Gosh, this was so inappropriate to be talking about.

"You've never had makeup sex?" Cece asked. "It's the best. Half of my relationship with Logan has been makeup sex. The other half was revenge sex."

"What's the difference?" I asked.

She looked up out of the corner of her eye for a second as if in deep thought, then laughed. "Not much. Logan and I have..particular tastes in the bedroom."

Not being familiar with sex, I really had no idea what she was talking about. I bit my lip for a second, pondering if I should ask what I really wanted to know. However, this wasn't really the setting for talking about this.

"Particular how?"

"Well, we get a little rough. Sex tends to be an olympic event for us. There's some slapping and biting, nothing too outrageous. I mean, we're not into whips and chains and stuff like that."

"People do that?" I asked, eyes wide.

The whole table turned to me in silence. I had a feeling I had just revealed my secret to everyone. Not that I was ashamed of being a virgin, but it's not something you just come out and tell a group of strangers. In fact, sex was never something that was discussed in my house growing up. Other than the basics of the birds and the bees, I really didn't know anything.

"I mean..of course people do that, but I've just never met anyone who did."

"Lillian, how experienced are you?" Cece asked.

"With what?"

"Sex, sweetie," she replied.

"Um..well I haven't actually ever..um, had sex." I replied hesitantly.

All the girls' mouths dropped open except for Alex.

"How old are you?" Maggie asked.

"Twenty-eight."

"And you've never had sex before?"

I turned to Harper and answered her with as much grace as I could muster. "I don't believe in sex before marriage."

"Then how do you know if you're compatible?" Harper asked incredulously.

"Marriage should be based on mutual love for one another, not whether or not the sex is good."

"But sex is a big part of marriage. If you can't make it work in the bedroom, how do you make it work outside the bedroom?" Cece questioned.

"I could say just the opposite. If you only have good sex, what's the point of the marriage? Look, I'm not judging. Those are just my beliefs."

"I get it. I wish I had waited. Before I met Cole, I tried to sleep with a few men to get it over with. When the nightmares started, they all ran. They weren't with me for any reason other than sex. With Cole, he wanted me for me and that's how I knew it was real for us," Alex said.

Sarah had remained suspiciously quiet through the whole thing. I could only guess that was because she had been pregnant with twins when she met Drew. I didn't know her story so I didn't want to judge.

"So, Sean came on to you and you shot him down, huh?" Harper said with a grin.

"Well, I didn't so much turn him down as he got irritated with me and it didn't take much from there for him to walk away."

"He was talking to you for less than five minutes. What could you have possibly said?" Maggie asked.

"I corrected his grammar."

"What?" A collective round came from the table.

"I'm an English teacher and I have a bad habit of correcting people's grammar. He said good when he should have said well. I told him as much and it pretty much went south from there."

"So, that must be why he walked out with Vira." Cece stated.

"I thought he and Vira weren't together anymore?" Sarah asked.

"They weren't, but then she was flaunting another guy in his face. What did you think he was going to do? I think she did it on purpose. She's been telling me that she was pissed at him that he couldn't accept their open relationship. I guess she got tired of waiting for him to change his mind."

The ladies continued to talk around me as I thought about what I had just heard. Apparently, Sean and Vira, the beautiful woman he walked out with, were having a sexual relationship. Now I knew that no matter if I had accepted a drink invitation from him or not, there would never be any way things would go further with us. Sean was obviously a man whore and there was no way I could ever be involved with someone that treated sex so casually.

CHAPTER 3

VIRA

I needed Sean to back off. I couldn't take any more of his insistence that things become more between us. I really loved his company and I had yet to find anyone that satisfied me the way he did, but I couldn't let it be more. I would never allow someone to work their way into my heart. That would lead to give and take and I most definitely did not give.

I got in the shower to wash off our sex marathon and felt the delicious warmth of the water wrap around me. I let the water run through my long, black hair and down my chest. Grabbing my loofa, I soaped up and started to wipe Sean's scent from my body. If I didn't, it would be even harder to make him leave. That's why I didn't do overnight stays. They made everything complicated.

I quickly finished in the shower and then stepped out to dry off. When I was dressed for bed, I steeled myself to go face Sean and kick him out so I could get some sleep. God knows I wouldn't get any sleep if he stayed. I opened the bathroom door, but he was nowhere to be seen. His clothes weren't on the floor and the bed was put back together. I walked toward the kitchen thinking that he was getting something to eat, but it was also empty.

"Sean?"

I was greeted with silence and for once, felt the pang of loneliness. I had wanted this. I had pushed him away, but part of me always thought that he would continue to come back to me. Tears filled my eyes at the realization that I had successfully pushed him away. I didn't cry. Especially not over a man, but Sean wasn't just any man. He was someone that made me feel things that I shouldn't be feeling.

I wasn't sure if what I was feeling was love or if it was just really caring about another person. I thought I loved him as much as I loved any friend, but as a boyfriend and lover?

Sean had stuck by me for a year and a half, never walking away from me. I had plotted against his friends and broken the law, but he didn't leave. When I was shot in the shoulder, he forced me to go home with him and he took care of me. I had been a huge pain in the ass and he still insisted on me staying with him.

But I continued to push him away. I just couldn't allow myself to slip into a world where my life revolved so completely around another person. I grew up in a life that dictated who I become and who I marry. I just couldn't allow that in my life. I had broken free and become the fun loving person I was today by avoiding anyone that could influence my life so greatly.

Shaking off thoughts of my childhood, I brushed the tears from my eyes and straightened my spine. I didn't need Sean. I didn't need his expectations and his demands. If he didn't want me for what I could offer, then I would find someone that did.

WALKING INTO THE UNDERGROUND, my face turned sour at the thought of spending my night here. I was the manager here and I hated every minute of it. The Underground was a gentlemen's club where rich, married men came to explore their sexual fantasies with the promiscuous women that worked here.

The club was very select in its clientele and you had to go through an interview process before you were admitted. Everything that happened here was kept one hundred percent secret. Every room of this club was designed to fit any man's needs. The women that worked here could choose what they were willing to do and worked the rooms that best suited their work needs.

The club was filled with light since the club didn't open for another few hours. Angie was at the bar stocking for the night and I gave her a quick wave as I walked toward my office. There were a few staff working to get the club cleaned before we opened and I saw that everyone was doing their jobs efficiently.

I was very specific in how I wanted the club cleaned every night. Everything had to be put back in its place after the club closed and then another crew came in the next day to clean and restock.

I spent the next few hours getting caught up on paperwork and getting payroll done. The club would be opening in an hour, so it was time for me to do my walk through and make sure everything was in place and ready. A knock at the door halted my mental checklist for the night.

"Come in."

Frank, one of our male bartenders, walked in with a big grin on his face. Our gentlemen's club catered to all proclivities, including men that were looking for man candy. Frank wasn't gay, but he had no problem working the bar and flirting with the few men that showed interest. Frank had been trying to get me to sleep with him for over a year now, but I wasn't interested. He was good looking, but I just had a feeling that he would fall short of fulfilling my needs.

"Vira, baby, how are you today?"

"Busy. I was just about to go walk through the club."

I had to admit, he looked good tonight. His black hair was slicked back and he wore black slacks and a black dress shirt that had been left open two buttons. However, the gold chain around his neck was too much and left him looking like an Italian mobster. He was a little on the short side for me, probably about 5'10", but he definitely said all the right things.

"You look damn sexy tonight. If you wear that in the club, all the men are going to think you're on the menu."

"They all know better than to try anything with me."

He stalked toward me and crowded me against my desk, his chest just inches from mine. He brought his hand up to brush my collarbone, running it up my neck lightly before grabbing a tendril of my hair.

"I wish you would give me a chance, Vira. We could be so good together."

My breathing hitched as I considered his offer. He was a handsome man and I should be attracted to him, but I just wasn't. I hadn't slept with another man since Sean a year and a half ago. I just allowed him to think I was sleeping around because it was easier to keep him at a distance. But I had done too good a job of that and Sean walked out this morning without so much as a goodbye.

All I wanted now was to not feel anything for Sean. I wanted to ease the hurt in my chest that was now there from my own stupidity. I leaned forward and lightly brushed my lips against his. He didn't waste a minute as he crushed his lips to mine. His hand snaked into my hair, pulling lightly as he guided my mouth the way he wanted me. I felt nothing. There was no spark, but I pushed through my negative thoughts, hoping that if I tried, something would happen.

His hands roamed my body and slid down to the hem of my short, black dress. When I didn't push him away, he slid his hand up my thigh to my panties. I wasn't even close to being wet, but I needed this. I closed my eyes and imagined Sean's hands on me.

It was Sean's lips that caressed my skin and burned a hot path along my neck. Suddenly, I was moaning with desire for the man I truly wanted. I could feel Sean's fingers on me, caressing me and giving me exactly what I needed. His whispers of my every desire rang in my ears as I came all over his fingers.

Then my dress was pushed up and my panties pulled aside. In one hard thrust, he was inside me, pounding into me and telling me how hard I made him. His warm breath tickled my neck as he pushed me higher and higher. I repeated his name over and over in my head as I slipped over the edge into oblivion. I felt him still as he grunted his release.

My breathing slowed and I finally opened my eyes, disappointed to see Frank and not the man I truly wanted. My eyes pricked with tears and I closed them before they could fall. I pulled away from Frank and put myself back together as I got my emotions under control. I couldn't be upset that Sean had left me this morning. I had pushed him away one too many times and he finally took the hint.

"Vira, baby. That was fantastic. Let me take you out sometime."

"Sorry, Frank. I don't do dates and I don't sleep with anyone more than once, but thanks for the release."

I patted his cheek with a smirk and walked away. I could do this. I could move on and be the woman I had always been.

———————

"So, what's going on with you and Sean? I thought you two were over?" Cece asked as we lay getting our massages.

"We are."

"Then why did he leave with you the other night?"

"I guess he hadn't had his fill yet."

"Vira, you know I love you, but you have to stop this. He's loves you and you're stringing him along."

That got my back up. I wasn't stringing anyone along. Cece knew me better than anyone and one thing could alway be said about me, I was always honest with men about what I could give. I turned my head toward her and scowled.

"That's bullshit and you know it. I never lead any man on. I told Sean from the beginning that I couldn't offer him more and he still came back to me. And let's not forget that you were the one that wanted me to seduce him in the first place so you could use him to get information on Logan."

Hurt crossed her face, but I didn't feel bad. I wasn't going to take all the blame for what happened between the four of us last year. I may have come up with the ideas, but she was a willing participant.

"I just mean that you know he loves you, yet you keep sleeping with him. It's not fair to him or you. You know he's going to keep coming back for more and the longer you accept him in your bed, the more it's going to hurt him."

"Sean's a big boy and he can make his own decisions. If he wants to come warm my bed, that's his choice. I've told him in every way possible that it'll never be more. What more do you want me to say?"

"I want you to stop sleeping with him."

"Why do you suddenly care so much about who I sleep with?"

"It was different before. We didn't know these guys, but now that I do, I don't want to see any of them hurt."

"But it's okay if I get hurt?"

She looked at me in confusion. I hadn't meant to say that last part. Crap. I didn't need her knowing how I felt about Sean. It would only turn Cece into some kind of matchmaker. I didn't even truly know what I wanted from Sean, so how could I even explain it to someone else?

"Why would you get hurt? You don't even care about Sean."

"Just because I don't want a relationship with him doesn't mean I don't care about him. I would never do anything to hurt him and I don't want anyone else to either."

"Then you should do the right thing and stop seeing him. He deserves to find someone who wants the same things as him and as long as you're in the picture, he will always want you. It makes it impossible for him to move on."

My brows furrowed as I thought about what she was saying. She was right. I could never give Sean more, and even if it hurt to let him go I would have to. My indecision would only make things harder on him and would eventually hurt me when I finally did cut him loose. I knew my heart was more involved than I cared to admit, so staying away would be best.

"Unless you've changed your mind about not wanting more with Sean."

Her words snapped me out of my thoughts. "No. Of course not. You know me, I don't ever settle for one cock."

She didn't look convinced, but didn't say anything more. We finished our spa day and then went to grab a bite to eat. There was a cute little restaurant on the outskirts of town that was fairly new, so we decided to try it. We pulled into the parking lot of *Grannie's Kitchen*. It was supposed to be a restaurant that served comfort foods and we were very excited to try it after our day of relaxation.

After getting a booth, Cece and I sat and talked about how things were going at home with her son, Archer. She had Archer a few months ago and he was getting so big.

"Logan was happy to stay at home with him today. He knew I just couldn't take it anymore. I love that kid so much, but he's been so difficult lately. I think he's already cutting teeth. He just screams nonstop."

I had no desire to talk about babies. I loved Archer so much, but I wasn't a mother and I didn't find baby teeth an interesting topic of conversation. Still, she was my best friend and I would do anything for her, including listening to her talk about her son for the umpteenth time today.

"He should stay home with the rugrat. You need a break, too."

"He's been working long hours, though. I feel bad that his one day off, he's at home taking care of Archer while I'm at the spa."

"Honey, you have to get that nonsense out of your head. Just because you're not earning money doesn't mean you aren't working. You're the cook, the maid, the daycare provider, and the wife all rolled into one."

"I know, but I still feel guilty sometimes. I was actually thinking about going to see if the guy renting Drew's property needs some help with the horse's."

"What would you do with Archer?"

"Well, my mom and Logan's parents would probably be willing to help out some. I don't know. Maybe I just need to give it more time. This might just be a phase. I mean, most of the time I love staying home with him. I'm just so frustrated right now."

"Honey, that's why Logan sent you on a spa day. He knew that you needed a break. Just enjoy it and forget about all the rest for one day."

"You're right." She took a deep breath and blew it out. "So, what's going on-" She was looking over my shoulder like she was trying to see someone. I turned around and saw a woman in cute jeans and a plain top. She was pretty, but didn't dress anything like I did.

"Who is that?" I asked as I turned back to Cece.

"That's the woman from the bar the other night. You know, the one Sean was hitting on before he went home with you?"

Crap. That was the last thing I needed.

"I should invite her over to eat with us. She's actually very nice, even if she is naive."

"What do you mean by naive?"

"Let's just say that she's more inexperienced than most of the people we know."

"Wow. She's got to be in her late twenties. Why hasn't she done the horizontal mambo yet?"

"She's twenty-eight. Apparently, she's waiting for marriage. She believes pretty strongly in that, so I could definitely see why she turned Sean down."

"I can't believe that Sean even went after her. He's not usually one to go for the innocents."

"He doesn't know. It was only by accident that we found out. Here she comes. I'm going to ask her to sit down with us."

I groaned.

"Be nice." She chided. "Lillian, hey. It's Cece from the other night. Why don't you come join us?"

Lillian. What kind of name was that? A virginal one for sure. I could just see her sitting at home with her cats while knitting a sweater.

"Hi, Cece. It's good to see you again." She turned to me with a smile. "Hi. I'm Lillian."

"Hi. It's nice to meet you."

She smiled again. I'd like to wipe the smile off her face. Damn. When did I become so bitchy toward other women? Lillian took the seat next to Cece which on the one hand was good because then I didn't have to sit next to her, but on the other hand, now I had to look at her face through lunch.

"I didn't meet you the other night at the bar. You were the one that left with Sean?"

"Yes. I am. My name's Vira."

"Vira?"

"Well, it's actually Elvira, but that's too long, so I go by Vira. A little more badass."

She gave an uncertain smile and turned to Cece. "So, what are you ladies doing today?"

"We were having a spa day. My son is driving me nuts, so Logan sent me on a spa day with Vira."

"That was really sweet of him. He seems like a great guy."

"He's the best."

"So, Lillian, are you seeing anyone?" I asked.

"Um, no. I was dating a guy, but I'm not after the other night. That's when I met everyone."

"What happened the other night?"

"Some guy was hitting on me and he just sat there. Harper came over and got rid of him. It was so embarrassing. Everyone in the bar was staring at us."

"Sounds like you need to get some backbone and learn how to deal with jerks by yourself." I sniped.

"Vira!" Cece admonished.

"No, she's right. I don't know how to handle myself with men. The way I was raised was very sheltered, so I really don't have much experience in dealing with jerks."

Now I just felt bad for the poor girl. There was nothing worse than not being prepared for the outside world. I was all too familiar with the world at that age. My parents had tried to marry me off to a man that was not only a cheater, but was a known abuser. They didn't care that he was a bad man. They only cared about his financial connections that he would provide our family.

"Just hang around with us. You'll pick up a few tips for sure," Cece said.

Great. Now Cece was inviting the competition to hang out with us.

"Order for Lillian?" A woman asked as she approached the table. Upon recognizing Lillian, she smiled and rested a hand on her shoulder. "Lillian, dear. I thought that was you. Not staying for lunch today?"

"No, Mrs. Waller. I have a lot to get done today."

"Well, you enjoy this and stop by next weekend. I really enjoy our scrabble games."

"I will. Thank you."

Lillian stood and smiled at us. "Thanks for the chat. I'll see you later."

"It was nice to see you again, Lillian," Cece said as Lillian picked up her food and walked away. I watched her walk out the door before turning back to Cece.

"Scrabble? Seriously? Did we just walk into the 1950's?"

"Be nice, Vira. She lives a very different life than us and I get the feeling she doesn't have too many friends."

"Not our age anyway. Who plays scrabble with little old ladies on the weekends?"

"You have no idea what her life is like. I think she's nice and I would like to hang out with her some more, so please be nice."

There was nothing I wanted to do less at the moment. Not only had she caught Sean's eye, but she was the exact opposite of me. What did that say about me that someone so boring could catch the eye of such a gorgeous man? Would he pursue her? Doubt began to creep in my mind for the first time that perhaps my life was not quite as brilliant as I thought I had made it.

CHAPTER 4

SEAN

What a goddamned pain in the ass this day was turning out to be. I got called to the school on another drug related incident and found a few baggies of weed in a seventh grader's locker. What seventh grader smoked weed? The kid walked into the principal's office and totally freaked out when I showed him the baggie of weed. Within a few minutes, I knew the name of his supplier and where they met up.

I called in another officer to take the kid down to the station while I contacted his parents and spoke with the principal. We set up a time for another drug search and then I went out to my car to run the dealer's name through the database.

Carlos Ramirez came up as a known drug dealer that had been in and out of prison over the last ten years. He had just been released six months ago. I put out a BOLO for his vehicle, a red 2014 Chevy Camaro. I made a few more notes on my computer and was just about to pull out of the parking lot and head back to the station when a car plowed into the back of mine.

Swearing, I got out of my car and went to see the damage. My whole back end was smashed in. Fuck. I looked up at the other driver to see a scared girl behind the wheel, probably no older than sixteen.

She climbed out of the car shakily and walked over to the front of her car.

"Oh my gosh, sir. I'm so sorry. My car started making this weird noise and then the car started doing this floppy thing and then there was this 'WHEE' noise. I got scared and let go of the wheel."

I pinched the bridge of my nose and asked for patience.

"Why would you let go of the wheel because you heard a noise?"

"Well it was loud and it hurt my ears, so I let go to cover them."

"So, you thought it was more important to cover your ears from a loud noise than steer the car to someplace safe and park?"

She wrung her hands together like she was nervous. "Well, I just panicked. I didn't know what else to do."

"Janie, are you okay?"

I turned to see the sexy teacher from last week standing on the sidewalk with a concerned look on her face. She was even sexier than the last time I'd seen her. Her dark brown hair was once again pulled up in a tight bun and she still wore her glasses which probably meant that she wore them at all times. She had on another pencil skirt, this one cream, with a lavender blouse. The killer was her shoes. They were old fashioned looking, like something out of the forties. Damn, they were sexy as hell.

She came running over to the student and wrapped her arm around her shoulder.

"What happened? Did you lose control of the car?"

"She let go of the wheel to cover her ears because the car was making a noise."

She looked at me like I was lying, but I just raised an eyebrow at her. "Janie? Is that true?"

"Well, it was loud and it scared me."

"Sweetie, someone could have been seriously injured. You should have pulled over." She breathed a big sigh. "Alright, let's call your parents to come pick you up."

"Whoa, whoa, whoa. Just wait a minute there. You think she's just gonna get picked up and that's it?"

"What are you planning to do? Drag her down to the station for getting scared?"

"Yeah!" I roared. The girl jumped a little and started picking at her lip. Sexy teacher walked over to me and pulled me slightly out of earshot of the girl.

"Detective. Obviously this girl is a jumpy driver. Wouldn't it be best if we called her parents and did the usual ticket and exchange of information?"

"And why would that be better?"

"She's just a kid. If you haul her down to the station, it will terrify her for life. Janie is a very shy girl and that would be cruel and unusual punishment for someone like her. I could see if she was a wild child, but she's not."

"And you think we should coddle her and make her feel better about herself. Maybe tell her she's not a bad driver and it'll get easier with practice."

She pursed her lips at me. "I didn't say that. I just think you should call her parents and explain to them what happened. I know her parents. They won't take it lightly and will most likely sign her up for another driver's ed course."

I sighed and ran a hand over my face. I really wanted to haul this girl down to the station just to put the fear of God in her, but the woman had me rethinking my bad mood.

"Fine. Let's get this taken care of."

My attention was divided over the next hour between the girl and her parents and the sexy teacher that stayed, most likely to hold me to my word. I wasn't actually planning on booking the kid or anything. That wasn't really what happened. I just wanted to put the fear of God in her so she wouldn't pull that crap again. She could have seriously injured someone.

When the parents finally talked the girl down from near hysterics, I issued the ticket and then put in a call to Jack, my buddy at the garage. He would need to tow the girl's car because there actually was something wrong with it. Jack couldn't get over for another hour because he was backed up with other jobs.

"Shit," I said as I hung up the phone.

"What's wrong?" The sexy teacher walked up to me and looked at me with concern.

"Tow truck won't be here for another hour, so I'm gonna have to get a patrol car to pick me up."

"I can take you over there. It's right on my way home."

"Are you sure you don't mind?"

"Not at all. I'm Lillian, by the way."

She held out her hand and I noticed how thin and delicate her hand looked. Dainty would be a better word. I would snap her like a twig if I had her in my bed.

"Sean. It's nice to call you something other than sexy teacher."

She reared back like she was highly offended by that, but didn't say anything. Instead, she turned on her sexy heel and marched to her car. I couldn't help that my eyes drifted to her ass as I watched her hips sway from side to side. I glanced around and saw several other male teachers that were leaving and all were staring at the gorgeous specimen in front of me. I quickly made my way to her car that looked more like a toy, in the hopes that no one would approach her if I was with her.

Once we got to her car, I buckled up and sat waiting for her to start the car. It was an honest to God five minute process. She buckled in, then checked all of her mirrors several times and adjusted where needed. Then she took out her sunglasses and gently put her glasses in the sunglass holder. After adjusting her seat, which I'm not sure why she would have to if she was the only one driving, she did another check on her mirrors.

Finally, we slowly pulled out of her space and drove the exact speed limit through the parking lot, which was now empty. She stopped at the stop sign and checked both ways down the deserted street twice before slowly pulling out onto the road. Her acceleration was so slow that by the time we got up to the thirty-five mile an hour posted speed, she had to break for the stop sign up ahead. I could have walked to the police station faster.

"You're a very careful driver, aren't you?"

"I just like to follow the rules. They're there for a reason."

I nodded and widened my eyes in annoyance at how slowly she pulled through the intersection. We made it to the highway that led to the police station a few minutes later. She was just merging with traffic when I saw the car that belonged to Carlos Ramirez.

"Speed up. That's my suspect."

"I'm sorry, what?" She asked, but didn't accelerate.

I glanced through the back window and saw that there were cars that would catch up in the merging lane if she didn't get over now.

"Quick, get over or we're gonna get stuck behind people."

She turned on her turn signal and glanced in the side mirror and then over her shoulder. As she started to merge over, she suddenly pulled the wheel back.

"What are you doing? We have to get over there. Merge!"

"I can't! There's a car coming," she shrieked.

"It's at least ten car lengths back. Merge!"

She let out a frustrated noise before checking her mirror once again and looking over her shoulder. She finally got onto the highway, but we didn't seem to be going anywhere.

"Step on it. We've got to catch up to the suspect."

Ever so slowly, she pressed her foot down on the gas pedal and we slowly gained speed. The speed limit was fifty-five and cars were flying past us. I called dispatch quickly asking them to send a car out to Highway 30 after spotting the BOLO suspect.

"Why are you accelerating so slowly? A grandma in a car ten years older just passed us."

"It's not safe to accelerate quickly. That's how accidents are caused."

"Lady, you're going to cause an accident if you don't put your foot down on the fucking gas."

"Don't swear at me. I didn't sign up for car chases."

"What car chase? The fucking car isn't even in sight anymore and you have to be going at least the speed limit for it to qualify as a car chase. At this pace, a turtle would outrun you."

"I'm going to take you to the station. You can have someone else look for your suspect."

"No, I need to catch this dealer or you're gonna have a lot more drugs in your school."

"Fine." She pursed her lips and we finally picked up a little speed. We were just about to pass a gas station when I saw the suspect pulling out from filling up with gas.

"Seriously, he had time to stop for gas. That's how slow you were driving."

"Whatever. I'm going the speed limit."

"You are now, but it took you five minutes to get to that speed. Drive a little faster. He's putting some distance on us."

"I'm not driving faster. It's against the law," Lillian said primly.

"You're with a cop!"

"But I'm not an officer. I could get pulled over and then I would get a ticket."

I stared at her for a second in disbelief. "Are you fucking kidding me?" I shouted. How did I possibly get stuck with the slowest driver in the world when I was after a suspect?

"Shit. Where'd the car go?"

"It didn't go anywhere. It's an inanimate object."

"What do you mean it's inanimate. It's moving!"

"But only because someone is making it move. It doesn't move on its own, therefore it's an inanimate object. So, it can't go anywhere. The correct way to say it is, 'where is the car'."

"Just pull over the fucking car and I'll walk. I can't deal with an English lesson while trying to do my job."

"I can't pull over. There's nowhere safe to do so."

"Then I'll jump from the fucking car."

"Now that's just silly. Do you realize how injured you could get?"

"At the speed you're going, I could probably land on my feet."

"Fine. You want me to speed up, I will."

"Thank you."

The car lurched forward as she pressed her foot all the way down on the gas and took off into the traffic. She barely weaved in and out of traffic, avoiding cars, but almost clipping a semi.

"Oh my, God!" she screamed. "I've never done anything like this before. This is so scary!"

"You're doing great. Just keep driving."

"Ahhh!" Her voice was a piercing scream and if I wasn't afraid she would step on the brakes, I would tell her to shut the fuck up. Another police car came from a side road and pulled in front of the suspect's car, slowing him down and then guiding him over to the side of the road. After they were stopped on the side of the road, Lillian eased the car over to the side of the road and put the car in park.

"Criminy Dick that was close."

"Criminy Dick? What does that even mean?"

"It's like saying 'oh gosh' or 'gee willikers'."

"Or you could just say 'oh fuck, that was close'. Even though that wasn't even nearing close. What exactly was close? It would have been close if you hadn't driven like a grandma the whole way. Oh wait, a grandma passed us! You are a terrible driver."

"I am not. I drive the speed limit. It's the law. How do you not understand that? You're a police officer!"

"But, you were driving with a police officer that told you to step on it."

"I'm sorry! I'm not used to high stress situations! Stop yelling at me!"

I wanted to yell at her some more, but she looked close to tears, so I did the only thing I could. I reached across the seat and grabbed her by the nape of the neck and pulled her in for a rough kiss. She hesitated for a moment, but then she moaned and kissed me back. When she opened her lips slightly, I took advantage and slid my tongue in, tasting her sweet flavor.

A pounding at the window made her jerk back from me, but I couldn't stop staring at her. My breathing was ragged as I tried to get myself under control. We stared each other down for a moment and her fingertips went to her lips, no doubt still burning from our kiss.

I wasn't sure what just happened, but what I felt was beyond anything I had ever felt for any woman, except maybe Vira, but those feelings were all jumbled with her lack of willingness to be in a relationship.

I wasn't sure how someone so infuriating could make my heart pound so wildly. There was one thing that was clear, though. I wanted to do that again to see if we both had the same reaction.

Pulling myself together, I stepped out of the car to talk with the officer that came to our window. There was another officer that was already at the passenger side of the suspect's car.

"Are you the one that called in the sighting?"

"Yeah, that was me."

"How did we beat you? You were quite a ways back."

"I was with the slowest driver on the face of the Earth."

I glanced at the car just as a shot fired and the officer fell to the ground. I pulled my weapon and started shooting, but the car was already peeling away and getting back on the highway. I ran around to the driver's side of the car and yanked the door open.

"Move over, Miss Daisy. I'm driving."

"Hey!" She wasn't happy with me, but she moved over and I threw the car into drive and took off after the car. The other officer had stayed behind to help his partner and radio for help.

"Sean, do you really think it's wise to bring a civilian along on a car chase? Doesn't this go against some protocol or something?" She asked nervously as I weaved in and out of traffic.

"Would you have rather stayed behind and waited for the ambulance?"

"Was he dead?"

"I don't know. It depends on where he was shot, but at that range, I sure hope he had his vest on."

"I think I might be sick."

"No time for that, Daisy. I need your help if we're gonna catch this guy."

"Stop calling me Daisy. My name's Lillian."

"That's a mouthful. Here, take my phone and hit speed dial one. It's the station. Ask to speak to Chief Jameson and tell whoever it is that we're chasing down the suspect that shot Officer Wheeling."

She reached for my phone with shaky hands. "Alright." She placed the call and relayed what I had said and then told them our current location. She continued to text our location to the chief as we drove since we didn't have the tracker from my car.

The suspect's car was a few car lengths ahead of us and I really wanted to take the fucker out, but traffic was still too thick. It would only cause more accidents and possible casualties. Until the station could get other cars here to help, I was on my own to stay with this guy.

"Lillian, you want to tell me why there's a battery indicator on the dashboard?"

She leaned over and looked behind the wheel where the speedometer was. "Oh, that tells me how much battery I have. This is an electric car."

"I know it's an electric car. Why the fuck are you driving an electric car?"

"It's better for the planet."

"Yeah, I'm not touching that one. When was the last time you charged your car?"

"Um..a few days ago. I usually don't have to charge it more than once a week because I don't drive very far."

"Shit."

"Why? How much power is left?"

"About five percent. I need to get ahead of this guy and cut him off, otherwise this car is going to die before we get help."

"Take a right up ahead."

"Why?"

"Just trust me!" She was getting really worked up and I was a little nervous to listen to her. If I followed her instructions and it got us nowhere, I would lose the suspect. If I didn't listen and I didn't get help soon, the car would die and we'd lose him anyway.

I swung the car right and followed her instructions as she shouted them out.

"Take the next left and we should be coming right at him."

"How do you know that?"

"The city started construction back here. Some of these streets were closed off as of yesterday."

I took the next left and was completely shocked when we were suddenly playing chicken with the suspect. I glanced over and saw Lillian texting furiously on my phone.

The car started to slow and no matter how hard I pushed the accelerator, it wouldn't speed up.

"Shit. How close is backup?"

"I don't know! They're not responding. Ooh. Okay. They should be here any minute."

"Any minute. Not fucking fast enough. We're going to either lose this guy or get run over in about twenty seconds."

The car continued to come at us, not realizing that we were now going about ten miles an hour and falling. I hit the button to roll down the window so that I could shoot at the car. The window slowly rolled down, dying about a quarter of the way along with the car.

"Oh shit. Hold on to something. This guy's gonna hit us."

"Well, tell him to stop!" Lillian screamed next to me.

"Sure, I'll just yell at him that we're in an electric car and can't move! Maybe you have his phone number!"

"Son of a haaamsteeer!"

I thrust my arm out in front of her and turned my face toward her. Her eyes were wide as she stared straight ahead. I heard the squeal of tires and looked ahead to see the car turn sharply to the left and come to a stop mere inches from our bumper.

I quickly opened the door and got out of the car, weapon pointed at the vehicle.

"Hands up! Use your right hand to open the door. Now step out of the vehicle with your hands up."

The suspect followed every word I said, his gun nowhere in sight. I had him cuffed moments later, making sure they were extra tight after the fucker shot a fellow officer.

"You better hope that officer lives or I'll make sure you become someone's bitch in prison. I'll make sure your life is short and filled with pain."

Several police cars came screaming down the street, blocking his car from the other side. Within minutes, the suspect was in the back of a squad car and I was filling the officers in on what had happened.

"What's going on with Wheeling?"

"Shot to the chest, but he had on his vest. Probably a few broken ribs."

"Thank God. That could have turned out so much worse."

Lillian was still sitting in the car that was now dead in the middle of the street. I saw her get out once the suspect was secure in the back of the squad car. She stood at the front of her car, not wanting to interrupt.

"Give me a second," I said to the officer, then I walked over to where Lillian was standing.

"Are you okay?"

"Yeah. I've just never done something that intense before. I mean..that was.."

"Intense."

"Awesome!" I pulled back in shock. I thought sweet, prim Lillian was going to freak out, but she seemed exhilarated by our adventure.

"Um..Okay. Well, I'm glad you enjoyed yourself."

"Oh, well. You know, it's not something I think I want to do again, but boy, what a rush."

"Did..Did you yell 'son of a hamster'?"

A big smile split her face and we both started laughing. I watched her face, seeing the sparkle that danced in her eyes and found that I really liked to see her like this. I couldn't imagine what it would be like if she actually let her hair down and enjoyed herself more often, but I decided that I really wanted to find out.

CHAPTER 5

LILLIAN

That was the biggest thrill of my life to date. I wasn't sure how I felt about that. Part of me was happy to step outside my shell a little, but the other part of me said that living that way just wasn't who I was.

The other thing I wasn't too sure about was the scorching hot kiss Sean laid on me. I was a little taken aback by it, but then I just seemed to melt into him. Still, we were so different and if he knew that I wasn't going to sleep with him, would he still be interested? Somehow, I really doubted that he would.

I waited around for quite a while for Sean to finish up with his fellow officers and then there was the issue of getting my car towed. Luckily, his friend Jack was able to pick it up and tow it to my house. He even got it plugged in for me after I gave him the code to the garage. I would have just gone home, but Sean said I would need to go down to the station with him and give my statement of what happened. Apparently, there was a lot of paperwork when a civilian tagged along with a police officer. Not that I really tagged along, more like I was dragged along.

I was pretty proud of myself, though. I was able to assist in catching a known drug dealer. Sean hadn't been aware that streets had been shut down in the warehouse district and without me, he would have run out of battery with my little electric car. Of course, if I hadn't offered him a ride, none of this would have happened to begin with. Perhaps Officer Wheeling wouldn't have been shot and the police would have apprehended Carlos Ramirez at his home instead.

When Sean was finally done at the station, we headed out to his truck in the parking lot of the police station.

"How about we grab a drink? I know I could use one after the day I've had."

"Sure."

We headed toward The Pub where I had met all of his friends the other night.

"I met your friends at The Pub the other night. They all seem very nice. In fact, Harper and Jack helped me out."

"Helped you with what?"

"A man came up to me and started hitting on me. It was getting a little out of hand and Harper came over to make him go away. Then Jack came over and they had some weird kind of foreplay argument." I shook my head, still not understanding exactly what happened. "Anyway, the guy took off and then I hung out with all of them. You know, your friends all had very strange ways of meeting up with their spouses. Except for Anna and Luke."

"Why is it weird? Not everyone just finds the person they're going to spend the rest of their lives with through friends or online dating."

"I just mean, it's all very intense. Cole and Alex especially. I mean, a serial killer is pretty intense. They didn't go into detail, but I got the gist of it. It had to be very stressful."

"It wasn't exactly a happy time for either of them, but they got through it together. My sister was actually targeted by the same serial killer. She just barely escaped with her life. She just started living her life again thanks to Drew and Sarah. They took her in and gave her a job as a nanny for their twins. She's not back to normal again, but it's definitely better than it was."

"What happened to the father of Sarah's twins?"

He seemed to hesitate just a minute before glancing at me. "She's never said."

"And Drew's okay with that? What if the father came back wanting custody? Isn't he at all curious about the man that just walked away from her?"

He pulled into the parking lot and shut off the truck before turning to me with a stern expression. "Frankly, it's none of your business. What happens between the two of them is between them. It's not our place to judge. Either you accept people the way they are or you don't. Sarah is an amazing woman and she doesn't deserve for you to pass judgement without knowing her."

I flushed at his accusation. Was that what I was doing? "I'm sorry. I never meant to.. I wasn't trying to judge."

"But you were. Maybe your life is all wonderful and everything is going as it should, but not everyone has that kind of life."

He stared me down and I swallowed thickly under his cold stare. I actually felt chills race down my spine and questioned the sanity of putting myself in the position to be spending time with this man.

"Let's go get a drink."

He got out of the truck and didn't wait for me as he walked toward the bar. Shaking myself out of my frozen state, I climbed out of the truck and followed him inside. He was already walking toward the bar, so I went and grabbed a bar stool.

"What can I get you?" The bartender asked.

"I'll have a white wine."

"Beer. Whatever's on tap."

We sat in uncomfortable silence as we drank our beverages. I didn't know what to say to him and I felt that my questions had put a strain on our..whatever this was between us.

When I was almost finished with my wine, he grabbed my hand and started pulling me toward the door.

"Let's go."

"Okay."

I assumed he was taking me home now since the night had become one giant bust. That was fine. I had work tomorrow and I had plenty to do before I went to bed. He pulled out into traffic, but he didn't head in the direction of my house.

"Um, where are you going? My house is the other way."

"I'm taking you to my house."

"And why would you do that?"

"Because, I can't stop thinking about how good your ass looks in that skirt. Now I want to see what it looks like out of it."

I blinked a few times completely stunned by the arrogance of this man. "I don't understand. You think that just because you want to see what my backside looks like, that I'll automatically go home with you?"

"Honey, don't pretend like you don't feel it too. I know you were as into that kiss as I was. There was definitely something there."

"Even if there was, why would you assume that I would just go home with you?"

"How long are we going to play this game?"

"What game?"

"The game where you pretend you aren't interested in sleeping with me so you don't seem like a slut. Don't worry, honey. I won't judge you."

I was absolutely mortified. I had never had someone just assume that I would sleep with them and I wasn't sure what kind of vibe I was sending off to make him think I would.

"Let me make one thing perfectly clear to you. I do not ever intend on sleeping with you. I'm quite sure you are not the man for me and I am not the woman for you."

"You don't have to be the woman for me. You just have to be the woman for right now."

I let out a frustrated sound. "When will you get it through your thick skull? I'm not playing hard to get, nor am I trying to seem less like a..slut. I simply do not want to sleep with you. You are arrogant, rude, you swear like a sailor, and you have very poor manners."

"What makes you think I have poor manners?"

"Well, for starters, not once have you attempted to hold a door open for me."

"Ah, so you want me to wine and dine you."

"No, I most certainly do not. I'm just telling you why I would never choose you to be my partner."

He pulled into a driveway and put the truck in park. When he turned to me, he looked truly confused.

"So, let me get this straight. You're not playing hard to get?"

"No."

"You don't want to sleep with me?"

"Not one bit."

"What about the kiss?"

I flushed as I thought back to how my lips tingled when he kissed me. I could still feel his tongue swiping against mine. I had never been kissed, and there were still things that I didn't understand about how my body reacted to it.

"See? The look on your face says that you remember every second of that kiss and you liked it. So tell me why we couldn't at least do more of that?"

"I think you should take me home. I really don't want to talk about this anymore. I told you I wouldn't sleep with you, so let's leave it at that."

Fifteen minutes later, Sean dropped me at my house and I bolted from the truck before he could question me further about any of it. I was so confused and I just didn't understand what I was feeling. I needed another woman to talk to.

AFTER MUCH TOSSING and turning the night before, I decided that I was going to call Alex. When I met her the other night, she seemed to really understand me and I thought I would feel comfortable talking with her. Luckily, I had grabbed her number before I left the other night.

After having my morning coffee, I finally worked up the courage to call her. When she answered I was a little hesitant, but when I finally asked to meet her, she seemed overjoyed to get together.

I went to school and made it through the day, only partially thinking about the events of the last twenty-four hours. I had to admit, my mind wandered to Sean quite a few times and I had to be asked questions several times when my mind wandered. I had never been this distracted in all my life, and all over a man that most likely would break my heart if I ever gave him a chance.

When the day ended, I packed up my stuff and headed to the address Alex provided. She lived in the country with Cole and assured me that he wouldn't be home until later. When I pulled up to their house, I was suddenly at peace. It was a beautiful home surrounded by the woods and I wondered why I had chosen to live in town over something so peaceful as this.

Then I stepped out of the car and my heel dug into the mud of the driveway. Clarity hit home and I realized that I was not made out for country life. I liked to dress in nice clothes and mud caked on my heels was not exactly something I could live with.

"Hi, Alex. Thank you for meeting me," I said when Alex greeted me with a warm smile.

"I'm so glad you called. It's nice to get together with a new friend."

"I know how you feel. Up until I met all of you the other night, I really didn't get together with girlfriends."

"Well, until I met Cole, I didn't really have any friends, but his friends all made me feel welcome and gave me a family, so I'm grateful every day for that. Please, sit down. What did you want to talk about?"

"Um..well, this isn't easy to talk about. I'm not really well versed in matters such as these."

"I'm guessing you're referring to sex."

"Is it that obvious?"

"I think it was obvious to everyone the other night, but that's nothing to be ashamed of."

"I feel like such an idiot. Sex was never discussed in my family. I was raised in a religious home and I still have those beliefs, but I never had any interest in learning any more."

"Until now."

"Well, yesterday I was out with Sean on a car chase, completely by accident, of course. There was this moment when we were arguing and suddenly he was kissing me. I felt things and things happened that I didn't understand."

"Like what?"

I cleared my throat. This was so difficult to talk about. "I felt warm and my heart was beating very fast. My lips felt like they were on fire when he kissed me."

"That's all a very good reaction. That's just a sign that you two have good chemistry. Have you ever had that reaction with other men?"

I picked at a small thread on my skirt. "I haven't actually um.." Tears filled my eyes at my sudden humiliation over having to admit this. I had never been ashamed to admit exactly how little experience I had, but then I had never discussed it with anyone either. I took a deep breath and looked up into Alex's understanding eyes.

"You've never kissed anyone before."

I shook my head slowly. She grabbed my hand and squeezed.

"Honey, there's nothing wrong with that. You shouldn't be ashamed because you haven't let men walk all over you."

"Walk all over me? I haven't even let them kiss me. I'm just so inexperienced and when I go on a date with a guy, if he doesn't make me feel something, I just hold back."

"Who cares? The right man won't care at all."

"I doubt Sean would feel that way," I grumbled.

"So this is more about how Sean will feel about your sexual status."

"No. He and I would never work, but.."

"But he's the one who kissed you and made you tingle."

"I saw him walk out with Vira the other night. He took her home with him. I could never do that. I'm not that girl and I never will be."

"Then tell him that. If he really wants you, then he's going to have to listen to what you want."

"But how could I tell him that? He would look at me as some conquest, not as a potential girlfriend, and that's if he even considered dating me. He's not exactly a nice man. Most of the time he's a total jerk."

"Look, Lillian. I met Sean when I first came to stay with Cole. I realize that he may come off as a jerk, but I'm not lying when I say that man is a really caring man. If you were to explain to him how you felt about sex, I know that he would be more understanding."

"He might be so understanding that he walks away."

"Well, that's true, but he is who he is. If he feels that he would only hurt you, he probably would decide to walk away."

I sat there and thought about what she said. I suppose that after last night, none of this might be an issue anymore, but if he did pursue me again, I would have to tell him why I wouldn't sleep with him. Otherwise, he wouldn't have all the facts, and if I wanted something more with him, he would have to know exactly where I stood.

"What's bothering you most? Is it that you need to tell him how inexperienced you are?"

"I don't think so. I think what bothers me the most is that he doesn't seem like someone I would ever date. I mean, he has a foul mouth and he never behaves like a gentleman. I guess I just always had an image of who I would end up with."

"When I first started staying with Cole, I was on the run from a man that had tortured me for months. Sean came to this house to try and help me. He didn't look at me differently, he just did everything he could to make sure that I was safe. He may not be the perfect gentleman or dress the way you like, but once you're a part of his life, there's nothing he won't do for you."

"I believe that."

"So, what do you need to know about dating or sex?"

"Okay, this is going to sound ridiculous, but keep in mind that the only thing I know about sex is from what I learned in health class." She nodded for me to continue. "When Sean kissed me, I got wet..down there. Is that normal or is there something wrong with me?"

She let out a little chuckle. "That's perfectly normal. That's your body responding to your attraction."

"So, will it always be that way?"

"That depends on how attracted you are to the man. I think that's a good indicator that you liked what he was doing."

"How do I find out more about sex? I mean, not the basics, but what it's actually like? Should I read a romance novel?"

Alex laughed out loud as she held her stomach. "Oh, Lillian, you're killing me. Romance novels will definitely tell you how most girls like sex, in varying degrees, but in reality, sex isn't usually as good as it's written in novels."

"So, what's it like with you and Cole? Is that overstepping?"

"No, not at all. Sex with Cole is everything you could ever imagine, but it's different with us. A lot of couples are together because the sex is good, but everything else is only okay, or vice versa. You expect the whole package to get better in time, but that's not the way it works. Cole and I have it all, which makes the sex explosive."

"I don't know why I'm even worrying about this. There's no way I could get a guy like Sean to wait around for me. He's already pointed out to me how irritating I am."

She gave me a devious smile. "You do realize that you're like forbidden fruit? That alone will keep him coming back for more. Now you just have to decide if you want to give him a chance or not."

———

AFTER FINISHING up with grading papers for the night, I took a long, hot bath and then got ready for bed. I pulled my nightgown over my head and looked at myself in the floor length mirror. My nightgown had a wide scoop neck that rested on the edges of my shoulders. It flowed in one long, wide layer down my body and had elastic at the wrists that flowed out into a long curtain around my hand. It was a beautiful, old fashioned look, but I loved the way it felt on my body.

As I studied myself, I realized that this was more matronly than sexy. What guy would ever be turned on by this? I didn't dress sexy and I didn't show off my body to men. I didn't own anything that could even be considered sexy lingerie. I huffed in irritation at my thoughts of ever keeping the attention of a man like Sean. Forbidden fruit or not, when he realized that I wouldn't sleep with him before marriage, he would walk away.

I climbed into bed and pushed thoughts of Sean from my mind. My life was fine the way it was and I wouldn't change myself for anyone.

I woke when something covered my mouth. I found it hard to breathe and I panicked as I realized that it was a hand on my face. My eyes flew open and stared at a black figure in front of me. My chest heaved with the exertion of trying to draw in a full breath.

"You tell your boyfriend to stop looking or I'll take it out on you."

Just as quickly as he spoke he was gone. I laid in bed for a few moments trying to figure out what just happened. I finally realized that I needed to call the police and report a break in. I grabbed my phone and went into my bathroom and locked the door.

"911, what's your emergency?"

"I need to report a break in."

"Is the intruder still in the house?"

"No. I'm pretty sure he left."

"Are you okay?"

"Yes. I'm fine. He came in and gave me a message, then left."

"What's your address ma'am?"

"421 Dolly Dr. I need you to contact a Detective Donnelly. The message was for him."

I hung up before I could think better of staying on the phone with the operator. I sat in the bathroom and waited for something. I wasn't really sure what to expect and I was a little freaked out that someone had just been in my house, but I was oddly calm about the whole thing. I hadn't been harmed, so overall the situation wasn't really that bad.

I heard banging and some yelling, so I calmly opened the door and headed toward the front door. I thought better of going in my nightgown and grabbed my robe off the door. When I was presentable I opened the door to two officers.

"Ma'am, did you call about a break in?"

"Yes. Please come inside."

After they stepped into the living room, I walked over to the couch and sat down. The officers followed me in and took seats on the opposite chairs.

"Can you tell us what happened?" The officer to the right asked as he held out his notepad.

"I was awoken to a hand covering my mouth. The person was covered in all black, so I didn't see a face."

"Alright. What happened then?"

"He told me that I needed to tell my boyfriend to stop looking or he would take it out on me."

"So, the voice was male?"

"Yes."

"The 911 operator said that you requested a Detective Donnelly. Are the two of you involved?"

I thought briefly about our kiss, but shook my head. "No. I was involved in a police chase yesterday for the police shooting yesterday.

I was in the car that Detective Donnelly was driving. I assume that's what this is about."

"And how would this man know who you are?"

"Honestly, officer, I think that's what the police are supposed to investigate."

A flash of anger crossed the man's face, but he quickly reigned in his temper. The second police officer leaned forward.

"Did you see how he exited the house?"

"No. I stayed in bed until I thought he was gone."

"Alright. We'll need to check the doors and windows." Both men stood and went to the front door. I stayed on the couch staring at the wall, not sure what else to do while they investigated. I heard Sean outside talking with the officers and then a knock sounded on the door. I got up and went to the door to answer.

Sean's face was quite hysterical when I answered the door and I couldn't help but laugh. He was scanning my body with an odd look, like he had never seen a woman covered quite so much.

"What's going on here? I got a call that I was mentioned at a crime scene. What happened and why are you laughing?"

"I'm sorry. You should have seen your face. Everything's fine. A man broke in and wanted me to give you a message. He said to tell my boyfriend to stop looking or he would take it out on me."

Sean's face turned to stone and he clenched his fist. "And what made you think he was talking about me?"

"Well, considering you are the only man I know that is looking into something and I was on that call with you, I assumed it was you to whom he was referring."

"But he didn't specifically say my name?"

"No."

I walked back inside and sat down on the couch, Sean following close behind. He sat down next to me and picked up my hand. I looked down at our interlocked fingers and scrunched my brows. He quickly pulled his hand back and ran his hand over his scruffy face.

"Alright, well you can either come stay at my place tonight or I'll get you a hotel room. It's not safe to stay here."

"Why would it not be safe? He came and delivered his message and now he's gone. I highly doubt he would come back the same night."

"Are you serious? The guy broke into your home and you're okay staying here?"

"I'm not going to be run out of my home. I didn't ask for this. I wasn't supposed to be dragged along on a police chase-"

"You could hardly classify what we did as a police chase."

"Forced to break laws-"

"What laws did you break?"

"You forced me to drive like a maniac on a highway full of people."

"You never topped sixty-five. Your driving was scarier than the actual speed."

"Or to be shot at-"

"Nobody shot at you."

"To have my car used for police business-"

"Your electric car that died during the supposed chase."

"Or to be targeted by an insane man that thinks I'm your girlfriend."

"We did share a pretty steamy kiss."

"Would you be serious for one minute?"

"I am. I'm just pointing out the flaws of your argument."

"The point is, I didn't ask for this and I'm not about to have my life turned upside down because of one day."

"Fine. Then I'll stay the night here. Tomorrow, I'll have Sebastian come and install a security system for you."

"I don't believe I asked you to take care of that for me. And I most certainly didn't ask you to stay the night," I said as I pulled my robe closed at the neck.

"Would you lay off? I'm trying to help. It's the middle of the night and I'm tired. Besides, you're dressed like someone out of the 1800's. I wouldn't be surprised if you were wearing a chastity belt."

Heat flooded my cheeks and I didn't know what to say, so I stomped off to my room and slammed the door. I heard Sean talking with the other officers a little while later and then a car drove away. I wondered if Sean gave up and went home, but then I heard him walking around the house. This was not the way I had thought I would spend my first night with a man.

CHAPTER 6

SEAN

I had just closed my eyes and was drifting off when I heard her screams.

"Oh my God. Where is it? It's gone."

I got up from the most uncomfortable couch in the world and ran toward her bedroom. I was only in my boxers because I couldn't get comfortable in my jeans. When I heard her scream, there wasn't time to put them on.

"What is it? What's wrong?" I asked as I burst through her door.

"My hand is gone." She was feeling all around the bed and tearing the covers from the bed.

"What do you mean your hand is gone?" I walked over to her and grabbed her by the shoulders, forcing her to look at me.

"I woke up and my hand was gone. It's gone! How can that be?"

She looked really tired and I wondered if she was actually awake. I put a hand on her cheek and gave her a few light slaps. Her eyes adjusted and she looked at me again.

"Why do you think your hand is gone?"

"I can't feel it. It's not there."

I lifted one sleeve and saw that her hand was there. I showed it to her and then lifted her other arm. Her hand was in fact missing, but I soon found it inside the elastic of her nightgown. I gently pulled her hand from her sleeve and saw relief cross her face.

"Did you maybe fall asleep on your hand?"

"I guess that makes more sense than me losing my hand."

I massaged her hand, trying to get the blood flowing once again. "You know, if you weren't wearing such a long nightgown, you would have seen that your hand was still attached."

"I like my nightgown."

I looked her over once again and saw that the neckline had moved and one shoulder was now exposed. I could see the swell of her breast peeking out and her nipples were now poking through the thin material. Her long, brown hair was brushing against her shoulder and I could see the silky strands hung down to the middle of her back. Suddenly, she didn't seem quite so matronly in this nightgown. She was more like a temptress revealing glimpses of the beauty hidden within.

I wanted to pull up the gown and feel her silky legs and run my hands up to her breasts. I wanted to run my hands through her hair and feel her come apart in my arms.

Damn. I was getting hard thinking about how good she probably looked underneath. I ran my hand up her arm to the back of her neck and leaned my forehead against hers. Taking in a deep breath, I closed my eyes to get myself under control.

"You have no idea how tempting you are, do you?"

"I'm not trying to be."

I leaned in and brushed my lips across her soft lips. I didn't want to push too much. I knew she wouldn't appreciate my advances. I was going to have to take things slow if I wanted to get anywhere with her.

When she didn't push me away. I kissed her a little harder and slid my tongue along the seam of her lips. When she moaned and parted her lips, I slid my tongue into her mouth in a gentle caress. My thumb brushed the pulse point on her neck and I could feel it's rapid rhythm under my touch. Not wanting to push too far, I pulled back and placed one more gentle kiss on her lips.

Her eyes were closed as she breathed heavily from our kiss. I leaned forward and pressed a soft kiss to each eyelid before stepping back from her touch.

"Sweet dreams, Lillian."

I turned and left the room, not wanting to jinx myself by turning back for one last look. I closed the door and then laid back down on the couch, knowing I wouldn't be getting any more sleep tonight.

By the time Lillian emerged in the morning, she was fully dressed and ready for school, her armor fully in place. I was disappointed when I saw that she was wearing a pantsuit today instead of one of her tight pencil skirts. Her hair was once again pulled up in a bun and her glasses in place.

"I already called Sebastian and he's going to send a crew out to install a security system for you. You'll have sensors on all your windows and doors. Hopefully, that will make you feel more secure."

"I suppose, but alarms won't deter someone that really wants to get in."

"No, but it may give you time to get a weapon. Do you know how to shoot?"

"A gun?" She asked in disbelief.

"Yes, a gun. I would feel better if you had one here for your protection."

"I don't know the first thing about using a gun and I doubt I could use one if I had it."

"Why's that?"

"Because I don't believe in killing."

"I doubt you would feel that way if it was kill or be killed."

"People say that all the time, but it goes against my beliefs."

"And what would those beliefs be?"

"The ten commandments."

"So, a guy comes to kill you and you won't fight back and use a gun because of the ten commandments?" I asked in astonishment.

"Not everyone understands. I believe very strongly and I don't know if I could live with myself if I took another life."

"So, what does that say about me?" I walked right up into her space. "I've killed a man before and there's not a single thing I regret about it. He didn't deserve to breathe the same air as anyone else around him. He was scum. So, do you think I'm a murderer, too?"

"That's between you and God. I can't say what will happen to you."

"But you think I'll go to hell."

"Not if you ask for forgiveness."

"I have to ask for forgiveness? Do you think God would have wanted me to let that asshole continue to rape a fourteen year old girl?"

She blinked rapidly and moistened her lips. I was guessing she'd never seen the underbelly of the world, never really had to see how truly evil people could be first hand.

"Where was God when my sister was captured by a serial killer? Or when that same man went after Alex? Should Cole have not put a bullet in his head after the man shoved a knife between his ribs? Or what about the man that attacked his wife in the bar? Should he have asked the man nicely to stop beating Alex with a liquor bottle?"

"I.." She stumbled over her words, trying to figure out what to say. "I can't..I don't understand why things happen the way they do, and I'm not trying to say you were wrong. But I can't suddenly change my beliefs after twenty-eight years."

"Well, let's hope you never end up on the receiving end of a madman's gun."

I walked to the door and headed out without another word. As much as I wanted that woman, I couldn't stand to be preached to about the moralities of my job.

"Sebastian, I'm gonna need someone to tail Lillian until I can get the evidence I need in this case."

"Do you want round the clock or just while she's out of the house?" His voice seemed a little distant on the other end of the phone. No doubt he was slammed with work right now. His company had really taken off in the last six months and the five men he hired didn't seem to be enough to keep up with the demand for their services.

"I need round the clock. It would be best if you could give me Lola, but if she's not available, just send whoever you think is best."

"Why do you want Lola?"

"Lillian won't like having a man stay with her, but she'll deal with it if she has to."

"Does Lillian know that she's going to have a bodyguard?"

"She will this afternoon. She doesn't have a choice in the matter. I fucked up and had her with me when I was chasing down a suspect. Someone broke in last night and threatened her."

"Shit. Where is she now?"

"I just followed her to the school. She should be fine until school lets out at three-thirty."

"Alright. I'll look at my caseload and see if I can send her. Give me a half hour and I'll let you know who I'm sending."

"Thanks, Sebastian."

I hung up and pulled out of the school parking lot and headed to work. The first thing I needed to do was go have a talk with my chief. This shit with Sawyer and Calloway had to stop before someone else got hurt. It was bad enough that Officer Wheeling got shot, but now Lillian was being threatened also.

"Chief, do you have a minute?"

"Yeah, shut the door." Chief Jameson waved me in and closed up a file on his desk.

"What's on your mind, Donnelly?"

"What's going on with the IA investigation into the missing drugs?"

"They're stalling. I can't get any answers from anyone."

"We have to close this case. The woman that was in the car with me yesterday was threatened in her home last night."

"Yeah, I heard about that. How did they find out about her? Do you think it was Sawyer?"

"Most likely. He's the one with the most beef to grind with me."

"Sean, I never asked what happened that he hates you so much, and I won't as long as you can assure me it has nothing to do with this case."

"Not at all."

"Alright. How's the girl?"

"She's fine. A guy broke in and had her give me a message to stop looking or he was going to go after her."

Chief Jameson sighed and leaned back in his seat. "Well, we can have patrols keep an eye on her."

"There's no need for that. I hired Reed Security to put someone on her."

"Is this your girlfriend or something? You've never done this for anyone else before."

I thought back to our moment in her bedroom last night and how much I wanted her and then about her comments this morning. I wasn't sure what was going on with us, so it was better to not say anything yet.

"No. I know her from the drug busts at the school. She offered me a ride back to the station yesterday after my car was hit, and I dragged her into this whole mess. I just want to make up for that."

He didn't look convinced, but didn't say otherwise. "The best way to get these two is to catch them in the act. Now that they know IA is involved, they're going to be more careful. This isn't going to be easy. I'll make sure they don't get called out to any more of your calls. We'll try to keep them in the dark as much as possible. Maybe we can force them into making a mistake."

"Let's hope so."

———————

I WAITED outside the school with Lola, hoping like hell Lillian would accept this help without throwing a temper tantrum. I had to get back to work and I didn't have time to deal with her fighting me on this.

"So, Sebastian told me that Lillian has some drug dealers after her. What does an English teacher have to do with drugs?"

Lola was a kickass woman and definitely looked the part as we stood leaning against my car. She wore form fitting jeans, a white tank, a military green jacket, and combat boots. Her hair was pulled up in a tight ponytail that swayed down her back. Her sunglasses made her seem relaxed, but Lola was always assessing and always ready.

"She's not really involved. More like wrong place, wrong time. She was with me and a drug dealer saw her. He assumed she was my girlfriend and he's trying to use her as leverage against me."

"But you aren't actually with her?"

I snorted. "I think I can say with one hundred percent certainty that I am the last person on the face of the earth that Lillian would want as a boyfriend."

"Why? You're a good guy."

"She's religious and apparently has a problem with my complete lack of regard for taking a life when necessary."

"Well, she's a civilian. She doesn't get it."

"And she never will. She's too innocent."

"For some reason, I get the feeling that you don't like that she doesn't understand you."

I ignored that comment as I saw Lillian emerging from the school with her bag that she always brought to school and her purse hanging from her shoulder. Her jacket from her pant suit was draped over one arm and the silky, short sleeved blouse perfectly accentuated her breasts.

She stopped when she saw me standing next to her car. When she glanced at Lola, I saw her eyes trace the scar along Lola's forehead and the horror that momentarily took over her features. I felt Lola tense next to me. Her scar was a big no go for topics of conversation. She never allowed anyone to ask questions or pity her.

"Detective. Are you here to borrow my car again? I'm afraid that I'm not really in the mood for a car chase today."

"I'm here to introduce you to your new bodyguard."

"My what?" Her eyebrows shot up and she glanced at Lola again before pursing her lips at me. "Why would I need a bodyguard?"

"You do remember the man that broke into your house last night, don't you?"

"It was actually this morning."

"Whatever. A threat was made against you and no matter how much of a jackass you think I am, I won't leave you unprotected when I dragged you into this."

"As much as I appreciate the thought, I don't need anyone to protect me. I'm sure you'll have this case wrapped up soon, and your friend went to my house today to install the security system. I think it would actually be a better deterrent if I wasn't seen with you anymore. The more that you appear at my house or place of work, the more the man will feel that I actually could be used against you."

"Irregardless-"

"Regardless."

I took a deep breath and closed my eyes as I blew out my breath. "I know I'm going to regret this, but..what?"

"You said irregardless. Ir means not or no. Regardless would be the equivalent of saying 'in spite of everything' or 'nevertheless'. When you put 'ir' in front of regardless, you are actually saying the exact opposite of the point you were actually trying to make. Therefore, you should actually be saying regardless."

Lola leaned over to me and whispered, "She's right, you know. It's not a word." She was trying to be quiet, but I saw the way Lillian's pursed lips spread into a thin smile that she was trying to reign in. I glared at Lola and then turned back to Lillian.

"Despite your objection.." I paused for effect. "Lola is very good at her job and I would appreciate it if you would accept my help. Staying away from you will not make a drug dealer think that you can't be used as leverage. If it's who I think is behind this, he knows that I would protect you even if you meant nothing to me, which you do."

That was probably a mean thing to say and I would be lying if I said I didn't feel bad when I saw the hurt flash across her face. After our morning, I really wanted nothing more than to get Lillian off my mind. Whether or not she brought up my wildest fantasies, I couldn't deal with someone judging me so harshly when she didn't know me.

"Detective, I think we need to get one thing straight. I didn't ask to be a part of this in any way and that now includes your offer of protection. If you have anyone follow me, I'll call the police. Now if you would be so kind as to move out of my way, I have somewhere I need to be."

She pushed past me toward her car and drove away three minutes later. Lola watched her go through her pre-driving checklist with a smile on her face.

"Well, that didn't go as planned. What now?"

"Shit. I don't know. If she doesn't want help, there's nothing I can do about is. She's not my woman."

"Well, I guess I'll head back to Reed Security. Give me a call if she changes her mind."

Screw it. If she didn't want my help, I sure as shit wasn't going to follow her like a damn puppy dog. I went home, having finished for the day, and grabbed a beer from the fridge.

Visions of Lillian in her nightgown crept into my mind. She was so buttoned up, but she was hiding the body of a vixen under all that material that she wouldn't share with me. She shared her mind with me, and I was sure that if I actually tried to get to know her, I would find that the woman was more than she seemed.

Then I thought of Vira and how simple things were between us for the most part. I got everything I needed sexually with her, but she kept me at a distance, never wanting to share herself with me.

A knock at the door pulled me from my thoughts. I walked over and pulled open the door to the devil herself.

"Vira. I thought we both agreed this was over?"

"That doesn't mean we can't have a little fun. Let's go dancing. It's been so long since we've gone and had some fun."

She stepped forward and ran her hand down my chest, looking up at me from under her eyelashes. I tried to not give in to her. I tried to think of any reason that I should stay home and not go with her, but the promise of rubbing my body against Vira for the rest of the night was just too much to take. I pulled her against me and kissed her hard.

"Let me change and we can grab some dinner before we head over."

I was temporarily distracted by her outfit. She had on a top that had a V that stretched down to her belly button and no back to it. I had no idea how it was keeping her breasts in, but I was damn sure gonna find out before the night was over.

CHAPTER 7

VIRA

This was my chance. I needed to reign Sean back in. He was trying to walk away from our arrangement and I couldn't let that happen. I wasn't ready for more and I didn't know if I ever would be, but if I let him walk away, I had a feeling I would never get him back.

He walked downstairs wearing a pair of jeans that hugged his ass and a tight, black t-shirt. His muscles rippled and stretched the arms of the shirt, making me remember just how wonderful those arms were when they were wrapped around me.

"Ready. Where do you want to go for dinner?"

"Well, seeing as how I'm dressed for the club, I guess we have to stay away from restaurants."

He stepped into my space and ran his hand in a gentle caress along the neckline of my top, following the V down to my belly. His fingers brushed my breast causing my nipples to perk in anticipation.

"Darlin', I would take you anywhere. The problem is that other men would want you also and I don't think my chief would be okay with me shooting random strangers because they looked at you like they wanted to fuck you."

He gripped my waist tightly as he pulled me into his bulky frame. I squeezed my legs together to lessen the throbbing that took over between my thighs. His lips hovered over mine and I could feel his warm breath caressing my face.

"Let's go before I fuck you against the door."

"I wouldn't be opposed to that."

"Neither would I, but I'm gonna drive you crazy at the club. I'm gonna have fun teasing you and making you want more until you're begging me to fuck you."

He stepped back and walked to the door looking calm as ever while I was panting and needing some cold water to calm my body. I grabbed his hand and went to his truck, wondering if I would ever have my fill of this man.

Two hours later, Sean had me panting on the dance floor. Not from dancing, but from the way he was running his hands over my body and whispering in my ear all the dirty things he wanted to do to me later. We had been at the club for only a half hour and I was already ready to leave and take Sean home.

He had requested several songs from the D.J., making sure each was dirtier than the last. It started with the most used sexual song I had ever heard, Marvin Gaye's *Let's Get It On* and then progressed to *Me and Mrs. Jones* by Billy Paul. For each song that was played, he swayed with me to the music and pressed wet kisses to my sweat dampened skin. The heat from his hands left goosebumps prickling all over my body.

He led me over to the bar where he ordered two shots of tequila and bent down and licked a hot trail between my breasts. He sprinkled some salt on the spot that was now wet and then leaned forward to swipe the salt off my heated skin.

I closed my eyes and dropped my head back as the salt spread roughly over my skin. His tongue didn't leave my body after he licked the salt from me. He continued to run his tongue up my neck until he was kissing behind my ear. My pussy clenched and I had to grip his biceps to keep myself upright.

He drank his shot of tequila and then ate the lime wedge before taking my mouth in a bruising kiss. As his tongue slid in my mouth, I wrapped my arms around his neck and pulled him as close as possible. His cock pushed against me, letting me know exactly how much Sean wanted me. I thought he might pull me out of the club, but instead, he picked up the salt and passed it to me.

I quirked an eyebrow at him, but took the shaker from his hand. I pulled his hand toward me and sucked his thumb into my mouth, taking extra time to get it nice and wet. I salted his thumb and then sucked the salt from his thumb, pulling him as deep into my mouth as I could. Swirling my tongue around his thumb, I showed him exactly what he could look forward to later.

He picked up the shot glass and drank it down, then grabbed my hand and pulled me to the dance floor. *Kiss You All Over* by Exile came on and Sean pulled my back to his front.

He wrapped his hands around me, one large hand pressing against my belly and the other skimming my breast before wrapping around my neck.

YOU'RE *my one desire*
  Gonna wrap my arms around you
  Hold you close to me
  Oh, babe, I wanna taste your lips
  I want be your fantasy, yeah

HIS LIPS SKIMMED my neck and his hot breath panted against my skin. He pulled my face to the side and crushed his lips against mine. I gripped the sides of his pants, pulling him tight against me. His erection pressed into my ass.

His hands continued to skim over my overly sensitized skin. His hand trailed down my leg, just barely brushing my inner thigh and then back up to my zipper where his hand rested.

You don't have to say a thing
  Just let me show how much
  Love you, need you, yeah
  I wanna kiss you all over
  And over again

His teeth scraped against my neck until he started sucking hard on my skin, sending quivers down my body. My eyes slid closed as I memorized the feel of his lips against me. His hands and mouth were all I could feel, all I could think about as he swayed behind me and pushed me toward ecstasy.

"Open your eyes, Vira." I obeyed and was vaguely aware of the crowded floor of people surrounding us.

"Do you see that man across from us? He can't keep his eyes off you. He wants to fuck you. He wants to be standing where I am and feel your soft skin in his hands, but he can't have you. You belong to me, Vira, and I'm going to show this whole club how much you belong to me."

His hand slid inside my shirt, pulling the sticky tape from my skin and grabbed my breast in his large hand. His fingers teased my nipple, bringing it to a stiff peak. My eyes slid closed again, but Sean's voice forced them open again.

"Keep your eyes open, Vira. Let him see the desire you have for me."

Love you, need you
  Oh, babe

I wanna kiss you all over

I WAS PANTING NOW, barely able to hold back the scream that was threatening to break free as Sean pushed me to orgasm.

AND over again
I wanna kiss you all over
Til the night closes in

HE CONTINUED to massage my breast as I came down from my high. The man across the room was watching in fascination and only turned away as the song died down. Sean turned me to face him and gripped the back of my neck, pulling me in for a steamy kiss. His tongue pushed into my mouth, commanding that I give him everything he desired.

Ten minutes later, Sean pushed me up against the door of his house, gripping the back of my leg and pulling me close to him. Our heavy breathing filled the night with the faint rustling of his keys.

"Shit," he said as he dropped the keys to the ground. "Fuck it." His lips found mine again as his fingers opened the zipper of my pants and pushed them down. I did the same for him, groaning when my hand met his thick erection. I started to bend down to suck him, but he gripped my hair and hauled me back up.

"Not now. I need your pussy. Push your shoes off."

I quickly stepped out of my heels and toed the ends of my pants to pull them down. He ripped the panties from my legs and thrust inside me, slamming me back into the door.

"Yes. Yes! Fuck me, Sean. Fuck me hard!"

With every thrust his breath puffed over my skin. "Vira, your pussy is strangling my cock. I won't last."

"I'm almost there. Harder, Sean!"

He slammed into me a few more times until I came with a scream that he quickly swallowed with his mouth. His body stilled as he came with a groan. He continued to kiss me as we both settled our racing hearts.

He leaned his forehead against mine until his breathing normalized. "I'm gonna need to do that again."

"Inside this time."

"Agreed. My neighbors don't need to see my ass."

I LAID on Sean's floor with my eyes closed, trying to catch my breath from the fuck fest Sean and I just had all over his house. After we came in the house, we made it to the stairs before starting round two. Round three was a few hours later in the shower. We took a short nap and just finished round four.

It was now morning and we really hadn't gotten any sleep. I desperately needed coffee because I had to work this afternoon. No nap would be long enough to recover from our night.

"I need coffee."

"Me too."

"Make me breakfast?" I asked.

"So, you don't want a relationship, but you want breakfast." At first I thought he was serious, but then a big grin split his face.

"Hey, there have been plenty of times that you've gotten breakfast."

"I would say I want you for breakfast, but I think you broke my dick a few minutes ago."

"As much as I would love another round with you, I have to get myself up and moving or I won't be able to make it to work later. I'm pretty sure I'm gonna need to soak in the tub so I'm not walking bow legged today."

"I like you walking bow legged. It shows all the other fuckers out there that I did that to you. Nobody will touch what's mine."

"But I'm not yours, Sean. We've talked about this."

As much as I wanted Sean to be mine, I knew that I couldn't make it a more permanent arrangement. He would start making plans that I just couldn't deal with.

"Here we go with this shit again. Vira, I tried staying away from you for two months. Neither of us was happy and you know it."

"That doesn't mean that I want to be yours. I like what we have, but I like my life the way it is. There's no room for a boyfriend."

"And why is that, Vira?"

"Because that's the way I want it! I've been living my life like this for so long and I don't want to change. Jesus, men don't change, why should I have to?"

"You're gonna end up with one sad, lonely life if you don't let someone in, Vira."

"That's my choice to make. You can't just expect me to change who I am."

"Right. You want to be able to go fuck other guys. Apparently, one man that gives you everything isn't enough."

"I'm gonna let you in on a little secret, Sean. There have been no other guys for the past year and a half."

"What? But-"

I held up my hand to stop him. "There have been no other guys because you were the best and all I needed."

"Then, why? If we're so good together that you didn't need to go find someone else, then why can't we have more?"

"Because I don't want it! How many times do I have to tell you that? We can continue like we are, sleeping together and only with each other. We can go hang out, but I will never be your girlfriend."

He stood up and put on pants while I sat on the floor, pulling the blanket over my naked body.

"I think you need to leave. I can't keep doing this to myself. You keep pulling me back in and I keep thinking things will change."

"I didn't pull you back in, Sean. You came after me, remember?"

"Yeah, I did, but then you showed up on my doorstep. This can't happen anymore. I need to stay away from you so I can move on."

I stood up, letting the blanket drop from my body. "Fine, but you know you'll be back for more. We're good together and it's only a matter of time before you come back to me."

"I won't come back to you because you're a selfish bitch."

"I believe you said that last time also."

I grabbed my clothes and headed for the bathroom where I quickly dressed. I may have been using Sean for over a year, but he always knew the way I felt. I never held back and led him to believe that I could someday want more with him. This wasn't on me and I wasn't going to stand around being called names because he couldn't' accept his part in all this.

CHAPTER 8

SEAN

I shouldn't have gone off on Vira like that. She had always been honest with me and I knew she didn't want more. I just hadn't wanted to admit it to myself. If I didn't pull my head out of my ass now, I was bound to end up pining away for Vira the rest of my life.

I had the day off of work and I didn't really want to be worrying about anything to do with police business today, but after Lillian had been threatened, I wanted to check in with her and make sure nothing else had happened. Lola was on standby, but she wouldn't be for long. Sebastian couldn't keep her hanging around waiting for a me to decide what to do. As long as Lillian was refusing protection, there was nothing I could do but have patrol cars swing by her place.

Walking up the sidewalk to her house, I noticed that everything about her house was perfectly in place. Her garden had fresh flowers and her yard was clean and well trimmed. The siding on the house looked like it had just been washed and I couldn't see a single speck of dirt on her windows.

I shook my head and knocked on her door. She answered wearing a nice pair of black skinny jeans and black flats with a pale blue blouse.

"Don't you ever wear clothes that you can just lounge around in?"

She looked down at her outfit. "What's wrong with what I'm wearing?"

"You look like you're going to teach. Don't you own jeans and a t-shirt?"

She crossed her arms over her chest and pursed her lips, her signature move with me. "I own plenty of relaxed clothing, but this was what I wanted to wear today."

I rolled my eyes at her. "Look, I just came by to make sure no one had bothered you."

"I'm fine, as I told you I would be."

I nodded and turned to go, but her voice stopped me.

"Why do you care about what I wear? You don't even like me."

I turned and looked her over again. She looked good, I couldn't deny it. This woman would look good in a potato sack.

"You look good, I just wondered if you knew how to let loose. You're always so buttoned up. You don't let down your hair. You follow the law to the fucking letter and you correct people's grammar. Don't you know how to have fun?"

"Despite what you may think, you know very little about me. Didn't your mother ever teach you not to judge people before you get to know them?"

"Care to prove it?"

"Prove what?"

"That you can break out of your shell and let your hair down."

She stood up a little straighter and pursed her lips again. "Bring it on."

Of course, it sounded ridiculous coming from her prim and proper, little mouth, but something about that was inexplicably sexy.

"Go get in some leggings and a long sleeve shirt with socks and tennis shoes."

She quirked an eyebrow, but did as I asked. I pulled out my phone and made a quick call to ensure she had the time of her life.

We were just about to leave ten minutes later when I noticed a problem.

"Do you have to wear your glasses to see?"

"Well, I don't have to, but it definitely helps. Why?"

"Hmm. I don't think we have time to get you something different."

"I have contacts if that will help."

"Perfect. Go put them in."

She came back a few minutes later, blinking and rubbing at her eye.

"Everything okay?"

"Yes. I just don't like wearing contacts if I don't have to. They irritate my eyes."

"Bring your glasses and lens case with. We can swap them when we're done."

Five minutes later we were on the road and headed out of town.

"So, where are we going?"

"You're gonna have to wait and see."

"Honestly, I can't believe that I came along to prove to you that I'm not some uptight prude that doesn't know how to have any fun."

"If you do what I have in store for you today, I'll stop calling you a prude."

"Normal people just talk to one another."

"Alright. We have about a half hour before we get to our location. I'll ask you a question and then you get a question."

"Fine."

"First question. Why are you such a rule follower?"

"I don't know. I guess the way I was raised. I wasn't taught that it was okay to bend the rules. They're in place for a reason."

"Sure, but still, you've never gone over the speed limit even by a few miles? I mean, everyone does that."

"I don't. Not intentionally anyway. I always watch my speed very closely."

"Okay, how about this. There are two rooms left at a hotel and you have three people. Both rooms have an occupancy limit of two. Do you tell the hotel that you have three people and pay for two rooms or do you sneak the third person in?"

"I tell them we have three people. It's not that I don't want to save money, it just wouldn't occur to me to lie about something like that."

"Why?"

"What if there was a fire? If you were trapped in that room, the firemen would only be looking for two people. Like I said, the rules are there for a reason, for the safety of everyone. I can't believe that as a cop you would question me on this."

"It's not that I'm against you following the rules, but you make sure every T is crossed and every I is dotted."

"Well, I am an English teacher."

I glanced over at her with a smirk. "Was that a joke?"

She blushed and looked away. "Okay, my turn. Why did you kiss me when you obviously hate me?"

"I don't hate you. As for the kiss, you are every man's fantasy."

When she didn't say anything, I looked over and saw her chewing on her lower lip, her eyebrows scrunched as she looked off in thought. A moment later she turned to me.

"I don't understand."

"The fantasy? Naughty school teacher? You wear those glasses and your hair's pulled up. You wear those tight skirts that show off your ass. Oh, come on. Don't tell me you don't know what you do to all those assholes you work with?"

"But..you always make fun of me for the way I dress."

"No, I make fun of you because you have the attitude to go with it. I just think you need to loosen up a little."

"I'm plenty loose."

"Darlin', I would love to have first hand knowledge of that."

Her face turned the shade of a lobster and she quickly changed the subject. "When are we going to be there?"

"Fifteen more minutes. My turn. How many men have you been with?"

"Excuse me? I hardly think that's an appropriate question. I hardly know you."

"Yet, I still asked."

She silently fidgeted, not looking at me for a few seconds. "I've had one boyfriend," she finally said.

No way. She was practically a virgin. Who only slept with one man by the time they were almost thirty?

"Aren't you like, late twenties?"

"Yes."

"How long were you together?"

"Less than a year."

"Damn. No wonder you're so buttoned up. You need to release that build up. I'd be glad to help you if you need it. I'm sure your vibrator could use the rest."

"You know, this is really not..I don't think we should talk about this-"

"Relax. Everybody goes through a dry spell. I'll gladly tell you my number if it'll make you feel better."

She turned toward me in her seat. "Fine. I have a question for you. What's the situation with you and Vira?"

"There is no situation."

"But you dragged her out of the bar the other night, and your friends made several comments about the two of you not being together anymore."

"We were never together. We were fuck buddies. I wanted more and she wasn't willing to give it. That night was a slip."

"And how many times do you slip?"

"One other time, but she's made it perfectly clear where she stands."

"So, even though you're sleeping with another woman, you're still flirting with me and trying to get me to sleep with you. That's the problem with relationships nowadays."

"What is?"

"Sleeping around. Even though you know Vira doesn't want

more, you continue to sleep with her. You don't mean anything to her, yet you don't look for someone who would truly care for you. In the meantime, you flirt with me, leading me to believe that even if I were to sleep with you, I would never have anything real with you. That's not what I want. I want someone that will cherish only me. I want someone that will give themselves to only me and vow that I would be their forever. Otherwise, what's the point in giving yourself to someone?"

The cab of the truck got quiet as I digested that little rant. Was that really what was happening with Vira? Did I really mean nothing to her? I had never considered that she was only using me for sex. I always assumed that she just wouldn't let me in because of something that had happened in the past. But if I looked at it from Lillian's point of view, that was exactly what was happening. If I was asking for more and she wouldn't give it, what was the point? Was she really worth a good time?

Lillian was also right that I was sending off the wrong vibes. If a woman I barely knew could see that I was hung up on another woman, but still flirted with her, she would also know that I was using her. How could I ever really move on with another woman if it was so obvious that my heart and head weren't available?

We drove the rest of the way in silence and arrived at the airfield ten minutes later.

"What are we doing here? Are we going somewhere?"

"We're going up."

WE WERE SITTING in the back of the plane while the instructor got Lillian attached to me. I had been skydiving many times, so I was comfortable with Lillian tandem jumping with me. Lillian looked a little nervous and hadn't said much since we entered the airfield.

She had very willingly listened to all the instructor had to say, but I couldn't be sure if it was because she wanted to jump or if she was determined not to back down. Now she kind of looked like she might puke.

She was now firmly strapped to the front of my body and the instructor was getting ready to open the door. He signaled a count down and I nodded, letting him know I was ready. What I wasn't ready for was Lillian taking a running jump as soon as the door opened. My body was quickly pulled behind hers as she bolted for the door of the plane and jumped with a scream as she catapulted us into the sky.

"Holy cannoli!" She screamed as we spread our arms and legs out, catching the wind beneath us. I linked my fingers with hers, happy that she was enjoying this. I wanted to make this special for her, so I wrapped my legs around her, pulling them together and then wrapped our arms toward her chest. I twirled us around as we moved faster and faster toward the Earth.

Her peels of laughter made my chest tighten knowing that I was giving her this joy. I didn't have much time left before I had to pull the chute, so I did a few more twirls before I flattened us out once again, allowing her to enjoy the free fall a little longer.

When our time was up, I pulled the chute and together we experienced the wonder of flying through the air for a little while. I maneuvered us to our landing site, feeling Lillian tuck her legs up as we landed. There was a guy waiting at our landing site to grab the chute and I was able to quickly unhook Lillian. She turned around with a huge smile on her face.

"That was amazing, Sean! Thank you so much!"

She jumped into my arms and laid a huge kiss on my lips that took me by surprise. When she didn't pull back right away, I wrapped my hand around the back of her head and held her to me as I deepened the kiss. Sliding my tongue against hers, I tasted the minty flavor that still lingered from her toothpaste. I had no idea how long the kiss lasted. I was still lost in the feeling of holding her in my arms. When she pulled back, she was panting and her face was filled with desire.

As with our first kiss, her fingers went to her lips, no doubt still feeling the lingering zing that electrified us.

WE STOPPED at a diner on the way back home for some lunch. While we waited for our food, I studied the woman in front of me that turned out to be quite different from what I originally thought. Sure, she was prim and proper to an extent, but she could let go. She just needed someone to have fun with.

"I may have misjudged you."

"Really, detective. And just what exactly did you misjudge?"

My cock tightened whenever she called me detective. I imagined her in some naughty lingerie, maybe a trench coat over it, wearing a patrol hat and calling me detective. Cuffs would be involved. A strip search for sure. I shook my head to clear away the images that started running through my mind.

"You have a bit of a wild side in you."

"Well, of course. Did you assume that because I like to dress nice and I use proper grammar that I don't like to have fun?"

"I may have assumed that."

"Well, I do like to have fun, when done in a safe way."

I grinned at that. "I didn't think you would consider skydiving as safe."

"I've actually always wanted to go, but I didn't have anyone to go with. I don't have a lot of friends and they're mostly work colleagues more than anything else."

"What about people you went to college with?"

"I went to the University of Pittsburgh. It was only an hour drive, so it was cheaper to drive there than to stay on campus."

"So you didn't have the whole college experience."

"No, and quite honestly, it wouldn't have suited me."

"You didn't want to go to parties and get wasted? Wake up with a hangover at noon the next day and then struggle to study for the big test you had Monday morning?"

"Rule follower, remember? I wasn't old enough to drink."

"Not even your last year?"

"I have a summer birthday. I didn't turn twenty-one until I graduated college."

I nodded in understanding. Still, who didn't want the college experience? It was part of growing up, kind of like an introduction to adulthood.

"So, tell me, detective. Why did you become a police officer?"

"Well, I went to school with absolutely no idea what I wanted to do. I studied criminal justice just because I thought it was interesting. I didn't know what I was going to do when I graduated, but then my sister was abducted by a serial killer. I went right to the academy after she was found."

"And now you're a detective."

"I made detective about two years ago."

"What kind of detective are you?"

"Well, since we aren't a huge department, we don't have different divisions of investigation. If you're a detective, you pretty much take anything handed to you."

Our food arrived and we ate in a comfortable silence. After I paid the bill, we headed back out to my truck and I completely surprised myself.

"So, what's it gonna take for you to agree to go out with me?"

"You mean like a date?"

"Well, I would kind of consider this our first date. I bought you a meal, we went and did something, and I got a kiss."

She blushed as she climbed into the truck, but I didn't let her shut the door.

"I'm waiting."

"Sean, I had a lot of fun with you today, but trust me when I say that I'm not the girl for you."

"Yet, there is definitely a spark between us." I moved closer so that I was in her space. "Don't deny it. I've kissed you twice now and both times felt like I was hit with an electric shock."

Her breathing hitched when I ran the back of my hand down her face. I leaned in for another kiss, dying to taste her again, needing to feel her body respond to me. My lips brushed hers lightly and were instantly electrified. I needed more of her. I pulled her against me and ravaged her mouth, pushing my tongue in her mouth to taste the sweetness within. My hands roamed down her waist, squeezing her side and then trailing up to her breast. Right as I was about to feel the perfect swells under my palm, she pushed me away and broke our connection.

"I'm sorry, Sean. I can't. This isn't me."

She turned in her seat and buckled herself in. I stood there for a moment in shock before shutting the door and walking around to my side. I couldn't believe it. There was no denying there was something great between us, so why was she pushing me away?

I started the truck and headed back to her house. The more I thought about it, the more it bothered me.

"Why won't you give me a chance?"

"I'm not what you're looking for, Sean."

"How do you know?"

"I saw the way you dragged Vira out of The Pub. That will never be me. I won't sleep with you just because we have good chemistry."

"What if I took you out with no expectations?"

"No expectations." She shot me a look saying what she thought of that idea.

"I can do no expectations. We could take it one day at a time and see where it leads us."

"But you will eventually want something from me."

"Lillian, there's not a day that goes by that I don't want you, but I am able to control myself. One date. That's all I'm asking. I'll take you out and we'll have a good time. Just like today. No strings attached. No expecting more. We'll just have fun and see if either of us wants more."

"I have a feeling more to me and more to you is quite different."

"Well, if we get to that point, we'll discuss it like adults."

I had a feeling that I was winning her over. I just needed her to agree to one more date with me. I didn't know how this woman had gotten her perfectly manicured nails in me, but she had and I needed to see if the few kisses we'd shared were really as spectacular as I thought.

"One date?" she asked.

"One date."

CHAPTER 9

LILLIAN

I couldn't believe that I had agreed to go out on a date with Sean. He was so sexy, and he was right, I couldn't deny that there was something between us. But he didn't know exactly how inexperienced I was. When he asked me about my sexual history, I was vague enough to make him think that I had a little experience. I didn't know why, but I wasn't ready for him to know I was a virgin. He obviously had a lot more experience than I did.

Our schedules worked well together for the most part, but he couldn't help if he was called out on a case. We set up a date for the following weekend, which left me the whole week to stew in anxiety over my attraction for him and what I would say if he asked more questions about my sexual history. I knew I needed to be quite frank with him if he asked again. He had to know that he was dating someone that wouldn't have casual sex, or even sex if we were in a committed relationship. I wondered how many dates it was appropriate to go on without him having that knowledge.

He called me on Friday to set up our date for the next day. All he would tell me was to dress in leggings, a sporty top, and sneakers. I didn't think he would take me skydiving again, so I spent the rest of Friday night going over a possible list of things we could do.

When Sean showed up on my doorstep at six the next morning, he looked absolutely mouth watering. He was wearing nylon shorts and a long sleeve shirt with tennis shoes. His muscles were still quite visible through his shirt and he had the most gorgeous calf muscles I had ever seen. He wore a baseball hat on his head and sunglasses that covered his beautiful eyes.

"You ready to go?"

"Uh..yeah. I'm ready."

I grabbed my purse and headed out to the truck with him. He opened my door and helped me into his truck, which I couldn't help but mentally check off on my list of things that I expected from a date.

"Where are we going?"

"Raccoon Creek State Park. I thought we'd go hiking."

"I love hiking."

"Good. I'm glad I didn't choose something you'd hate."

"Do you go out this often or is this just because you're taking me on a date?"

"You mean doing outdoor activities? I don't get to do them as often as I'd like, but that just means you're the perfect excuse. I was thinking about what you said about not having friends to go out and have fun with. So now I've made it my mission to take you out to do as many fun things as you like for as long as we're dating."

"That's very sweet of you."

"Don't let it get around. I've got a reputation to maintain as an asshole. Could you imagine what criminals would try to pull if they thought I was sweet?"

I smiled at his banter, thinking maybe I had misjudged him as much as he had misjudged me.

We arrived at the park about forty-five minutes later and spent the day hiking the many trails the park offered. Sean had brought two hiking packs, food, water, an extra hat and sunglasses for me, and hand towels. He seemed to have thought of everything.

About mid-day, we stopped in a nice, quiet section of the park that had a nice patch of grass to sit in. Sean had even brought a blanket to sit on, which he laid out on the ground for me. I laid down and looked up at the sunny sky through the trees, giving my body a much needed break. It was a gorgeous spring day and the faint sound of birds and the breeze lulled me into a sleepy state.

I woke to the feel of feather-light kisses being placed on my eyelids and cheeks. When my eyes fluttered open, Sean was leaning over me with a breathtaking smile on his face.

"Sorry. I couldn't help myself. You looked so beautiful that I had to kiss you."

"I'm sorry I fell asleep on you."

"Don't be. It's peaceful out here. A perfect day for a nap in the park."

I couldn't tell if he was feeding me lines or being genuine, though I wanted to believe that this was the real Sean I was seeing. He seemed more relaxed out here and I wondered if he was this relaxed around everyone. Part of me secretly hoped that he was just this way with me.

"How long was I sleeping?"

"About an hour."

"Oh my gosh. I'm so sorry. You must have been so bored sitting here."

"Actually, it was nice to sit here and enjoy the quiet."

"Are you saying I'm loud?" I said with a laugh.

"Not at all. I did like watching you sleep though." He laughed and then rubbed his face. "I just realized how creepy that sounded."

We laughed and then he pulled out some snacks for us to eat. After we had finished, we packed up and headed back. It had been a perfect day and I was a little nervous to admit that I wanted more time with Sean.

"So, next weekend?" He asked as he walked me to my door.

"Are you going to tell me what we're going to do?"

"Not a chance." He leaned forward and gave me a light kiss on the lips before smiling and walking away. I wondered why he hadn't kissed me more, but then decided that I was fine with the pace we were taking this. I walked in my house and then realized I was going to have to wait a whole week before I saw him again. When did I become the girl who waited around for a man?

CHAPTER 10

SEAN

Surprised couldn't even begin to describe what I was feeling right now. After spending the day with Lillian, I found that I really enjoyed her company. She still corrected my grammar, but it didn't bother me so much anymore. It seemed to be just a natural reaction for her, not that she was pointing it out to be snooty.

She was a genuine person and I liked that I didn't feel she was ever putting on an act for me. With Vira, I always felt that she was putting on a face to seem tough, and while I liked that about her, I wished that she didn't need that with me. I got tired of always trying to figure out what she was running from.

While I liked hanging out with Lillian and I was extremely attracted to her, I wasn't sure I could hold out for her. I still craved Vira and even though I had told her we were over, if she just came to me and offered more of herself, I would be with her in an instant.

Since it didn't look like that would happen, I could still have fun with Lillian in the meantime. I had an idea of something I'd like to do with her, so I looked into it and found that it would be perfect for next weekend.

Work was getting stressful because I had yet to get any more leads on the drug cases I was currently working. Carlos Ramirez wasn't giving up any information and even when he was offered a deal in exchange for information, he didn't take it, which most likely meant that he worked for some seriously bad guys. There had been no more threats against Lillian, but then Sawyer and Calloway had been left out of the loop and had no idea what was going on in the investigation.

I was at work going over case reports when my phone rang. I smiled when I saw it was Lillian calling.

"Hey, Lillian. You miss me already?"

"Sean. You need to go down to the hospital. A kid collapsed at school today and I overheard someone saying that they hoped it wasn't from the drugs he'd been taking. The principal is speaking with the student now."

I was up and out of my chair as soon as she said drugs.

"I'm sure the principal will be calling as soon as he gets something out of the student, but I wanted to give you a heads up."

"Thanks, Lillian. I'm on my way to the hospital now."

When I got to the hospital, I showed my credentials and talked with the intake nurse. A student had been brought in presenting with signs of a drug overdose. I waited around for two hours before a doctor came out to speak with me.

"Detective Donnelly?"

"Yes."

"I'm Doctor Emanuel."

I shook his hand and we walked over to sit in the empty waiting area. "What can you tell me about the student that was brought in?"

"I'm afraid he didn't make it. We're informing the family now."

"Was it a drug overdose?"

"Yes. We won't know what exactly until the labs come back. I can send over the results when they come in."

"That would be great. I'll also need the child's name and his parents' names."

"I'll have the nurse gather all the information you need. The parents are not in town at the moment, so we had to tell them over the phone."

I sighed and ran a hand over my face. I hated cases with kids. It was always so damn difficult.

"Alright. I'm going to head over to the school." I pulled out my card and handed it to him. "Please send all information directly to me. Only the chief or I are able to accept the information. Do you understand?"

"Of course."

I headed over to the school where the student that made the comment was still waiting, along with his parents. The principal came out to talk with me before leading me into the office.

"It seems that this student, Samuel Markham, gave the pills to Daniel because Daniel was in pain from an ankle injury. Daniel's parents hadn't taken him to the doctor and Samuel felt bad for him. Samuel saw Daniel crushing up the pills before he took them."

"Jesus. Where did he get the pills?"

"He took them from his parents. Apparently, they were in a prescription bottle, so he assumed they were safe."

"Well, Daniel's dead now, so they'd better start talking."

I stormed past the principal and proceeded to take the parents and kid to the police station for further questioning. By the time my paperwork was done, it was well past ten o'clock at night and I was beat. I was about to head home, but then I thought that maybe Lillian would like an update. I drove to her house and thought better of it as I was pulling onto her street. I was going to drive past, but then I saw her lights on and decided to stop anyway.

When she opened the door, she had on the same nightgown she wore a couple of weeks ago. She didn't have a robe on and the cool air was making her nipples poke through the thin material. She seemed to realize that she wasn't dressed properly because she quickly crossed her arms. I tore my gaze from her chest and looked at her flushed face.

"Sorry to stop by without calling. I just thought you might like to know what was going on."

"Sure. Come on in." She held the door open and held her arm out for me to enter. I sat down on her couch, glad when she took the seat next to me.

"The kid died."

"Oh, I'm so sorry. Do they know what killed him?"

"Drug overdose. That's all I can tell you at this point. Thank you for calling me this afternoon."

"Of course. Is there anything I can do for you now?"

"Just talk to me."

So that's what she did. She talked to me for a good hour at least about random things. She told me about her family and growing up. She told me how her mother always corrected her English when she spoke and that's where she got it from. I listened intently until the sound of her sweet voice lulled me off to sleep. When I woke in the morning, I was lying on the couch covered in a blanket and the smell of coffee floated through the air. I sat up and rubbed my eyes, knowing that I had slept better here than most nights I did in my own bed.

I made my way to the kitchen and found Lillian dressed in her sexy teacher clothes and making lunch. Breakfast was already on the counter and there was a second cup of coffee next to the second plate.

"Good morning." My voice came out rough and I had to clear my throat to work the sleepiness from my throat. Lillian turned around with a bright smile on her face.

"Good morning. I hope you slept well. I know that couch isn't the most comfortable."

"It was fine. I actually slept really well."

"Good. I'm glad. I made you breakfast and there's coffee in the pot."

"Thank you. I appreciate that."

"I'm also making you some lunch to take with you. I wasn't sure if you normally brought your own lunch, but I didn't want you going hungry."

"You made me lunch?" I asked in bewilderment. Nobody had made me lunch since I was a kid in school.

"It's nothing special. Just a roast beef sandwich and some chips."

I was stunned. I hadn't had anyone take care of me in so long, I wasn't quite sure how to react.

"Thank you."

"You're welcome," she said with a smile. Then she turned and went back to making my lunch. I sat down and ate my breakfast after I grabbed a cup of coffee. I could definitely get used to this.

CHAPTER 11

LILLIAN

Sean seemed completely dumbfounded by me making him breakfast and lunch. Was it really that odd? Had I overstepped some imaginary line? I was just treating him the way my mother would treat a guest. I didn't understand it.

I finished getting ready for the day and then gathered my stuff at the door. Sean had finished eating and then rinsed and put his dishes in the dishwasher, which I thought was very thoughtful of him.

He walked toward the door and grabbed me around the waist. He kissed me deeply and then pulled back.

"Thank you for last night and this morning."

"Any time. I'm glad I was able to help."

We both went our separate ways and I spent the rest of the week waiting for the weekend when I would see him again. I didn't hold any illusions that he would make a habit out of what happened last night and frankly, I didn't want him to think that I was okay with sleepovers, but for one night, it felt wonderful.

When Saturday morning came, Sean was at my house bright and early. What I didn't expect was the whole group of people with him.

I was a little shocked when I opened my door and saw all of his friends parked in the driveway waiting for me.

"Um..what's going on?"

"Sorry about this, but I told Jack my plans with you for today and suddenly everyone was coming. I hope this is okay with you."

"It's fine, but I do think it's a little weird that all your friends know where I'm going on a date with you before I do."

He smiled at me and guided me toward the truck. "We're going to Kennywood Amusement Park!"

"Like rollercoasters?"

"Yep."

"Oh my gosh. That's fantastic. I've always wanted to go on a rollercoaster!" I started jumping up and down, not caring at all that his friends were probably staring at me like I was crazy.

"You've never been on a rollercoaster?"

"Nope!"

"Well, let's get going so we can pop that cherry."

I blushed, understanding the reference. Little did he know the most important cherry I had yet to pop. We got to the amusement park and went right to the fastest ride there was. We stood in line for about forty-five minutes before finally being seated. I was a little nervous, just as I was on the plane, but I did an excellent job of hiding it. Sean must have sensed my nervousness because he reached over and grabbed my hand.

"I don't get it. You took a running leap out of a plane, but you're scared of this when you're strapped in?"

"On the plane, it was my choice to go. Right now, I'm waiting for them to get the ride moving. I have no control over it."

He laughed and gave my hand a little squeeze. A minute later, we started the steady climb to the top of the track. When we were just reaching the top, the coaster fell over the hump, taking us on a wild ride. I screamed the whole thirty second ride, delighting in the crazy ride I was on. Sean did this for me. He brought fun to my life and helped me experience things I had missed out on.

CHAPTER 12

SEAN

I couldn't stop looking at Lillian. She looked so carefree today and it made me want to always put that happiness on her face. She was over at the food stand grabbing our lunch with a few of the girls. The guys had offered to stand in line, but the girls couldn't make up their minds what they wanted, so it was decided they could just take our money and get whatever they wanted.

Lillian was laughing as she talked with Harper and Alex. She turned toward me and waved with a huge smile on her face. I couldn't help but wave back and then instantly looked around to see if the guys saw how whipped I was. They had. Every single one of the guys was staring at me with some sort of bewildered expression.

"What?"

"What was with the finger wave?" Cole asked.

"That wasn't a finger wave. It was a normal wave. A manly wave."

"Sure it was. I always waggle my fingers when I wave at people," Ryan said.

"You are so whipped," Jack said with a laugh. "It won't be long before you'll be joining the club."

"And what club is that exactly?" I questioned.

"The one we're all a part of where you do everything possible not to fuck up so your girl doesn't threaten to cut your balls off," Jack replied.

"Hey, I'm not a part of that club," Ryan said with disdain.

"Sure, but you did bring Cassandra along today. You've been trying to get in her pants for a year and a half," Logan said as he clapped Ryan on the shoulder.

Logan and Ryan worked on a project with Cassandra and Ryan instantly had a hard on for her, but she wasn't giving in to his advances. Much like a woman I knew.

"The one thing you guys are missing is that Lillian doesn't use that kind of language, therefore my balls will never be in danger."

"Sure, you watch. Within two months, she's literally going to have your balls in a vise," Sebastian said, putting in his two cents.

"I highly doubt that since she knows nothing about engineering tools."

"Dude, I wasn't suggesting that she was actually going to put your balls in a vise."

"But you did. You said she would 'literally have my balls in a vise'. If that's not what you meant, you should have said figuratively."

Shit. Now all the guys were staring at me. I had just corrected Sebastian's grammar. What was Lillian doing to me? Luckily, I was saved from further ridicule when all the girls walked back over with the food. Nothing would shut up a bunch of guys like food.

After we were done eating, the girls all headed to the bathroom, but Alex stayed behind. She tugged on my sleeve and motioned me to the side with her head. I followed, curious as to what she needed to talk to me about.

"How are things going with Lillian?"

"Good. What's up?"

"Sean, I want you to be careful with her. She's not like Vira in any way."

"I'm well aware of that."

"No. I mean..she's innocent, more innocent than you could imagine. Just don't hurt her."

That was ominous. What would compel Alex to come over here and warn me about Lillian. Still, there was nothing I would ever do to hurt Lillian, so I said the only thing I could.

"I won't."

CHAPTER 13

LILLIAN

"Thank you for today. I haven't had so much fun in a long time, and your friends are great."

Sean was walking me to my door after a wonderful day. He was so great and I was surprised at how natural things felt with him. Maybe this could go somewhere with him. Now I just had to find a way to tell him my biggest secret.

"I'm glad you had a good time. I don't want to wait for next weekend though. How about you come over tomorrow morning at seven and we'll go somewhere. I have to arrange a few things, otherwise I'd pick you up."

I smiled up at him, happy that he didn't want to wait. "Sure. That sounds great. Clothing?"

"Optional, of course."

I laughed and smacked his chest. "Stop. You know what I mean."

"Casual."

"Okay. I'll see you at seven."

I really wanted him to kiss me, but I wasn't good at saying what I wanted so I turned to let myself in the house. He grabbed me around the waist and spun me back into him, kissing me feverishly. I wrapped my arms around his neck, loving that he obviously wanted to kiss me just as much. When he finally pulled away, I felt dizzy with lust for him and had to pull myself together so I didn't maul him.

"I'll see you in the morning."

I smiled as he turned away and headed to his truck. I unlocked the door, completely lost in the magical world that was now my life. It seemed I had greatly misjudged Sean.

CHAPTER 14

SEAN

I headed home and made arrangements for Lillian and I to go out on a friend's boat tomorrow. It was going to be just the two of us. I was lucky enough to have connections that would show Lillian exactly how great life could be, if she just let go and have fun.

I was replaying the day in my head, thinking of the way Lillian laughed with my friends or the way she gripped my hand on the rollercoaster. She was quickly working her way deeper into my life.

The doorbell rang bringing me out of my thoughts. I walked over and was shocked when the devil herself stood at my door.

"Vira. What are you doing here? We're over. You shouldn't be here."

"It's Anna, actually." She shoved past my stunned body and walked into the living room. "And you decided we were over. I never did."

Who walked into someone's house and dropped a bomb like that on someone? After a momentary pause to wrap my head around what I just heard, I shut the door and turned to face Vira. Or Anna.

Vira was wearing black dress pants and a black vest that most women would wear a shirt under. It had big silver buttons on each side of the vest and the V dipped down to the middle of her breasts, leaving quite a fair amount of cleavage showing. Her black hair had purple strands peeking out from underneath.

There was no denying my attraction for her. I was getting hard just looking at her and it had been too long since I had touched her. Any thoughts of the anger I felt toward her the last few weeks were gone and all I could see was the woman I wanted standing in front of me.

"What do you mean your name is Anna?"

CHAPTER 15

VIRA

It was now or never. If I didn't try to open up to Sean, I was going to lose the one man that finally made me feel something after all these years. If Cece could do it, so could I.

"It's actually Anna Belle Covington, but I don't go by that anymore and if you tell a single soul that my name is Anna Belle, I will cut off your balls and shove them down your throat."

"Why do you go by Vira Williams?"

I snorted and looked to the side. I really hated sharing shit with people. I had kept it all in for so long that I didn't really know how to share anymore. Not even Cece knew this stuff about me.

"I grew up in the south and my family was very rich and pretentious. I didn't want that life for myself, so I left and changed my name. Seriously, who names their daughter Anna Belle? Like I could ever be a wilting flower."

"Why do I get the feeling that you just glossed over a whole shit load of information?"

"Because it's not important. It's not who I am and I never will be again."

He crossed his arms over his chest and stared me down. His gaze bore holes into me. "So why now? What made you finally come tell me this?"

I took a deep, huffing breath and rolled my eyes, but I couldn't look at him. "Because you needed more and you were going to leave."

"So you want more, too. Otherwise, you wouldn't have shared with me."

I finally looked at him and narrowed my eyes. It was one thing to share. It was another to feel like I was being stripped bare. "I gave you that much. Don't ask for more right now."

"One more question and I'll let it go."

"What?"

"Did you ever sleep with Sawyer?"

That was not what I was expecting. I had never considered that he would be jealous of Sawyer. "No. He was a flirtation to get what I wanted."

"Does he know that you screwed him over? Because he's a loose canon right now and if he finds out that you used him, there'll be hell to pay."

"As far as I know, he doesn't know a thing. I told him that Cece was getting back together with Logan and asked him to stop. Then his career went up in flames and we haven't spoken since."

He walked toward me and pulled me into his arms. I almost sighed at the feel of being in his arms. Almost. But I kept up my armor, not quite ready to give everything to this man.

"Well, it's not everything I want to know, but it's a start. Are you sure you want to do this? There's no turning back from here. Once you're mine, I'm not giving you up."

I nodded. I could do this. I would do this.

Then his lips were on mine, ravaging my mouth and making me moan in pleasure. I had missed this with him. I needed to feel his arms around me, wrapping me in his warmth and protecting me from all the shit in the world.

He grabbed me under the ass and lifted me in the air. I wrapped my legs around him as he carried me upstairs. He laid me down on the bed and kissed me as his hands caressed my body. I felt his fingers move to my vest and push the buttons through the holes. When he reached the bottom, he pulled back and slowly opened one side, revealing my breast. He leaned down and took my nipple in his mouth, his warmth sending chills down my spine. Then he opened the other side and repeated the process.

This was beginning to feel too intimate. I didn't do intimate. I fucked and Sean knew that. I grabbed him by the face and forced him to look at me.

"Sean, fuck me. You know how I like it, so give me what I want."

"Anna-" I flinched at the name. I didn't ever want to hear that name again, but he just stared at me, waiting for me to accept it. "Anna. Let me love you. That's all I've ever wanted. Just give me this."

His lips brushed mine softly and for a moment, I felt tears building inside. I swallowed them down and closed my eyes, just feeling his hands and mouth on my body. He licked his way down my waist and when he reached my pants he slowly undid the button and lowered the zipper.

My breathing accelerated as he pulled my pants from my body, sliding them over my heels. I laid on the bed in my black panties and heels as his gaze burned over my skin.

"You are so damn sexy. I tried to push you out of my head, but you were always there. You were under my skin from the moment I met you and I don't think there's any way I could ever work you out of my system."

I didn't know what to say. I needed Sean and I was willing to bend for him more than I cared to admit, but I wasn't sure how deep my feelings were. I hadn't allowed myself to care about anyone else in so long, that I wasn't sure I would know love if it smacked me upside the head.

I wasn't sure if he had taken my panties off or if he had just moved them to the side. I didn't realize that he had even gotten undressed. I was so lost in my thoughts that I barely registered his presence next to me until he thrust inside me in one long thrust.

"Oh, God. Sean."

His thrusts were long and slow. This wasn't our normal way of fucking. He was making love to me. This was the first time I had ever made love with someone and allowed this level of intimacy. I couldn't move my eyes from his. Even when my eyes slid shut, I forced them back open so I could see his intense eyes staring back at me.

When he pushed me over the edge, he came moments later and then kissed me lovingly before wrapping me in his arms.

"I love you, Vira. I've been waiting for you for so long."

It was all too much. I couldn't think. I couldn't breathe. I needed to get away and pull myself together, but I didn't want to hurt Sean.

"Sean-"

"Don't say anything. I know it's a lot for one day."

I laid there and tried to stay calm when all I wanted to do was run, and that's exactly what I did in the early morning. I couldn't stay here with him. He would wake up and want commitment or to pretend we were now some couple. What had I been thinking coming here and offering more?

I slipped out of the house and headed for Logan and Cece's house. I knocked several times and finally Logan answered the door in a pair of low hanging jeans with a cloth draped over his shoulder. I pushed passed him, only briefly checking out his sculpted abs before I looked around for Cece.

"Where is she?"

"Well hello to you too, Vira. It's a pleasure as always."

"Oh, shut up. I need to talk to Cece. Where is she?"

"She's nursing Archer."

"That baby's still on the tit?"

"Plenty of mothers breastfeed until the baby is a year old, sometimes longer."

"You'd better get used to saggy boobs then." I headed toward the baby's room and opened the door without knocking, relieved when I saw Cece sitting in the rocker.

"I am such a bad person."

"What'd you do now, Vira?"

"I offered Sean more and then he made love to me and told me he loved me and I ran."

"You did what?" I heard from the doorway. I turned to see Logan standing in the doorway with his arms crossed over his chest. He looked pissed.

"This is none of your business, Logan."

"You've been dragging Sean around by his balls long enough. How could you do that to him? You had to know that he felt more for you."

"I didn't think he was going to tell me he loved me! I thought we were just going to take baby steps. He acted like I was all the sudden going to commit to him and we were going to get married."

"What exactly did you offer him?"

"That's not-"

"Goddamnit, Vira!" Logan had never raised his voice to me. I looked at Cece who looked equally as shocked, but didn't say anything.

"I told him my real name."

"Your real name?" Cece looked at me in confusion.

"Look, it's a long story and I'll tell you another time. Right now, you have to tell me what to do."

"Jesus, Vira. Did you really think that giving your real name, that you've been hiding from everyone, is a small piece of information? Of course he assumed you were offering him more. A lot more." He huffed out a breath and took a deep breath. "You really are a bitch sometimes." Then he walked away, leaving me alone with Cece. I turned to see her still stunned and staring where Logan had stood.

"Cece, say something."

"I'm still trying to get over the fact that you have another name and you never told me. Why?"

I sat down on the floor, leaning against the dresser and let out a sigh.

"I came from a very rich family. I hated everything about them, so I left them all behind along with my name. I became someone else."

"And you didn't think I'd understand?"

"I didn't think it would matter to you."

"It doesn't, bitch. Which is why you should have told me."

"I'm sorry. I left that girl behind a long time ago."

"So, is that why you don't have relationships with people?"

"Initially. That had more to do with the fact that my parents wanted me to marry an abusive asshole for his money and what his connections could do for us. I guess I figured that if I never had a relationship with anyone, no one could ever use me in that way."

"You know that Sean would never do that to you."

"I know. I'm just stuck in my ways at this point. It really doesn't even have to do with my family anymore. I've been living my life this way for years and I really like it. I don't want Sean to leave, but I don't know that I can give him what he wants. That was what I was hoping we would talk about, but then he pulled out the L word and it was just too much. Before he woke up this morning, I ran."

Cece sat there nursing her son and didn't say anything. It was starting to make me nervous. Cece and I never judged each other, but I was beginning to think that her personal relationships had changed her attitude toward me.

"Say something. Do you hate me?"

"Of course not. How could I judge you? You do remember what I did to Logan, right? I was just thinking about how this would turn out for you."

"And?"

"And I think you have to go back to him. Tell him it was too much."

"That would hurt him."

"And what do you think will happen if you keep seeing him, but push him away? Either way, you're going to have to tell him what you think about his declaration. It's not fair to drag him along for a ride he may not want to take."

"You think I should have stayed away."

"If you really wanted to make something with him, then you know I'd be behind you one hundred percent, but you can't keep him as your play thing forever."

"Shit. I hate it when you're right."

I walked over to her and gave her a side squeeze and then headed to the door. Time to pay the piper.

CHAPTER 16

SEAN

I t was like a bad dream. I knew it when I said the words to her last night that it was over. I felt her tense up and knew that she didn't feel the same way and wasn't ready for what I had to give. I felt like an idiot as I laid here in bed, the same bed that she snuck out of forty-five minutes ago. I felt her get up and I snuck a peek. I saw her eyes and how frantic she was to get away.

As mad as I was at myself, I was even more pissed at her that she would come here and offer something only to run away. I told her she would be mine and she didn't tell me no. I had to be done with this. I couldn't take it. No matter how many times I let her back in, it always ended the same way, with me being the jackass that couldn't accept the person she was and always would be.

The doorbell rang downstairs and hope flared in me that she hadn't actually left me. Maybe she just ran out for breakfast. I quickly threw on pants and ran downstairs, flinging the door open with a grin on my face.

Lillian was standing in front of me with tears in her eyes that she was desperately trying to hold back.

"Lillian, what's wrong? You look like you're about to cry."

"Can I come in for a minute?"

"Of course."

I opened the door wide for her and stepped to the side. I followed her into the living room and took a seat next to her. I reached for her hand but she pulled away.

"I need to ask you something and I need you to be honest with me."

"Sure. Anything."

"I came here this morning for our date.."

Fuck. I closed my eyes and my head dropped back. I had totally forgotten about Lillian. I glanced at the clock and saw that it was almost eight o'clock.

"I saw Vira run out of the house as I was pulling up to your house. She didn't notice me, so I pulled over and waited. I kept telling myself that I needed to talk to you first before I assumed that she spent the night here. I mean, I know we're not in a committed relationship or anything, but I didn't think you assumed that I would be okay with you sleeping with other women while we were dating. So, I need you to just be honest with me and tell me if you slept with Vira."

I had fucked up so bad. There was no way Lillian would ever forgive me for this. Now that Vira was gone, I wasn't sure why I had even given in to her last night. I was so stupid to assume that things would be different between us. Now Lillian, the one woman that had ever really made me really happy, was sitting here on my couch and I was going to have to hurt her because I couldn't lie to her.

"Sean. Please, just tell me the truth."

"Yes, I slept with her."

A few of the tears in Lillian's beautiful eyes fell down her cheeks, leaving glistening trails that I wanted to wipe away. I couldn't do that though. I was the one that hurt her and I knew she wouldn't accept comfort from me.

"I don't understand. Did you ask me to come here so that I would see her leave? Did you plan this?"

"No. I swear I didn't. It was all a horrible mistake."

"A mistake? I don't understand? You dropped me off yesterday and kissed me like you needed me to breathe and then you went home and had sex with another woman hours later. How does that even happen? Am I really that forgettable?"

"No! You are not forgettable."

"Yet, you forgot about me."

"It wasn't like that. Do you remember that day that we went skydiving and we were asking each other questions in the car?" She nodded. "You said that I didn't mean anything to Vira, but I didn't look for someone who would truly care for me."

"I remember."

"The reason I kept going back to Vira was because I loved her, or at least I thought I did."

"Why would you date me if you were in love with another woman?"

"I wanted Vira, but she kept pushing me away. Then I met you and you were just so much different. You were open with me and I was attracted to you. I wanted to know more about you. I didn't think about Vira at all when I was with you."

"Gee, that's comforting."

"What I mean is, if I was forgetting about her then maybe it wasn't love."

"But you still slept with her when you were dating me. All it took was her coming over here for you to decide I wasn't worth it."

"She told me she wanted more. I thought I finally got through to her. I thought she really wanted me."

"Well, I hope you two will be happy together."

"You don't understand. I told her I loved her and she ran. I don't think she would ever accept what I wanted to offer her. It's over."

"How can you be sure?"

I sighed and ran a hand over my face. "I kept going back to her over and over after I broke up with her. Every time I expected a different outcome and every time she let me down. When I told her I loved her, she changed and I just knew that no matter how many times I tried, she would never give me what I needed. I just knew it was done. There was no point left in trying. I think it was the obsession of wanting something unattainable."

"That may be, but you also destroyed whatever was happening between us."

I reached for her hand, forcing her to let me hold her.

"I know I screwed up. Give me a chance to make it up to you."

"Do you honestly think a few dates will make it up to me? You chose a woman who used you as a play thing over a woman that wanted to build something honest with you."

She pulled her hand from mine and stood, heading toward the door. I sprang to my feet, not ready to let her leave yet.

"Lillian, don't go yet. I know I fucked up. I wish I could go back in time and see that she was playing me, but I can't. Please say you forgive me. I need you to know that I would never have hurt you if she hadn't fucked with my head."

"Sean, I do forgive you. I don't understand it and I don't like what you did, but I can't be mad at you either. We never had a commitment to each other. I feel sorry for you that she messed with you and treated you like you were worthless."

My hopes lifted that she would come around. I just had to make her understand how misguided I'd been.

"Any normal person would feel bad about the way you've been treated. Forgiving you doesn't mean that I have to stick around though."

She opened the front door and was stepping through when she turned and looked back at me. Her sweet face was covered in tears, but she did her best to hold it together.

"I actually had a really good time with you and I'm glad I got to know you. Despite the situation, you really are a good guy. I won't forget what you did for me."

She turned and walked out the door. No yelling. No calling me bad names and swearing at me. She didn't threaten to cut my balls off or have me killed. That wasn't Lillian's style though. I'd gotten to know Lillian well enough over the past few weeks to know that her religion anchored her and made her the person she was.

I slammed the door as she drove away and went to sulk on the couch. How had I fucked this all up so much? How had I let Vira sink her claws in me again? I didn't know how long I sat there replaying the past twenty-four hours in my head, but when I heard the knock at the door, my heart leapt that Lillian had come back.

It was like deja vu. I was once again staring down the she devil that had now ruined my life. She actually had the nerve to stand there and look ashamed. I wanted to slam the door in her face, but before I did, I was going to make it perfectly clear that things were over between us.

"Hi, Sean. Can I come in?"

"Not a chance in hell."

"I guess I deserve that."

"You deserve a hell of a lot more, but I don't have the time for you in my life anymore."

"I didn't mean to run out on you. I got scared and I just couldn't do it."

"You know what, Vira? I have given you so many opportunities to have something with me. I always came back to you and last night turned out to be the worst mistake of my life."

She flinched slightly, but didn't say anything.

"I was dating a good woman and we were doing well, but then you walked back into my life and pretended like you wanted something-"

"I did-"

I held up a hand to stop her. "You played me again. I told you that if you and I got back together, you would be mine. You didn't deny it. You didn't tell me no. Then you ran out of here and left me. Again. I'm not sure why I didn't see it before. I knew you were selfish and I knew that I was only going to get hurt, yet I still went after you. I hoped that you would realize how good we had it. Now I'm starting to think the only thing good between us was sex. There never really was anything else, was there?"

"I think I wanted there to be. I'm sorry. I know that's not enough. I wanted more with you, but when you told me you loved me, I think I just couldn't see how it would work. We want different things."

"Well, I'm glad you finally came to that conclusion. It would seem we're both a little slow on the uptake."

She nodded and looked down. "I'm really sorry I hurt you and that I ruined things for you."

"Too little, too late for both of us. I'd like you to leave now."

She looked up at me and her armor was in place. It was like nothing could touch this woman and it made me see how horribly wrong we really were for each other. I closed the door and went to the liquor cabinet. It was five o'clock somewhere.

CHAPTER 17

LILLIAN

After I left Sean's house, I went back to my own to sulk. This day had gone to total poo. I was supposed to be off doing something fun with Sean and instead I was coming back to my lonely house, with my lonely life that now seemed awfully dull.

Sean had brought so much fun to my life. He helped me experience life on the wild side, or as much on the wild side as I would allow. His friends were wonderful and treated me like one of the girls without any questions. There was no judgement or seeing what I was like first. They just accepted me for who I was and that was the best feeling in the world.

After moping around the house for a few hours, I decided what I really needed was a drink. I headed out to The Pub and asked for a glass of white wine. I just needed something to take the edge off. While I sat in the empty bar and drank my wine, I thought about calling Alex. She seemed to understand me, but then I decided that wouldn't be a good idea since she was friends with Sean.

I was about halfway through my second glass when the door opened and Logan and Ryan stepped in. Being that I was on my second glass, I was a little tipsy. I didn't drink a whole lot, so the wine went to my head a little faster than I expected.

"Logan! Ryan! Hey! What's going on!" Everything came out happy and cheery, just the opposite as I was feeling. I got up to walk to them, but instantly tripped over my own feet, falling to the ground. I started laughing at how I had gone from prim and proper to falling down drunk in a matter of weeks.

Ryan walked over to me and wrapped his hands around my arms and pulled me to my feet.

"Hey, Lillian. You doing okay?"

"I'm fantas-s-stic. I just decided to have a little drink, seeing as how it's a S-sunday afternoon and I don't have anywhere to be."

I was proud that I was able to get most of that out without slurring.

"I thought Sean was taking you out today?"

"Oh, well! Let me tell you something. I went over there this morning and Vira was slipping out the door. Seems Sean and Vira were knockin' boots last night, if you know what I mean."

Ryan and Logan looked at each other with some sort of weird look that I couldn't interpret. Maybe they didn't understand.

"You know, having relations? Coitus? Fornication? Mating? Copulating? The horizontal mambo? Getting jiggy with it?"

"Yeah, I think we get the idea," Logan interjected, stopping me from throwing out a few more euphemisms.

"So, anyway, I decided that I could really use a drink, cuz I was sitting at home thinking about Sean and Vira having sex, and that's-s a little weird, right?" I said with a laugh. "I mean, really, I can't compete with a woman like Vira. I mean, I'm sure she's all fur and no knickers, as the British would say."

"I don't think that means what you think it does," Ryan said.

"I'm sure she does things for Sean that I could never do. I mean, I don't beat the bishop-"

"Again, not what you think it means."

"Or partake in buggery-"

"I'm not sure what exactly that means," Logan said as he rubbed a hand over his face.

"It's anal sex-x," I said as I held up a hand to my mouth to whisper the answer to him.

"Please call one of the girls and make this stop," Logan said to Ryan, but I didn't care. I was feeling pretty good as I downed the rest of my wine. I held my hand up for the bartender to refill my drink.

"I'm not into dogging and I probably have a growler."

"Where is all this British terminology coming from?" Ryan asked.

"I got a guide to dirty British slang as a Christmas present last year. I never thought I'd actually get to use it though."

Logan stepped to the side and pulled out his phone. The bartender had placed a new glass of wine on the counter for me, so I grabbed it and let the fruity flavor fill my mouth.

"I love wine so much. I wonder why I've never allowed myself more than a glass before?"

"Lillian, have you had any food today?" Ryan asked.

"Ummmmm..let me think. I had a protein bar before I left the house this morning and saw that skank walk out of Sean's house."

I covered my mouth as I realized that I had just said something so horrible. "Holy cannoli, I should not have said that. That was a horrible, horrible thing to say about another person."

"I'm pretty sure you've said worse with your British slang."

"Still, it was not a nice thing to say. If they want to shag, that's their business and I should bloody well mind my own."

"Is anyone coming?" Ryan asked Logan. "It's turning into British trivia over here."

"Alex is on the way. I think the others will be coming soon."

"Thank God."

"Yes! Thank God! You're right. I should be thanking God because I still have my dignity, which is more than I can say for that slag."

"What?" Logan asked.

"Whore," Ryan deadpanned.

"You guys are too cute." I patted each of them on the cheek before taking another drink of my wine.

I walked over to the jukebox and looked through the list of songs to play. I squealed when I saw one that I wanted to play. I dug through my pocket, not finding any quarters so I walked over to the bar where I had left my purse and pulled out a twenty.

"Bartender!"

He walked over with an annoyed look. "Sorry, but I didn't catch your name."

"It's Sam."

"Sam, I need some quarters so I can sing about my man that cheated on me with his twat of a girlfriend. Can you help a girl out?"

Sam smiled and took my money, changing the twenty for quarters.

"That's gonna be a mistake," I heard from behind me.

I turned around, but didn't know who had said it. "Just you wait. I'm a great singer."

"I'm sure you are, sweetheart," Logan said with a grin.

I strutted my stuff over to the jukebox and put the quarter in. I saw there was a little stage with a mic. Walking up to it, I turned on the mic and was pleased when Sam flipped on the lights on the stage. I was surrounded by pinks, blues, and greens. Adele's *Rumor Has It* filled the bar and I sang my heart out. I had never felt so loose and I found I really liked it.

I shook it on stage, letting the music flow over me. My behind was shaking all over and I heard Sam whistle from the bar. I had it going on. I looked up when I heard the bar door open.

"Alex! Come join me!" I waved her over enthusiastically and ignored Cole. I didn't need more men. Right now I needed women around me. Alex walked hesitantly toward the stage, looking like it was the last place she wanted to be.

"Sam! My girl needs a drink! Give her a bourbon!"

"Wine. I'll have wine," Alex corrected. "How many have you had so far?"

"Three."

"You've only had three glasses of wine? In how long?"

"Oh, it's been about three hours now."

"And you're this drunk?"

"I know! I can hardly feel a thing! This is great!"

"Maybe you should slow down."

"Now way! Sam, bring me another wine!" I ran over to the jukebox and put on *Bye Bye Bye* by Nsync.

"I love this song!" I turned to see Harper and Cece running toward me. "Babe, grab us drinks!" Harper shouted to Jack as she ran onto the stage.

Harper, Cece, and a reluctant Alex joined me on the stage to perform our rendition for the men standing before us. Halfway through the song, Sarah and Maggie came into the bar with Drew and Sebastian. Cassandra was a few steps behind. I didn't know Cassandra that well, but considering that she was kind of an outsider like I was, I jumped off the stage, stumbling slightly and falling into some chairs before I ran up to her and dragged her to the stage.

The song had ended and I looked through the playlist, trying to find out what song to play next. As I glanced back at the room, the answer was simple.

It's Raining Men filled the room. The girls all screamed and the guys groaned. All the girls were singing at the top of their lungs. Harper and Cece jumped down from the stage to pull the guys up to us. Jack and Logan came a little more eagerly than the others. We pulled them up and started pulling their shirts off. Jack and Logan started doing their own little strip tease, for their wives, but I had eyes and could appreciate their bodies.

I was slightly disappointed at this point that I was the only woman without a sexy man to dance for, but then I turned to the door and saw Sean standing in the doorway. I was broken hearted, yes, but right now, I didn't want to feel a thing. I wanted to dance with a sexy man and feel something close to what the others were feeling.

I got off the stage and pulled him over with the other men. My eyes locked with his as I danced with him, letting my body say what I couldn't.

I FEEL stormy weather moving in
  About to begin
  With the thunder don't you lose your head
  Rip off the roof and stay in bed

ALL OF THE girls dropped to the floor of the stage as the men started gyrating their hips above us. The guys now had their shirts off and were dancing dirty for us. I fanned myself at the sight of Sean dancing above me, his muscles rippling and pulling as he moved. I had never wanted a man so much before. In fact, I think was the first time in my life I would have ever considered breaking my pledge to stay a virgin until I was married.

All The Single Ladies came on and all the girls jumped up and started doing their best Beyonce impression. The guys all stepped back down, putting their shirts back on, making all the women groan in disappointment. The guys headed over to the bar and I couldn't help but watch every move Sean made. I wanted that man and no matter how much he hurt me, I couldn't deny that he was the only one I wanted.

CHAPTER 18

VIRA

I felt like complete shit for what I did to Sean. I tried to play it off like I didn't want him as much as I thought, but it was a lie. He didn't push back this time and tell me he would keep chasing me, and it was probably for the best. The look on his face said that I had destroyed what we'd had.

I didn't know why I'd run. I could have easily stayed in bed with him and he probably would have calmed me if I had only told him what I was feeling, that it was too much. Sean was good at that, seeing through my bullshit. It was like he didn't care anymore. I was the boy that cried wolf one too many times and he was through with me.

I wanted to go back to Cece's and hang out with her, but Logan would be there and he was pissed at me. I didn't want to cause any tension between the two of them. I missed the days when it was just Cece and me. I knew that was selfish, but I desperately wanted my friend back.

I was out walking through town, trying to clear my head and I ended up walking past The Pub, our hangout. The music was pumping inside, which didn't normally happen. It was usually a pretty low key hangout. I looked in through the window to see what was going on and was surprised to find our whole group of friends in there. All the women were up on stage with the men dirty dancing above them.

Sean was there with *her*. I couldn't have been more insignificant if I tried. Obviously he didn't love me as much as he said or he wouldn't be dancing with the little priss like that. Then my eyes caught sight of Cece and my heart broke a little. She was there with all of them having a good time. My best friend in the world was hanging out with the other woman, having a good time while my heart was breaking. Granted, it was of my own doing, but friends were supposed to be there to support one another.

She hadn't even called me after I left her house earlier to find out how I was. She hadn't wanted to know how it went after I talked to Sean. I was feeling really low now. My only friend was becoming friends with the one person I could never live up to.

I walked away from The Pub, vowing that I wouldn't let this get me down. I just needed to find another man for the night. It had been too long since I'd been with anyone but Sean. Maybe that's what my problem was. I was blinded by lust. I headed toward the club feeling renewed. I would find another body to fill my bed tonight and I wouldn't let Sean or Cece bring me down ever again.

CHAPTER 19

SEAN

"How long has she been like this?" I asked Logan as I took a pull of my beer.

"When we came in, she was already a little tipsy. She just kept ordering, so we called the girls and told them to get over here. They just joined her instead of trying to get her to slow down. Fuck. It just spiraled out of control. Now we're all gonna be carrying their drunk asses home."

"You should have called me sooner."

"I don't think she would have liked that. Now she's too drunk to care."

"Should I cut her off?"

"Are you kidding me? Have you ever seen her let loose like this? Let her enjoy it," Logan said. "Besides, she's pretty funny when she's up there. You should have seen her earlier," He said with a laugh. "She was singing along to some girly song, and she's a pretty good singer, but she has the worst dance moves I've ever seen."

Damn. I wish I had seen that. Although, seeing her dance to Beyonce was pretty comical.

"So, who had the bar closed down?"

"We all did. When the girls started coming and joined her on stage, we knew this wasn't going to be something the public should see. Sarah talked to Hank about having us rent out the bar for the rest of the day."

"Let me know how much I owe you."

"Are you kidding me? If you hadn't fucked up, I wouldn't be watching a bunch of drunk women sing and dance on a bar stage. This is better than football."

Sam walked over with another round of drinks for the girls and they all eagerly grabbed them.

"This must be the first time in a while that one of them wasn't pregnant. At least they can all let loose," I said, thinking back since all the girls met.

"Well, maybe one of us will get lucky and get one of them pregnant tonight."

"Cheerio! Oi! Whatcha!"

"What the fuck? Is she using a British accent?" I asked.

"She got a dirty British slang book for Christmas."

"Before I get in a kerfuffle, I have enough marbles not to be miffed over what that tosser tried to take from me. While I'm taking the piss, I'm going to absobloodylootely enjoy myself before I fall arse-over-tit!"

Lillian laughed at her British accent and went to put more money in the jukebox.

"She's been doing this all night, but now she's added the accent," Logan laughed.

"And if you don't like it, you can piss off," she shouted.

Jolene by Dolly Parton came on and Lillian started singing along, surprisingly good for how drunk she was. The girls got down from the stage, leaving Lillian up there to belt out her song.

"You do realize that these songs are for you, right?" Harper said as she staggered up to me.

"What do you mean?"

"Hello? She's singing a song about a woman taking her man. All the songs are for you, and she's wasted enough that she doesn't care that you're witnessing this."

"I thought she was just having fun."

"Men are so dense sometimes. You're lucky she's not me or you'd be wearing a cup right now to protect the family jewels."

"Oi! Ladies, get your arses back up here!"

I walked over to the stage and grabbed Lillian's hand pulling her in closer to me. "Lil, maybe you should come down and have some water."

"Bugger off! I'm having a knees up with my mates!"

She pulled her hand free and went back to the mic. All the girls started singing along to what I thought was ABBA.

THERE'S NOT a soul out there
   No one to hear my prayer

GIMME GIMME GIMME a man after midnight
   Won't somebody help me chase the shadows away
   Gimme Gimme Gimme a man after midnight
   Take me through the darkness to the break of the day

THE GIRLS WERE all doing hip thrusts and moving in seductive ways. Lillian, however, looked spastic in her movements. I had to smile though, she looked like she was really having fun.

The day turned into night and the girls managed to get Lillian to drink some water, so hopefully she wouldn't feel too bad tomorrow. She had school though, and I was guessing she would have to call in sick.

Lillian slowly turned from happy drunk to sad drunk and it showed in her song choices. When she sang *The Winner Takes It All,* I figured it was close to time to leave.

. . .

THE WINNER TAKES it all
The loser standing small
Beside the victory
That's her destiny

I HATED SEEING Lillian like this. While it'd been fun to see her let loose and have fun, now she just looked defeated and I had done that to her.

I WAS in your arms
Thinking I belonged there

SHE DID BELONG with me and I had fucked it up. I would make this up to her somehow. I wouldn't let her run from me. I would have a hell of a time earning her trust, but I could take it. I would do whatever I could to earn the love of this good woman.

BUT TELL ME, does she kiss like I used to kiss you,
Does it feel the same when she calls your name
Somewhere deep inside you must know I miss you,
But what can I say, rules must be obeyed

"I REALLY HOPE you have a plan for getting her back. She's amazing and you'd be a fool to let Vira get between the two of you again," Logan said standing next to me. We were both mesmerized by Lillian. In fact, as I looked around, I saw all my friends watching her in awe. She really did have the most amazing voice.

"Vira and I are over."

"Yeah, I've heard that before."

"I'm serious. When she left this morning, it suddenly dawned on me how much of an idiot I had been. She was always using me, even if she didn't mean to. She doesn't know how to love someone."

"Dude, I could have told you that," he spat.

"Then why didn't you?"

"You needed to see it yourself. How could you not see how much better it was with Lillian? She's awesome."

"I see that now."

"Well, you'd better hope it's not too late."

IT WAS FINALLY morning and Lillian had been sleeping for a few hours. I spent the better part of the night holding her hair back as she sang to the porcelain god. She was so sick and was crying about never drinking again. She ended up sleeping on the bathroom floor because she was getting sick so often. When she made it an hour without being sick, I carried her into the bedroom and put her to bed.

Knowing that she wouldn't want me in her room with her, I laid down on the most uncomfortable couch in the world and closed my eyes. Since it was now seven in the morning, I was assuming the worst was over. I got up and called the school, letting them know that she had a nasty bug and wouldn't be in today and possibly tomorrow. When someone got as drunk as she did and wasn't used to drinking, it sometimes took a few days to recover.

I went to her kitchen and saw that she was pretty much out of groceries, so I left her a note that I had run to the store and would be back soon. I made sure to get enough groceries to fill her cabinets and fridge for the next week, but when I got back to her house, she was still passed out.

It was well after noon before she came stumbling out of her bedroom, moaning and holding her head.

"What did I do last night?"

"You pretty much drank all the wine at The Pub."

She screamed and then held her head when it obviously hurt. She moaned and then stumbled over to the couch.

"What the heck happened last night?"

"You don't remember?"

"I think I went to The Pub, but that's all I remember. What are you doing here?"

"Someone had to drive you home. You weren't exactly going to make it on your own."

"What did I drink?"

"White wine. A lot of white wine. I'm pretty sure they had to order more this morning."

"I'm so nauseous," she said as she leaned back into the cushions.

"Well, we can fix that. I'll go get you some water and some toast."

I went to the kitchen and gathered up a little for her, along with some pills for her head.

"Here. Eat this," I told her as I walked back into the living room. She picked up the toast and took a small bite.

"Okay, tell me what happened."

"I got a call from Logan that I needed to get down to The Pub. He said that you were a little tipsy when he got there and he called the girls to come hang out with you, but that turned into a dance party. When I got there, you were dancing with all the guys on stage, along with their wives. Then you pulled me on stage and had me dance with you."

She groaned. "Please tell me the only people in the bar were our friends."

"Yes, they were. Logan asked Sarah to rent out the bar for the night. It's a good thing he did because it wasn't exactly PG 13 in there."

She had a look of horror on her face. "Oh dear. Did I do something bad?"

I laughed at the look on her face. "Lil, you didn't do anything you would be too horrified about. I mean, you spoke in a British accent for the better part of the night and I really couldn't tell you what you were saying. Although I think you had a few choice words for Vira."

I was laughing at the memory, but Lillian just looked mortified. "Don't worry, Lil. I wouldn't let you do anything that would have embarrassed you."

She cleared her throat and swallowed thickly. "Did I..say anything in this British accent that could be classified as.."

"Dirty?"

"Yes."

"There was some definite swearing, but honestly, I didn't understand half of what you said."

She set her plate down and put her head in her hands. "Oh my gosh. I can't believe I let that happen."

"That wasn't even the best part. You were singing up on stage with the girls. You never told me you had such an amazing voice, although, maybe you should reconsider a dancing career."

"Stop. Oh my gosh. I can't believe I did that."

"We had to tempt all of you to leave with a trip to the ice cream shop and you climbed across my seat to order in your British accent. That was the best part of the night."

"Please. I think I've got the picture." Then she seemed to remember why she had gone drinking in the first place. "I think you need to leave. I think we said everything we needed to yesterday."

"I'm not leaving."

"I have to get ready for school."

"It's two o'clock in the afternoon. I already called in sick for you."

"That was so irresponsible of me," she groaned.

"Everyone has one day like that in their lives."

"Not me. I'm not that person. I don't go drink copious amounts of liquor-"

"Wine."

"Dance around on a stage-"

"I'm not sure that was dancing."

"Say horrible things about people in weird accents-"

"You were using slang. No one understood you anyways."

"Anyway. Adverbs can't be plural."

"See? A few hours of sleep and you're back to your old self."

"Sean. I really think you need to leave. Thank you for making sure I got home safe, but now I need to be alone. Nothing has changed from yesterday."

"Before I leave, I need to tell you something."

"I don't think I want to hear this."

"Well, too bad. I'm going to say it. What I did was absolutely horrible and there's not an hour of the day that I won't regret what I did to you. But it's done and over with. I can't change it and I can't take back the hurt I caused you. I know that I broke your trust and you probably think I'm some horn dog that can't keep it in his pants-"

She shot me a look that said my actions spoke louder than words.

"But you have to understand that I thought Vira and I had something real. I didn't just go out and fuck some random woman because I didn't get it from you. Vira knew that I was moving on and she used my feelings for her against me. After you left yesterday, she stopped by and I made it clear to her that I never wanted to see her again."

"You were so willing to throw us away yesterday. How did the sudden realization that Vira was using you make our relationship any more significant?"

"It didn't." Her shoulders slumped. "It just made me realize that what I had with Vira was never real. Everything we did was always a good time, a manipulation on her part. Everything you and I had was just you and me. We had conversations and got to know one another. You didn't hide anything from me. I know I don't deserve a second chance, but I'm still asking because I want to see what we could have had. I'm asking you to put your trust in me that I will never hurt you again, and I will work every day to make sure that trust is earned back. I will never see her again. I just want a chance. Please tell me I have a chance."

She was silent and seemed to be mulling over my declaration. I hoped that what I had said was enough, that I had made her realize how much I wanted her.

"If I give you another chance, there's something you need to know first."

"Okay." I was nervous. My palms were sweating while I sat here and wondered if I would get my chance.

"I've already told you that I wouldn't sleep with you."

"I'm not expecting-"

She held up her hand. "Please let me finish. There's a reason for that and you need to know before we take this any further. I don't believe in sex before marriage."

That dropped like a bomb in the room. It wasn't that I was upset by that revelation, more that I realized she had never had sex before. I had made multiple attempts to lure her into some kind of sexual embrace. I had dragged her out of a bar with the intention of taking her home and fucking her. I felt like such a shit.

"Oh my God." I grabbed my head in my hands and scrubbed my face.

"I figured that would be a turn off for you."

My head shot up. "No. I just can't believe how many times I tried to get you to sleep with me and I never really listened to what you were saying."

"Well, I just wanted you to know. I won't change my mind on this. It's something I feel very strongly about and I know it isn't everyone's way of thinking in this day and age. If you really want to give this a try, you have to be sure you're okay with this. I'm not suggesting that we're going to get married someday, I just don't want you to get your hopes up."

I nodded, not really allowing the information to really sink in. "I appreciate that."

"Look, this is a lot to take in for both of us and I really need some time to think about this and make sure I can move on from what happened. I don't want to give you false hope. Can you give me a few days to think this over?"

"Of course." I stood and made my way to the door in some sort of weird haze. I was just about to leave when it dawned on me that I hadn't said goodbye and it would appear I was running. I turned back to see she was lying on the couch with her eyes closed. I walked back and pressed a kiss to her forehead. Her eyes popped open and her lips parted.

"Make sure you drink plenty of water and keep eating or you won't feel better. Get some more sleep."

She nodded and I backed away, her beautiful eyes following me the whole time. On the drive home, I really let her words sink in. I had to decide if I wanted to move forward with a woman that wouldn't give me herself unless I married her. What if we weren't compatible in bed? On the other hand, no other man had had her and that was something that was very appealing to me. If things went well between us, some day she could be in my bed and I would be the only man to bring her pleasure. She would only ever have my cock. I would be the only man to touch her curvaceous body and hear her moans.

That wasn't the only thing that was appealing about Lillian. She made me feel good. She opened up to me and talked to me about real things. I didn't always agree with her, but she was always honest, which was something I was sorely lacking with previous partners. The fact that I just wanted to spend time with her to help her experience something new was probably the thing that clicked with me most.

Then and there I decided that whether or not Lillian and I ended up together in the future, Lillian was definitely a woman I would be willing to wait for.

CHAPTER 20

LILLIAN

I spent the rest of the day in a miserable state of nausea and confusion. My stomach wasn't settling and my conversation with Sean was playing on repeat in my head. I had already forgiven Sean for sleeping with Vira. We had made no commitments to one another, so technically he hadn't done anything wrong, or that's what I was telling myself.

The question that swirled through my head was if I could trust Sean again. I had already started to fall for him and I could see that we could have had something special. He made me feel alive and introduced me to the best friends a girl could ask for.

Around five o'clock, the doorbell rang and I reluctantly dragged my butt off the couch to answer it. I was shocked to see Harper and Alex standing on my doorstep.

"Sean told us that he had to leave, but asked us to stop by and check on you," Harper said as she shoved past me into the house. That was so sweet of him.

Harper and Alex carried a few handfuls of bags back to the kitchen and were unloading by the time I got there.

"We brought some food for you, but I see you already have a ton of food," she said as she went to put the food away.

"What? I hadn't gone shopping yet."

"Well, looks like Sean did it for you. So, tell us what's going on there. We didn't exactly get a chance to talk last night."

I sat down at the table and the girls joined me. I wasn't sure I wanted to talk about it with them. This was private and I didn't know them that well.

"Lillian, you don't have to worry about us saying anything to Sean. We just want to help." Alex had grabbed my hand and gave me a reassuring squeeze.

"Well, basically, Sean and I have been dating. I was supposed to meet him at his house yesterday morning and when I got there, Vira was walking out."

"That bitch!" Harper slammed a hand on the table as she stood.

"I thought you were friends?" I asked in confusion.

"Well, we're friends because of Cece, but she only comes to hang out when Cece's around and she's a lot of fun. That doesn't mean I'm okay with her hurting one of my friends."

"Don't worry about Sean. From what he's told me, he laid into her after what happened."

"Lillian, I was talking about you. I don't even know what happened yet. You're a good person and I don't like seeing a woman like her stalk in and hurt you."

I was a little shocked. While I had hoped I was making friends, I hadn't realized they would defend me against someone who was already a part of their group.

"So, did you go yell at Sean when you saw her leave?" Alex asked.

"Well, I was hoping I was wrong, so I sat in my car for a while and tried to be rational about the whole thing. I was hoping she had just stopped by. When I finally worked up the courage to go confront him, he answered the door half naked. That kind of answered my question. Still, I asked him about it, and he confirmed that he slept with her."

Alex's hand flew to her mouth. "I'm so sorry. I never would have thought Sean would do something like that."

"Oh, please. Don't be naive, Alex. Vira has had him wrapped around her finger for a year and a half. He was half in love with her and she kept dragging him along. I'm sure she said something to reel him back in again," Harper said.

"Something like that." I replayed my conversation with him in my head. The sadness when he realized how badly he screwed up. "The thing is, I believe that's exactly what happened. He said that when she snuck out in the morning, he realized that she was always using him. When I was at the door, he knew he had screwed up."

"I don't know that she was using him," Alex said. Harper glared at her. "What I mean is that I saw the way she looked at him. She did feel something for him. I think she just didn't want to. That's probably why Sean believed whatever she said. He could see it, too."

"Well, whatever happened, he was pissed when she walked out on him. He told her he loved her and she left."

"Ouch. So now you don't know if you want to give him another chance," Harper stated.

"Exactly. I don't believe he hurt me on purpose. I think she dug her nails into him and he couldn't resist. I just don't know if I can trust him again. I want to, but his behavior isn't anything I'm used to. Would you date someone that slept with another woman and tossed you aside?"

"When I was first dating Jack, he saw me talking with Luke, Anna's husband. We were at The Pub and he had just proposed to her. She was meeting us there and I was giving him a hug. Jack stalked over and called me a slut in front of the whole bar. I was mortified. We were apart for a while and honestly, I was miserable. It's not the same, but I understand where you're coming from. Jack and I were pretty new at the time, so I decided that I would give him a second chance. He apologized and promised never to hurt me again."

"Cole and I broke up because I couldn't remember him. I had

blocked out everything from the previous six months after I was attacked. I just couldn't deal with it. I kept pushing him away because he wanted to pick up where we left off and I wasn't ready for that. We were apart for months, but when I needed him, he was there for me."

"Okay, but those are your situations. That's not what Sean and I have."

"How do you know? When we were out together, he seemed to really like you," Harper said

"And yet he slept with another woman."

"Touche."

"I think you should give him another chance, but that's me," Alex said.

"Why?"

"Well, mostly because I don't think you should let Vira ruin what the two of you could have had. I think Sean genuinely wants to be with you and he made a mistake. Like you said, you two weren't committed. You move on with the understanding that you won't tolerate that behavior and he has one chance with you."

I thought about what Alex said and I had to admit, it made sense. A big part of me wanted to give him another chance.

"I think what we need is a girls night," Harper said as she stood. "We're not going to sit around here and make dinner. Let's go out to eat!"

"Ooh! I'll call the girls to meet us," Alex said.

Within a half hour, all the girls had found sitters for the kids and we were on our way to Maggie's Diner. When we walked in, I was shocked to see all the girls already sitting there, even Cece who was friends with Vira. I knew they were coming, but seeing all of them gather to cheer me up really shocked me.

"I figured that we needed to stay away from alcohol tonight," Harper said as we took our seats among the girls

"I'd appreciate that. I'm not even sure I'll be able to eat anything.

"Lillian, I want you to know that while I'm friends with Vira, I don't condone what she did. She's always been a little wild and she got me through some rough times, so it's hard for me to be too upset with her, but I don't like that she hurt you or Sean," Cece said as she sat down next to me.

"Thank you. I appreciate you saying that."

We ordered food and talked about anything and everything, except Sean. Maggie told us how she won Sebastian over after they broke up. My eyes widened with every detail of her story.

"So he let me throw the grenade out the window and I agreed to only work on research," she said with a shrug.

"You threw an actual grenade at a moving car?" I questioned.

"Yep. It was awesome! I still go to the shooting range with Sinner, but Sebastian doesn't like it. He wants me to stay all holed up at Reed Security, never seeing any action."

"You want to see action?" I asked again. This baffled me. How did one go from being a reporter to wanting to blow up cars?

"I wouldn't want to do it without Sebastian. We worked well together."

"Don't you miss being a reporter?" Harper asked. "I mean, I don't think I could give up writing for anything."

"Well, I still write the occasional story for a paper in Pittsburgh, but it's not my main focus anymore."

When we finished eating, we all headed outside to our cars when we heard voices coming from the alley. I glanced to see a man handing over a small baggie of something to the other man. The second man gave the first man something. I couldn't pull my eyes away from it.

"I bet that's a drug deal. It's been getting worse around town. Before I moved here, I was investigating Sean because of the missing drugs," Maggie whispered in my ear.

"Why Sean?"

"Well, he was always working a scene when drugs would go missing. I assumed it was him that was taking the drugs, but now that I know him, I know there's no way it was him."

"Maybe we could find out some information for him," Harper said from behind me.

"What do you mean?" I asked. "How could we find out anything?"

"We could pose as a bunch of girls wanting a good time. Maybe score some drugs and find out where he usually deals."

"Is that safe?" I asked.

"If we're all together, we should be fine."

"Let's do it!" Maggie said excitedly.

"Okay, but I don't think we should all go over there. I think a few of us should stay over here. Otherwise, we'll draw too much attention."

"What are we doing?" Anna asked.

"We're gonna go buy drugs from that drug dealer to try and help Sean on his case."

"Harper, Jack is gonna be so pissed."

"Only if he finds out."

"Really? You think there's a chance he won't find out about this?"

"Okay, so who's going over there?" Cece asked.

"I'm definitely going," Maggie said.

"I'm going too," Harper said, raising a hand.

"If anyone is going to help Sean, it's going to be me. Besides, these drugs are in the schools. I want to help if I can." I said with more confidence than I had.

"Fine. Cece, Anna, Alex, and Sarah will stay over here and pretend to be waiting on us to bring back the drugs. Harper, Lillian, and I will go over and play the ditzy girls looking for a good time," Maggie said excitedly.

"Well, you'd better get your asses over there quickly or he's gonna leave," Anna said. "Jack is gonna kick my ass for letting you do this." She held up a hand to Harper. "I know. No one *lets* you do anything."

Harper tugged on my hand and before I knew it, the three of us were approaching a drug dealer to buy drugs and obtain information from. What the hell had happened to my life?

"Hey. We're looking for a good time. Do you know where we might be able to find something to give us a lift?" Maggie asked.

The man, short and scrawny looked at us warily. "What kind of lift are you looking for?"

"We're willing to try anything."

The man looked at us suspiciously. "I have rules for new clients. You have to try out the merchandise in front of me."

"What?" I squeaked. Harper nudged me, letting me know I was not being cool.

"Sure. What do you have for us to try?"

"All I have on me is pot. Is it just the three of you?"

"No, my girls over there want some also."

"Call them over. Either you all try or I'm outta here. Payment up front."

"You got it!" Maggie pulled out a large roll of bills and handed it over. "You'd better have the good stuff or you won't have us as repeat customers."

Harper called the other girls over and soon we were all receiving our joints in a dirty alley next to the diner. This was such a bad idea. I had never even had a cigarette before.

"I'm not sure what to do. I've never done something like this before."

Maggie took a drag off her "doobie", as she called it. I watched in fascination and then repeated what she did. I started coughing immediately, wishing I hadn't gone along with this crazy scheme. After everyone had taken a hit, Maggie turned back to the dealer.

"So, where can we find you next time?"

"I'll give you my card." He pulled it out and handed it over. "If you ever bring the cops around, you'll be in deep shit, you understand?"

"Of course. We're just looking for a good time. Do you have anything else we can try next time?" Harper asked.

"What are you looking for?"

The dealer eyed me with suspicion, so I took another long drag off the doobie. Gosh, I was doing drugs in an alley with a drug dealer and a bunch of girls I had just met in the last month. What was becoming of me?

I blocked out the rest of the conversation as I tried to keep my feet under me. The ground didn't seem to be level anymore and my head felt really strange. The dealer came up to me, swirling in front of me in some weird pattern.

"Finish that off before you leave the alley. I don't want any traces coming back to me."

I took another drag as he stared me down, the effects really hitting me hard. I was so screwed. The distant sound of sirens made me whip around looking for lights. The dealer swore and ran down the alley. I wasn't sure if I could run if I tried, and frankly, I wasn't sure why he was running. What were we doing here anyway?

I looked at the girls and they were all laughing at each other, except for Alex. She seemed just as dazed as I felt.

"Oh my God! Let's go back in the diner and get some food. I'm so hungry!"

I wasn't sure who was talking. They all seemed to be saying things all at once.

"Police! Put your hands in the air!"

We all raised our hands, doobies held high for all to see.

"What the fuck? A bunch of women getting high in the alley. Call in backup."

"Oh my gosh! He's calling the police. We're going to jail and we'll have to wear those ugly, orange jumpsuits," I cried.

"Some woman named Bertha's gonna be my bitch," Harper said.

"I think it's the other way around. Isn't it that you're going to be a bitch for Bertha?" Maggie questioned.

"I told you this was a bad idea, Harper. Jack's gonna kick your ass," Anna said with a laugh.

"Harper? Harper Huntley? Hey, Calloway! Remember this broad? She's the one that attacked the guy with a poster!"

"Hey! I gave him a shit load of paper cuts! I bet he thought twice before breaking into someone else's house!"

The other police officer walked forward and got in Harper's face. "You're also the woman that attacked someone with a chicken."

"It was a turkey, jackass!"

"I'm going to jail, aren't I? Sean will never date me now. He won't want to be seen with a felon. I'll lose my job at the school!"

"Relax, you don't go to jail for smoking a joint," Cece said.

More sirens sounded and it wasn't long before I heard the voice I dreaded. Although seeing his face was a little different. I was still swaying and couldn't make out faces that well, but his voice was strong and steady.

"Lillian? What the hell is going on here?"

"These women were all smoking weed in the alley. They're under arrest for possession."

Before I knew what was happening, all of us were handcuffed and taken down to the police station. They put us all in a holding cell until the effects wore off. Alex and I sat on the floor holding each other's hands, while the other girls laughed and begged the officers to bring them some food.

"I am so going to hell. Why did I agree to go along with that plan? Sean wouldn't even look at me in the alley. He probably hates me. I'm a druggie now in his eyes!" I cried.

"Yep. A hardened criminal if I ever saw one," Harper laughed.

"Harper! What the fuck were you thinking?" Jack roared as he walked back to the holding area.

"Hey, Jack!"

"Don't 'hey, Jack' me. What were you thinking buying pot in an alley and then sticking around to smoke it?"

"I'm confused. Are you upset that I smoked pot or that I didn't go home to smoke it?"

"Both!" He roared.

"Relax, Jack. We were trying to help Sean."

I heard a groan and looked up to see Sean, Logan, Luke, Cole, Drew, and Sebastian all standing behind Jack looking equally pissed. Alex must have just noticed the men also because she jumped up and ran over to Cole.

"Cole! You have to get me out of here!" Cole's face went from furious to concerned." "I need food!"

"You're hungry?" He asked with a confused look.

"Ooh. That sounds good. Could I get some chips and salsa?" Maggie asked.

"Maybe some Doritos!" I staggered to my feet and walked eagerly toward the bars as if the food was already there waiting.

"I want a hot dog with everything on it," Cece piped up.

"You'll get your hot dog alright. You're just gonna have to wait until we get home," Logan said with a grin.

"Ladies! What are you thinking?" Anna asked.

"Finally, a voice of reason," Luke said.

"We need donuts!" she shouted.

We all cheered along her idea, Sarah stepping forward to speak to Sean. "You must have a lot of donuts around here."

"And why is that?" Sean asked as he crossed his arms over his chest.

"Well, duh. You're cops. Aren't donuts cop food?"

Maggie leaned forward against the bars, pulling Sebastian closer. "Baby, you're good friends with the chief. Can you please go get us some donuts?"

"And why would I do that?"

"Well, I've been a good girl."

"Freckles, how in the hell could you see this situation as being good?"

"I didn't bring my gun, so I couldn't shoot anyone. I didn't raid your stash and get any grenades, even though I now know how to use them. And when the drug dealer ran away, I didn't chase him down like I normally would have. I'd say all in all, I've been excellent tonight."

"Well, I guess you can't argue with that logic," Sebastian said shaking his head.

"Can we get back on point here? How on earth did you girls think you were helping me?"

"Ooh! I've got the answer to that one! Call on me!" I said, jumping up and down with my hand raised.

"Lil, we're not in school. You don't have to raise your hand."

"I was just making sure it was my turn to talk."

"By all means," he said as he gestured for me to continue.

"We overheard these guys doing a drug thingy in the alley and Harper thought we could help. Then she suggested we go over and pose as women looking for a good time and see if we could pull any information out of them."

"And did it work?" Sean asked.

"Um. I'm not sure. That dealer was staring me down and I got nervous. I think I smoked the whole joint, so I don't really know what happened."

"We got his card and he told us that he usually deals around the diner during the week," Harper said triumphantly.

"How did all of you get roped into this?" Drew asked.

"Well, he wanted us to try it first and so we called the girls over to join us," Maggie said. "We had to make it realistic."

"Freckles, do you ever just say to yourself, "Sebastian wouldn't like this. I should walk away."

"Hey, it's not like we're married or anything. I can still do whatever I want."

"Jack likes to think he can control me, too," Harper snickered.

"Logan tries, but he's the one that ends up tied up." Cece said casually as she examined her nails.

"Don't remind me," Sean groaned.

"I feel like I'm missing out on a lot of information here." I sat down on the bench next to Cece and rested my head against her shoulder.

"Don't worry, you have another few hours to tell each other stories while I sort out this mess."

Sean stalked away and the guys followed, grumbling about their women and how we all needed to be put on short leashes.

"Where are you going? Are you bringing us donuts?" Maggie shouted.

————————

AFTER GETTING a major scolding from the police chief, we were all released and sent home. He decided that while our actions were horrible, our intentions were well meaning and he dropped the charges based on the information we were able to obtain. Sean let me know on the way out that we really hadn't gotten them much of anything useful and the chief was really just being nice. He also suggested that I take tomorrow off of work and get my head on straight. I got the distinct impression that he was upset with me.

CHAPTER 21

SEAN

I walked into the station a few days later, only to be called right into the chief's office. He told me that Carlos Ramirez was ready to talk, but only to me.

From that moment on, my day was chaotic. Ramirez didn't have a smoking gun for us, but he did have supply routes, shipment dates, and the guy he reported to. We agreed to take him into protective custody with his continued cooperation. Sebastian agreed to let the department use his safe house on the outskirts of town since we didn't have our own. I was taking Ramirez over there to meet up with his security detail that was getting everything set up.

After grilling Carlos all day and getting paperwork in order for his protection, I was beat and wanted to get home, but I still had to drop him off and it was never as simple as a hand off.

I also hadn't dealt with any of the shit that had happened the other night with the girls. They could have gotten in some serious trouble. Lillian could have been fired from her job. Any of them could have been hurt if the dealer had gotten spooked. I still couldn't believe they did something so stupid.

I needed to cool down though before I went to see Lillian. That wasn't our only issue at the moment. We still hadn't discussed what was going on with us. I wanted to make things work with her, but I hadn't been able to find out where her head was. I wanted to give her space to think, so I hadn't contacted her over the past few days.

I pulled up to the safe house, noticing that the two men on duty for the night were inside and seemed to be setting up. One of them came to the door and headed down to meet us. I recognized him immediately. He was a few years younger than me and a damn good cop.

"Hey, Stevens. All good?"

"Yeah, it's been quiet so far."

He glanced around the yard, not seeing anything and walked toward the car.

I closed the car door and walked around to Ramirez's door, opening it after I scanned the area. Not seeing any threats, I allowed Ramirez to step out. Stevens took up a position on the other side of him and we headed for the house. Movement out of the corner of my eye had me drawing my weapon, but it was too late. Something hard smashed into my hand and then moments later, my ribs. The wind was knocked from my lungs as I bent over trying to suck in a breath. Pain spread through my side as I was hit multiple times until I fell to the ground.

My head lulled to the side as I verged on blacking out, but I forced myself to stay awake. Lying next to me on the ground was Stevens with a bloody face. It didn't look like he was conscious. I heard grunting and forced my head to turn. There were three men standing over Ramirez, each of them taking a turn beating him with bats. He would be dead soon if they didn't stop.

Gunshots fired from the front of the house and the men took off down the driveway. I looked around and saw my gun within in reached and grabbed it with my left hand. Sucking in a breath as best I could, I fired off several rounds. Two of the men dropped to the ground, but the third disappeared into the night. I had no idea if any of my bullets connected or if it was from the other officer. I couldn't hold my head up anymore as each breath I drew became more painful. I vaguely heard someone shouting and a face came into view, but I was fading fast.

I MANAGED to get a call in to Chief Jameson before I passed out for good in the back of the ambulance. When the paramedics arrived and started jostling me all around, I came to my senses enough to realize that I needed to let the chief know what happened and get officers to the hospital to stand watch outside Ramirez's room. That's if he made it.

I had been at the hospital for six hours now and I was getting pissed just lying around, waiting for X-rays. I already knew my ribs were at least cracked. I had heard them breaking with every swing of the bat. I didn't have the luxury of walking out, though. I was injured on the job and I had to follow procedures.

No one but the chief had been allowed into my room, though I suspected it wouldn't be long before Cara came back. She was my emergency contact, so I was sure she would be nagging the nurses to be let back very soon. No doubt she would have called Sebastian and informed him of what happened. Soon enough, all my friends would be here and that was the last thing I needed. I just wanted to go home and lick my wounds in peace.

The nurses had given me something for the pain, so I had been able to relax a little, but I asked her not to give the full dose because I didn't want to be completely out of it. Call me paranoid, but it was always a possibility that someone could come back to finish the job.

"Alright, Detective Donnelly. We're going to get you down for X-rays now." The nurse looked to be in her sixties, but wore her hair like she was already eighty. She had tight curls that looked like something my grandma used to get when she went to the salon.

"I can already tell you I have cracked ribs."

"Oh. Well, I'm so glad you were able to make that diagnosis for me. I'll just write you a prescription for pain medicine, how about the strongest I'm allowed, for the next two months and you can be on your way. Imagine if all my patients were as talented as you. I wouldn't even have a job."

She pursed her lips and gave me a stern look that said to shut up and do as she said.

"Fine."

"Fine what?"

"I'll shut up."

"You'll shut up what?"

I rolled my eyes as the woman treated me like an eight year old boy that had sassed his momma.

"I'll shut up and do as you say." She raised an eyebrow. "Ma'am."

"I'm so glad we could come to the same conclusion. Now, let's get you moved on down to x-ray."

An hour and a half later, I was back in my room with a diagnosis of three broken ribs and a broken hand. Luckily, none of my ribs had caused any further damage, so I was able to leave in the morning.

My hand was splinted soon after with strict instructions for aftercare and follow up appointments. I was just settling back into my bed when I heard commotion outside my room. As expected, Cara was yelling at the nurses and the police officer stationed outside.

"I'm his sister. You let me through right now or you'll be wearing your balls as a necklace."

I rolled my eyes at my sister's antics. She'd obviously been hanging around with the wives for too long. She pushed into the room and stopped in the doorway, her hand flying to her mouth. I prepared myself for the tears, but they didn't come.

"You asshole. What were you thinking?"

I quirked my eyebrow in confusion. "Um..what?"

"You are my only brother and you went and got yourself beaten. I thought you were a better officer than that."

"Cara, it's not like I asked for a fight. They snuck up on us."

"Right. My brother, the badass that doesn't let anything past him, found himself on the receiving end of a baseball bat."

"I love you, too, Cara."

"Don't you ever do that again. Do you have any idea what it's like to be called and told that your brother was injured on the job and is now in the hospital?" She shrieked.

"Gee, Cara. I would imagine it's not nearly as bad as finding out that your sister has been kidnapped and then was gone for ten days." I shouted as much as my ribs would allow.

I groaned when I finished my rant, knowing I shouldn't have done that. Cara rushed to my side and held my hand.

"I'm sorry. I didn't mean to yell at you. You just had me worried."

"I know, but I'm fine. Now I get to lay around the house all day and watch TV. Every man's dream, right?"

"Well, I wouldn't bank on laying around watching TV. There's a whole lobby full of people out there that are worried about you."

I sighed. "Yeah, I figured there would be. You can go out there and tell them I'm fine. I'll be going home in the morning, so tell them to leave."

"Even Lillian?"

"What?" I jolted up in the bed, instantly regretting the movement. "Why is she here?"

"I think the better question is why have you not introduced me to her? She's very nice. Not really the kind of woman you go for, but definitely an improvement from Vira."

"Can we not do this now?"

"What? You don't want to tell me about the perfectly nice woman that you started dating and then screwed over when Vira came back to you?"

"She told you that?" That didn't sound like Lillian.

"No, but the room full of women out there were very willing to fill me in on what's been happening with you recently."

"Can you ask Lillian to come back here? Tell everyone else to go the fuck home. They can come see me in a few days."

"Fine, but this conversation isn't through."

She leaned over and gave me a kiss on the cheek before leaving the room. I couldn't believe Lillian had shown up. I figured that she was still pissed at me. More than that, I didn't think any of my friends would think to call her.

The minutes ticked by and my eyes started to droop as I waited for Lillian to come back. It was taking forever and I was finding it harder and harder to force my eyes to stay open. Something soft touched my cheek and I willed my eyes open, not remembering where I was. Lillian's beautiful face was inches from mine, concern showing deeply in her eyes.

When her hand came up to cup my cheek, I turned my face into her hand, relishing in the comfort of having her so close.

"When Sebastian called me, I completely freaked out," she whispered softly.

"I'm fine. Just a few broken ribs and a broken hand. Nothing time won't heal."

My eyes continued to drift open and closed. I grabbed her hand in mine and held on tight. "About our situation-"

"Not now. We can talk about it later. You just need to rest and get better."

I nodded and finally let sleep take over. I hoped that she would be there in the morning. I hoped that she would say we could make this work, but I also knew I had a long way to go before she would give in to me.

"I AM NOT SITTING in a damn wheelchair. I can walk out of this hospital on my own and there's nothing you can say that will make me change my mind. Now move," I growled at the nurse.

"Sir, this is against hospital policy."

I was in a pissy mood. When I woke up, Lilian was gone and it was now almost noon and I had yet to hear from her. Maybe she had been a figment of my imagination. I was on painkillers last night, so it was very possible my mind had conjured her out of thin air.

"Listen, lady-"

"Sean! What are you doing?" Lillian stood outside the elevator looking horrified. She looked beautiful, wearing a fifties style dress in a deep blue that made her blue eyes even more vibrant. She rushed over to me and wrapped a hand around my upper arm. "Why are you not in a wheelchair?"

"I don't need a damn wheelchair. I can walk out of here on my own."

"Sean, please. Sit in the wheelchair. You scared me last night and I can't deal with anything happening to you. What if you collapsed?" Her voice caught and I noticed tears in her eyes. Damn. I couldn't stand to see her so upset.

"Get the damn wheelchair."

Lillian gave me a watery smile and then helped me into the wheelchair the nurse brought over. I sat down and was actually happy it was here. I wouldn't admit that to anyone, of course. Lillian bent over and gave me a kiss on the cheek, but when she stood, I saw she sent a wink over to the nurse. Goddamnit. I'd been played. Who knew Lillian had it in her?

She wheeled me to the elevator and then out to a vehicle that Sebastian was standing next to.

"I didn't think you had it in you, Lillian."

"It took hardly any effort at all."

"What are you talking about?" I questioned Lillian.

"Sebastian didn't think I could get you down here in a wheelchair."

"Well, I would have walked out of there if you hadn't started the waterworks," I said a little breathlessly. I stood and was surprised at how much effort it took. Even the few steps I'd taken had really taken its toll on me. I was relieved when Sebastian came over and took my arm. Every step was agony and that was most likely because I had refused any pain meds this morning. Getting into the SUV proved even more painful and I had to stop several times to take a few short breaths.

"Didn't take any pain meds, I see," Sebastian quirked an eyebrow at me. "We have to stop on the way to your house for your prescription, so you're gonna have to tough it out for a few more minutes."

I laid my head back against the seat and closed my eyes. Sweat had beaded on my forehead, but I didn't have the energy to wipe it away right now. Lillian had climbed in the backseat and her hand threaded through my left arm, momentarily squeezing before she sat back. Sebastian got in the driver's side and took off.

The drive was painful to say the least. I felt every bump in the road and holding myself so my right side didn't get bumped was exhausting. I kept my eyes closed to keep the nausea at bay. I was almost ready to ask Sebastian to drop me at home first, but then he pulled through the drive thru at the pharmacy, nixing that idea. When we finally pulled in the driveway, Sebastian turned to me with a grin.

"You can thank me anytime."

"For what?"

"The ride. I'm guessing it was long and painful. I really doubt you'll be going without your pain meds any time soon."

He got out and walked around the SUV while Lillian snickered in the back.

"Asshole," I muttered under my breath, causing Lillian to laugh harder.

When I finally got inside, I went right back to my bedroom, not wanting to be upright any longer than I had to. I was just getting comfortable on the bed when Lillian walked in with a bottle of water and my pills. There was a whole handful of them that I had to take for a while and I grudgingly swallowed them down. I laid back, ready to drift off.

"Hey, sleeping beauty. Before you drift off to lala land, your chief wanted me to let you know not to bother going in to work until you got the all clear from the doctor."

"Thanks." I couldn't give two shits at the moment.

"Thanks for the help, Sebastian. I'll take it from here."

"Do you need anything?"

"I'll need someone to stay with him for a little bit this afternoon so I can go home and get some things."

"Sure. I'll send someone over around dinner time with food."

"I appreciate it."

I opened my eyes and looked at Lillian. She was walking Sebastian out, but returned moments later.

"Why do you have to go get things?"

"Because I'm going to stay with you."

"You really don't have to do that."

"Well, if I don't take care of you, who's going to? I really don't think you want your sister here."

"I don't need anyone to take care of me. I'll be fine."

"Sure you will, but I would feel better knowing that someone is here to help. Besides, the more you're able to rest and not overdo it, the faster you'll heal. I'm guessing that by the end of the week, you'll be ready to get out of here."

"How are you going to be here when you have school?"

"I took off a week with my sick days. We'll see what happens after that."

"Lillian, I don't want you using up your sick days on me. Really. I'll be fine."

"I'm confused. Do you not want this time with me to convince me that we should be together?"

She was right. I was a dumbass. I was trying to convince her to leave when this was the perfect opportunity to patch things up between us.

"Does that mean you're willing to give me another chance?"

"That means I'm willing to hear you out."

"Any chance you'll dress up in a sexy nurse's outfit?"

THE FIRST FEW DAYS, I basically slept and did my exercises so I didn't catch pneumonia. The pain pills were taking it out of me and I hated that. I tried to get up and move around at least a little bit every day. By the fourth day, I made a point to hang out more in the living room so I wouldn't be a comatose lump in bed. I was missing out on all my good time with Lillian and I needed to find out where her head was before she left.

We were watching TV when I decided to broach the subject with her. I just didn't know how. I didn't want to just blurt it out, so I decided to sidle my way into it. When a commercial came on for cave exploring, it gave me my opening.

"You know, Laurel Caverns is pretty cool. I think it's only about an hour drive from here. We should go see it."

"Up for cave diving already?"

"Maybe in another month. I could take you down there for another adventure."

She looked back at the TV for another minute and I was afraid she was just going to ignore me, but then she turned back to me.

"How can you want me back? You just told Vira you loved her and now you suddenly want to be with me. I don't understand it."

"I thought I loved Vira, but when she walked out on me, I guess it finally hit me that what we had wasn't love. If I really loved her, I probably would have fought for her when she showed up on my doorstep later. Instead, I was just over it. Maybe I was more in love with the idea of being with her. I don't know. I guess I really didn't know her."

"If I give you another chance, that's all you get. I mean, obviously we won't always get along, but I won't tolerate what happened before."

"Understood."

"We would be exclusive."

"I agree."

"And you have to be patient with me."

"Always. I have a few stipulations of my own."

"Such as?"

"My grammar is not a reason for you to leave."

A slight smile touched her lips, but she straightened her face again, pursing her lips and reminding me of the woman I met that first day in the school. "Anything else?"

"I do the driving."

"When you get clearance from the doctor," she amended.

"Noted. And finally, I don't want to ever see you in the police station again for smoking weed, trying to help me out on a case." Her smile brightened the room. "As you have seen, this case is a little more dangerous than it appeared."

Her face shuddered and I instantly regretted saying that last part, but I needed her to understand that I wasn't okay with her putting herself in harm's way to help me.

"Is it always like this," she finally asked after a minute.

"Is what always like this?"

"Your job. Is it always this dangerous?"

"Well, this is the first time I've landed in the hospital, but I'm not going to lie to you. Every time I go to work, there's a risk that I might not come home. It's just something every officer has to accept."

She swallowed loudly and then cleared her throat. "I guess I just hadn't really thought about it until this happened."

I grabbed her hand. "Hey, it's not like this is an everyday occurrence."

"But it's still a risk. You could be shot any day you go into work."

I nodded. "Yeah, but it's my job and I love it. That's not something I'm going to change, not even for you."

It was a harsh thing to say, but I needed her to understand that I wouldn't be manipulated later on into giving up my job for her.

"Maybe that's something you need to think about before we take this any further. I want to be with you, but if you're not okay with my job, it's better if we don't take this any further. For both of us."

"I will, but maybe in the meantime, we can take things one day at a time."

"Sure."

We sat on the couch and held hands for the rest of the afternoon. I desperately wanted to pull her into my arms, but my body wouldn't allow it at the moment. When I went to bed that night, I desperately wanted to ask her to come sleep in my bed, but I knew she wouldn't be okay with that. She went off to her room and I went to mine. We felt even further apart now than when we got up this morning.

CHAPTER 22

VIRA

The last week had been absolute torture. I had spent almost every night in the arms of a different man, each one as unfulfilling as the one before. I tried everything I could think of to wipe Sean from my brain. He was taking up so much space in my head and I had never allowed that to happen before.

When Cece called me the other night and said that Sean was in the hospital, I wanted to run to him so badly. I wanted to be there to make sure he was alright, but Cece said it wasn't a good idea. The whole night I worried about him. I prayed to God that he was going to be okay. When Cece stopped by the next day and told me the extent of his injuries, I actually broke down in tears. Cece looked horrified, having never seen me so emotional before.

She held me while I cried and I told her how horribly I had screwed up. I told her about my relationship with my parents and how they basically ignored me growing up unless I could be useful to them. I told her about the man they wanted me to marry and how that had spurred me on to becoming someone else.

I couldn't blame any of my actions on that, though. I had become this person of my own making and no amount of daddy issues would change that. I knew what I wanted to do, but I wasn't sure if it was the right thing. I called Cece over in a state of panic, hoping that she could guide me through this.

"Cece! Thank God you're here." I pulled her into my arms for a big hug. She rubbed my back and then pulled back, studying my face.

"Vira, you know I'll always be here. What's going on?"

I pulled her over to the couch to sit with me. It was sad that I questioned the validity of her statement. "I'm going to get Sean back."

"Vira, that's not a good idea. You know I love you, but you hurt him and he's done with you."

"All of that shit that I spout all the time about not wanting a man in my life? It's all bullshit. I just didn't realize it until now. Sean was almost killed. The one man that made me feel again. He looked past my bullshit and owned me."

"But Vira, you didn't let him in. He told you he loved you and you threw it in his face when you walked out."

"Look, I know that I've been shitty to him. I'm not a hearts and flowers kind of girl and I never will be, but we could have something together. I need some time. I mean, it's not like I changed over night or something and I know myself well enough to know that I can't give him exactly what he wants, but in time, I may be able to."

Cece sighed and rubbed her forehead. "I know you want to believe that you guys can work this out, but I don't think you're the one he wants anymore. I'm sorry. I'm not saying this to hurt you. I just don't want to see you hurt anymore."

"But, he could forgive me. Everyone makes mistakes. Look at you and Logan. He looked past what you did and he married you."

"That's true, but you and I are very different people even if we looked the same for a while. I was never the girl that was made out to live the glamorous, partying lifestyle. Deep down, I was the same girl I was back before he broke my heart. I had a lot of fun with you over the years and you taught me so much about myself, but that was never really me."

I was a little offended by that. I had seen her through so much and I felt like now it was all being thrown in my face.

"So, you think I'm some party girl that doesn't deserve love?"

"That's not what I'm saying. You chose this life to get away from someone you didn't want to be. I chose it to try to escape feeling inadequate. There's nothing wrong with the way you live your life. It's fun and full of adventure and for a time, it was great for me. Sean isn't like that though, and you shouldn't give up the way you want to live for someone who will never appreciate who you are."

"You think I should walk away."

"I think if you go after him again, you're only going to hurt yourself. I'm not sure I can watch that. You're my best friend and I don't want to see you hurt, but Sean is also my friend. I'm asking you not to do something that will hurt both of you."

"I can't believe you're not with me on this."

"Vira-"

I stood up and started pacing the living room. Anger from years of being left behind poured through me. This wasn't fair.

"No. I was there for you with Logan. I was there to help you and now you've got what you want." I turned to her and pointed an accusing finger at her. "I saw you the other night with them. You were in The Pub with all of them hanging out, laughing with Lillian. After all we've been through, you chose them. For once in my life, I want someone to choose me! Is that too much to ask? I wanted my parents to choose me over money. I want Sean to choose me over Lillian. I want you to choose me over your new friends. Is that really too much to ask?"

"VIra, I'm not choosing anyone over you," Cece said as tears ran down her face.

"Then why are you asking me to leave Sean alone? Why do you spend more time with them than you do me? It's like you've got your new family and your old one no longer matters."

She walked over to me and wrapped me in a big hug. "I love you so much and you gave me everything when I needed you. I will always be grateful for that, but I can't sit by and watch you hurt your-self. When you realize that you and Sean aren't meant for each other, I will still be here for you."

She had pulled back and was holding my hand tightly in hers. I stepped back and crossed my arms over my chest.

"What I need is for someone to feel like I'm enough. It may be wrong to go after Sean, but I feel something with him. Hell, I prob-ably love him. I need to see if I can convince him that we could be good together."

"I think you need to start with *you* knowing that you're enough. I can't stop you from going to Sean. You've always done what you wanted. So if you need to tell him how much you want him, that's what you'll do."

She picked up her purse and walked out the door. I felt like I had just lost my best friend. I sat down on the couch and cried. I never cried, but Cece had always been the one person I could count on and she had just walked out of my life.

I KNEW this was a stupid idea. Sean had told me not to come see him ever again, yet here I was on his doorstep ready to knock on his door. I just wanted to make one final plea to him. I wanted one more chance to do the right thing, to say the right thing. If I didn't, I knew I would regret it the rest of my life.

Before I could lose my nerve, I knocked on his door and waited for the scowl that would be on his face when he opened the door and saw me. It took a few minutes, as I figured it would based on the injuries he had.

When he finally answered the door, he looked tired from the effort. His face was a little pale and his right arm was wrapped protectively in front of his waist. My throat closed up as the scowl I expected appeared.

"What do you want? I thought I told you I didn't want to see you ever again."

"You did, but I wasn't honest with you last time and I need to set the record straight before I lose my nerve."

He was taking shallow breaths and he looked like he was in pain.

"Look, can we talk inside? You look like you could keel over at any moment."

"Fine, but make it quick."

He walked over to the sofa and sat down slowly. I sat across from him, needing space from the anger that was radiating off him. I tried several times to start talking, but each time, my throat closed up.

"Vira, for fuck's sake. Just say what you have to say and leave."

"I love you," I blurted out, but once it was out, everything else flew out behind it. "I'm sorry I didn't tell you sooner. I don't think I was really sure about it until I heard about what happened to you. Then I started imagining you never being in my life again and it was like a knife to my chest. I couldn't breathe. I know that I may not be able to give you exactly what you want, but I'll work on it. I'll try every day to open up to you and show you how much I want to be with you. I know with a little patience, I could get there."

"Vira, what exactly are you asking for? You want to date me? You want to fuck me? What do you want?"

My hands got clammy at the thought of dating, of having a boyfriend, but I could do it. I swallowed down the nausea churning and continued.

"I'll take whatever you'll give me. I know that my version of love isn't what you're looking for, but I'm asking you to accept me for who I am. I'm asking you to love me for me. I know that I'm not exactly wife material, but I do love you and I will always do what I can to make you happy. So I guess I'm asking you to pick me."

Tears had filled my eyes as I poured my heart out to him, but this was my moment. My one chance to win him back was now and I had to put it all on the line for him.

"Pick me, Sean. Pick me."

I couldn't stop saying it. I just wanted one person to want me. I closed my eyes as I repeated it over and over in my head. I felt the air shift and then Sean was sitting on the ottoman in front of me.

"Vira, why now?"

"Because I can't lose you."

"You've said that before and then you walked out on me."

"I was scared. This is so new to me. God, my head is so fucked up. I'll tell you everything. I'll tell you why I left. I'll tell you why I'm this way. I'll tell you everything. Just tell me I'm not too late."

He lifted his left hand and brushed a tear from my face. "Part of me wishes I could, but I can't Vira. Our moment passed. You had so many opportunities to open up to me and you chose not to." He wasn't harsh, just matter of fact and that scared me more than anything because it sounded so final. "There was a time that I would have revelled in the fact that you wanted to tell me about yourself, but right now, none of it matters. I don't want to hear your story anymore. It won't change a thing at this point. I'm moving on with my life and I'm trying to build something with Lillian. I'm sorry, but you and I can't see each other anymore. It's not fair to Lillian and frankly, it doesn't make it any easier on me."

I wiped the tears from my face and looked to the side, trying to figure out what to do next. I came here and gave it my all and it wasn't good enough. I stood and headed for the door. Sean stayed seated on the ottoman.

"Vira." I turned back to see him looking at the ground. "Someday you'll meet someone that you want to talk to. It won't take you a year and a half to open up to him. It'll feel natural. You'll want to tell him your secrets and you'll want more with him. When you meet him, don't make the same mistakes you made with me. That's the man you were meant to be with."

He finally looked up at me and I could see in his eyes that we were truly over. There was nothing more to say. Telling him I loved him one last time would only make me seem pathetic. He'd told me that I was too late and he didn't want to hear anything more from me.

I walked to the door and stepped out into the sun. After sliding my sunglasses in place, I walked to my car with no regrets. I had taken a chance on love, but I was too late, and though it didn't work out, I was proud of myself for trying.

I had to find a new path in life. My job was unsatisfying, my friends were lacking, and I had lost the only man I ever loved. It was time to move on.

CHAPTER 23

LILLIAN

It was the last week of school and I only had to finish entering my students' grades for the semester. I was glad that the year was over. I loved to teach, but I was excited to get to spend more time with Sean. There wasn't a whole lot we could do, but I could talk to him and we could get to know each other better.

Sean was doing better after the first couple of days. He had exercises that he had to do regularly and they seemed to be helping, though he was still a long way from going back to work, which I was secretly happy about. We hadn't talked any more about being together or the fact that his job was dangerous. I really wasn't sure what to think about it. I didn't want to worry about him all the time when he was at work, but I knew I would if I stayed with him.

I headed to his house after school like I had been doing all week. Some of his friends stopped by during the day to check in on him and see if he needed anything. When I got done with school, I went to his house and spent the night in his guest room. He insisted that I didn't need to stay with him, but I was so worried that he would try to be macho and do something he wasn't supposed to. I needed to be sure he was okay.

"Sean," I called as I walked into the house. I didn't see him anywhere, so I started walking through looking for him. I found him in the laundry room hunched over a laundry basket and holding his side, taking shallow breaths.

"Are you okay?" I asked as I rushed to his side.

"Fine," he bit out through clenched teeth.

"You don't look fine. What did you do?"

"I was just doing laundry."

"You know that I would have done it for you."

"I'm perfectly capable of doing my own damn laundry."

"And that's why you're hunched over, barely able to breathe."

"I was lifting the basket and it pulled at my ribs. Just give me a minute and I'll be fine."

"Of course," I said, trying my best not to laugh. "Would you like me to take the laundry basket for you?"

He glared at me. "I told you I could do it."

I held up my hands and backed away. "Alright. I won't offer to help you again."

I went and sat in the living room for a good five minutes before I heard shuffling, like something was being dragged across the floor. Sean appeared in the living room moments later, slowly kicking the laundry basket into the living room. It had to hurt just as much to do that, but Sean was stubborn. When he finally got close to the couch, he gave up and sat down. He had sweat beaded on his forehead, which I thought was a little unusual considering the progress he had been making.

"Are you feeling okay?"

"Just peachy."

"Then why-" It hit me then that he looked the same way as when we left the hospital. "So you decided to stop taking the pain meds again."

"I was only taking half the dose anyway. I figured I could go without. They make me sleepy and I don't like that."

"Well, you're not supposed to like it. You're supposed to take them to help give your body time to heal. You know, it's not just about getting rest. When you take the pills, it allows you to move your body more freely, which helps stretch the muscles. It's all part of helping your body heal."

He grunted at me, but didn't say anything more. Lord, he was stubborn. I got up from the couch and headed toward the kitchen.

"So, what do you want for dinner?"

"I think you should go home."

I poked my head back into the living room, not having heard what he said. "What's that?"

"I think you should go home."

"Why would I go home?"

"Because I don't want you here anymore."

I wasn't sure what to say to that. I was trying to help him, so I wasn't sure why he wanted me gone. I thought he wanted me to be here so we could get to know each other.

"I'm confused. I thought you wanted me to stay. I thought I was helping you."

"Goddamnit. Why does there have to be some reason behind it? Isn't it good enough for me to say that I want to be left alone?"

"I just thought-"

"Well, that's the problem, don't you think? You thought. I never asked you to stay here with me. I never asked you to move in and take over my life."

My eyes filled with tears at the accusation in his voice. I felt like such a fool. I was trying to help him because I cared about him. I thought he wanted me back, but right now, he was doing everything he could to push me out of his life.

"Okay. I'll just make you some dinner and leave."

"I don't need you to make my fucking dinner," he roared. I could see it had hurt him to yell and like the nitwit I was, I felt bad that I had caused him to get so upset that he hurt himself. I quickly slunk off to my room, no, his guest room and quickly gathered my stuff. I willed myself to hold back the tears until I left. I didn't want him to see how badly he'd hurt me.

I grabbed my bag and headed for the front door, ignoring Sean sitting on the couch. He didn't try to stop me and he didn't look my way. I shut the door behind me and headed for my car. I didn't know where to go, but I knew I didn't want to be alone right now. I called a few people and finally Sarah answered. I begged to stop by and she must have sensed how upset I was because she insisted I head to her house right away.

When I arrived, Sarah was waiting for me on her porch. "What happened?"

I broke down in tears and let her hold me. She guided me inside and sat me down on the couch. "Sweetie, tell me what happened. Is Sean okay?"

I let out a sarcastic laugh. "Oh, he's perfectly fine."

Drew walked into the room holding a beer. "What's going on?"

"I don't know. Lillian's upset, though." I saw her signal for Drew to leave the room and then she turned back to me. "Tell me what happened."

"I really don't know. I went to Sean's house after school and he was in the laundry room trying to do laundry. I offered to help because it looked like it was hurting him, but he insisted he could do it. When he came back to the living room, it hit me that he had stopped taking his pain meds. He told me he didn't want to take them because they made him sleepy. Then I told him I was going to make dinner and he blew up at me."

"That's it?"

"Yeah. I don't get it. He told me that he didn't want me there anymore. That he didn't need my help, but he obviously does."

"That's so strange. Most men would give their left nut to have a woman waiting on them hand and foot."

"I know. I thought I was helping him. He even said that me staying with him would give him a good chance for us to get to know each other."

"So why would he push you away? I don't understand men sometimes."

"I don't know. Is Drew ever like this?"

"Not really. I mean, when I first met him, we didn't exactly get along, but he was still grieving for his wife. I don't think he intentionally pushed me away. I think it was more that he was at war with himself and didn't know what he wanted."

"See that's what I don't understand. Sean has been telling me all along that he wants me, that he wants this to work, so why all the sudden is he acting like he doesn't want me?"

"Oh for fuck's sake. Will you two just stop? It's not difficult to get if you just think about it for a minute," Drew said as he walked into the room with his beer.

"If it's so simple, then why don't you just tell us so we can stop guessing."

"Obviously, he's feeling emasculated. He's having to let his woman do everything for him. You said you walked in on him doing laundry and he had hurt himself?"

I nodded. "So he can't even do his own fucking laundry. Then you were going to make him dinner."

"Why is that so wrong? He likes my cooking."

Drew rolled his eyes. "Because you have to do it for him."

"So he's upset with me because I'm trying to do things that he can't do himself?"

Drew grunted in frustration. "He's not pissed at you, he's pissed at himself. Let's have a little history lesson here. Way back in the caveman days-"

"The Paleolithic Era," I interjected.

"Right. Anyway, back then, men were hunters and gatherers. Women prepared the food and took care of the home."

"I don't think they had actual homes back then, but I understand your point."

"Would you shut up and let me finish?"

"Drew!" Sarah admonished.

"I'm trying to make a point, not giving a history lesson."

"But you did in fact say that you were giving a history lesson," Sarah pointed out. "But please continue."

"Men need to feel useful. He probably didn't mind so much at first because he was in a lot of pain and it was nice to be taken care of, but as time went on, he just felt inadequate. I mean, come on. He has trouble doing his laundry. That and the fact that he's not working, he's probably feeling unproductive. Guys don't deal well with that, and the more time that goes by, the shittier he's going to feel about it."

"So what am I supposed to do about it?" I asked.

"Nothing," he said as he took a pull on his beer.

"Nothing? I'm just supposed to let him talk to me like that? To treat me like a pest?"

"Well, if you want to push him further away, by all means, go confront him."

"But I can't help him if I don't go see him. He needs someone to help him," I said in frustration.

"Look, leave him alone and he'll eventually figure out how good he had it. He's going to see how difficult it is to go it alone and he'll come crawling back to you. It may take a while, but it'll happen. If you go bug him, he's just gonna push you away until one of you says something you can't take back."

I looked at Sarah questioningly. "Do you think he's right?"

"Well, he has all the same functioning parts as Sean, so I guess he has more insight into his behavior than we do. I'd say listen to Drew on this one."

"Do you really think this is going to work, Drew?"

"Fuck, I'm not a psychologist. I can't say for sure that it'll work, but if it were me, I'd be doing the same thing at this point. No man wants to feel like he has to rely on his woman for everything."

"Why don't men just tell us this stuff instead of making us guess?" Sarah asked.

"Because, we expect you to just understand that we're simple people. We don't have deep emotions. We're pretty much black and white."

"I wouldn't agree with that, but you think what you want," Sarah said.

So I went home and did my best to not think about Sean for the next two weeks. I didn't call him or go see him. I didn't ask any of our friends about him. I didn't even drive past his house once. I was holding out pretty well, but it was killing my sleep. I worried about him every night when I laid in bed and often stayed up for hours just wondering how he was doing. He'd better get his head out of his butt soon or I was going to need sleeping pills.

CHAPTER 24

SEAN

"So, when's the last time you saw her?" Drew asked.

"Saw who?" I pretended to have no clue who he was talking about.

"You know who, asshole."

It was our poker night and since I wasn't cleared to drive yet, everyone came to my house. Part of me was relieved that I didn't have to go anywhere and the other part of me was pissed that I had to be catered to.

"About two weeks," I grumbled.

"So why the fuck haven't you called her?" Jack asked.

"Because I don't feel like it. When I want to talk to her again, I'll call her."

That wasn't true at all. I knew I'd been an asshole to her, but I just didn't have it in me to apologize yet.

"You're such an asshole. You had it good. Now look at you. You haven't shaved in two weeks and your face looks like Cole's ass," Logan said.

"Hey, I don't have a hairy ass, and if my ass looked like that, you can bet I'd be getting a wax."

"I don't shave because I don't want to. I've got no one to impress, so what's the point?"

"You don't have anyone to impress because you were a jackass," Drew retorted.

"How do you know it was me? Maybe she just got on my nerves. A man needs space sometimes."

"She came to my house you jackass. She couldn't figure out why you threw her out. She was crying. I had to sit there and listen to a woman, who wasn't my wife, crying over my friend because you were too much of an asshole to tell her that you were frustrated."

"Frustrated about what? You had a woman taking care of everything for you," Logan questioned.

"She was taking over the damn house. Her shit was all over my bathroom. She insisted on doing every last thing for me. I wasn't allowed to do my laundry or cook dinner," I exclaimed.

"Yeah, that sounds rough, man. I sure wish that my wife would let me do the cooking and laundry. Maybe I could get her to let me clean the house." Jack turned to me with a crazed look. "Said no man ever. What the fuck is wrong with you? Is it time to turn in your man card?"

"I just wanted some fucking space. She was here every day after school just taking care of everything."

"So, she left during the day, but came home at night to take care of your every need? Yeah, that sounds like a shitty deal," Logan replied.

"Fuck you. You guys don't get it."

"You think we don't get it? Do you remember coming over to my house and dragging me out of bed every day for two months? I couldn't take care of myself and I had to have other people force me to take a shower. I'm still fucked up, but guess what? You man up and get over it. She's trying to help you," Cole sneered at me.

"I don't want any fucking help. I can do shit on my own. I don't need a woman here to take care of me."

"Is that why your house is trashed? No food in the cabinets? Piles of laundry all over the place?" Sebastian asked.

I looked around my filthy house and grumbled. "Whatever. I'll get to it." I had stopped taking my pain pills completely a week ago, so I was drinking as much as possible tonight. I didn't need to hear about how sad my life was without Lillian and I didn't need the guys ragging on me because my house had turned to shit.

"Man, you have to call her. Beg and plead for her to come back. This place stinks," Sebastian grimaced.

"I can't call her and ask her to come back and clean for me."

Ryan rolled his eyes at me. "I don't even have a girlfriend and I know that you don't ask her to come back to clean your shit up. You call her and tell her you were a complete asshole. You tell her you were feeling shitty because she had to do everything for you and you took out your frustrations on her."

"Whoa. I don't get into all that mushy crap. I'm not a flowery guy. I don't share my feelings." I couldn't believe Ryan was even suggesting that.

"You may not, but that's what a woman expects to hear. So as much as it pains you to tell her what you're feeling, you do it so she'll come clean up your shit," Ryan said, as if it was the most obvious solution in the world.

"And you all agree with his assessment?" I asked everyone.

They all gave me looks like I was a dipshit. Jack shook his head at me. "Remember when I called Harper a slut in front of the whole bar? I had to say all kinds of shit I would never let any man hear me say just so I could get her back. And it was worth it. I couldn't imagine not having her in my life."

"I snapped at Sarah one night because she was taking up time that I wanted to myself. I was an asshole and I had to make it up to her. We weren't together yet, but I needed her to understand why I needed my time alone at night. I bared my soul to her that night, and it made it easier for both of us. I didn't have to keep explaining myself to her. Once she understood, she knew to give me my space."

"Cole? I'm assuming you had to at one point with Alex?"

"Fuck yeah. When Alex lost her memory, I was a complete dick to her a number of times. Grovel had become a permanent part of my vocabulary."

"Sebastian, come on. You and Maggie don't do this kind of shit, right? I mean, Maggie's so level headed."

"She is, but I'm not always. When Cal died, I blamed myself because I couldn't see the shooter out of my left eye. She pushed me until she knew why I was blaming myself and then made me realize what an idiot I was being. Sometimes, you've gotta bite the bullet."

"Logan?" I asked hopefully.

"Shit. Don't look at me. If you all remember, Cece was the one that screwed me over. The only groveling done was by her. But you, you should definitely consider getting down on both knees and begging for forgiveness. That woman is not one you want to let go of."

"It's just 'let go'."

"Let go of what?" Logan questioned.

"Your sentence should be, 'That woman is not one you want to let go'. Putting of at the end of the sentence is an unnecessary preposition."

"Okay, I stand corrected. She needs to go. Bring our Sean back and get rid of the Sean that corrects our grammar on poker night," Jack said.

I GROANED as I rolled over on the hard floor. Fuck, I must have fallen asleep here last night. I didn't remember much beyond my in depth conversation with the guys. After that, I decided it would be best to drink myself into oblivion. I finally peeled my eyes open to see six grown men lounging about my house in the most uncomfortable positions.

Jack and Drew were curled up on the floor next to each other and Jack had his arm slung around Drew's waist. Cole was passed out in his poker chair, head hanging to one side. Logan was sleeping in an armchair with his legs hanging over one arm. Then I looked at the couch and saw Ryan, the little fucker, taking up the whole damn couch, sleeping peacefully.

As my eyes adjusted, I noticed that there was something different about all of them. They had something sparkly on their faces. I looked closer at Ryan to see he had on eye shadow, blush, and lipstick. I started laughing, but then groaned when my head started pounding.

"I see you're finally awake."

I looked up to see Harper standing in the doorway to the kitchen. A big smile spread across her face and she started laughing. Then I heard more peels of laughter and saw the faces of all the other women. Soon the laughter was so loud that I thought I might throw a lamp at someone.

"What the fuck? I'm trying to sleep," Drew grumbled. I heard Sarah and Harper laugh even louder and then Drew fully woke up. "What the fuck! Jack, get the fuck off me."

Drew jumped up from the floor, flinging Jack's arm off him. "I was trying to sleep," Jack grumbled.

"You had your fucking arm around me!"

"Relax. It was the best sleep you've gotten in a while and you know it," Jack groused.

"Dude, why the hell are you wearing makeup?" Logan asked as he stretched in the armchair.

"Damn, my neck is killing me. I haven't slept like that since I was in the military," Cole said as he rubbed his neck.

I leaned over and smacked Ryan, jerking him awake. "Why the hell are you sleeping on my couch? I'm the one who's injured."

"I thought you didn't need any help with anything? Seems that you can sleep on the floor, too." He finally turned to me and shot me a dirty look. "What is all over your face?"

"What are you talking about?" I rubbed a hand over my face, coming away with a mix of pink and glittery shit. "What the hell?" I glanced around again and saw the women snickering by the kitchen. "What the fuck is this? Why are we all wearing makeup?"

The women burst out laughing as we all examined each other's faces. "Dude, pink is definitely not your color," Cole said to Jack. "Maybe you need more of a mauve."

"Harper, this has you written all over it. What did you do?" Jack asked.

"You called me last night completely wasted and told me that you were all having a sleepover. The girls and I decided to come over early this morning and see exactly how drunk you had all gotten. I brought the makeup just in case. Turns out it was a lot of fun to give you all a makeover. We all painted your nails different colors though. You know, to be distinctive," she smirked.

I looked down to see my nails were painted fire engine red. Red was a manly color, right?

"Purple? Really? I look like a hooker," Logan rumbled.

"Better than the sunny yellow I've got," Drew said as he examined his nails.

"I kind of like mine. I could pass as a goth kid," Ryan said as he held his hand out in front of his face to examine.

"Dude, Ryan." Drew shook his head. "No."

"Well, when you ladies are finished admiring our handiwork, you can come in for breakfast. I bought out the grocery store to feed you," Harper said.

"They let you in the grocery store?" Jack asked.

"Harper, I told you not to go in there again," I admonished.

"Don't worry. I wore a disguise. I dressed like Jackie O."

She flitted off to the kitchen and I shook my head at Jack.

"Shit. I'm supposed to be at the office at ten," Sebastian said as he jumped up. "How do I get this shit off? Freckles! Get this shit off me!"

"I'm sorry, Sebastian. Did you say something?"

"Freckles, don't mess with me. I'm meeting with all the teams this morning. I need this shit off me."

"There's a washcloth in the bathroom. That should take care of the makeup."

"What about the nail polish?"

"Oh, that's easy. You just need nail polish remover. I know I brought some." She looked through her bag and then snapped her fingers when she came up empty. "Darn it. I could have sworn I brought some with me. Oops."

"Freckles," Sebastian warned.

Maggie laughed. "Serves you right. Maybe next time you won't get wasted and stay out all night."

She laughed as she walked away into the kitchen. Sebastian turned to me with a look of panic. "Do you have any remover?"

"Me? Why the fuck would I have any?"

"This is all your fault. None of us would have gotten so drunk if you could just learn to communicate with your woman."

I laughed sharply at his reasoning. When I got up and headed into the kitchen, all the girls turned to look at me.

"Yes?" Sarah asked.

"Do any of you have nail polish remover?"

"Sorry. We didn't think to bring any," she said innocently. "Maybe it's about time you call Lillian and apologize to her."

I glared at her and then walked out to the living room. "Which one of you fuckers is giving me a ride to the store?"

An hour later, all of us except for Sebastian were sitting around wiping nail polish off our nails with the smelliest shit ever. Why women did this to themselves I would never know. It took me a half hour to find the shit in the store because I didn't want to ask anyone where it was. Then I grabbed ten bottles because I had no clue how much it would take to get it all off. Sebastian had to leave before we got back, so he ended up going to his meeting with the nail polish still on.

"When you ladies are done doing your nails, we need to get this place cleaned up. If Sean's going to win Lillian back, he can't be living in a shit hole," Cece said.

Logan flipped her the bird and went back to rubbing his nails. Cece narrowed her eyes.

"I saw that, Logan."

Something weird passed between them and I could swear the temperature in the room increased ten degrees. Cece turned and walked away, while Logan rubbed his hands together.

"Oh yeah. Tonight's going to be good."

"You two are fucked up, you know that?" Ryan asked.

By the afternoon, the house looked like normal again and the women all dragged their spouses home. They had all left their kids with family and had to get back. I sat down on my newly cleaned couch and stared at the empty house.

I had been absolutely miserable without Lillian the past two weeks. I'd known I fucked up, but I was too much of a chicken shit to do anything about it. That was about to change. I needed to get my shit together.

CHAPTER 25

LILLIAN

"You're sure this is going to work? It's been two days since you were over there and I haven't heard a word from him," I asked Harper. We were out for lunch because Agnes, Jack's mother, took the kids for a few hours. Since I was off of school, I was now free to go to lunch with friends in the middle of the day.

"Don't worry. We've got this all taken care of."

"Got what taken care of? I still don't know why you insisted I dress up like this."

Harper had asked me to wear a sexy but casual dress. Since I didn't do sexy, I wore a summer dress that was a sunny yellow with a boat neck. I wore my mother's pearls because they went with the dress and drop earrings. My hair was pulled back in a chignon.

"Okay, don't freak out, but I asked a friend of mine to meet us here. He's going to be your lunch date."

"My lunch date? I thought you and I were having lunch?"

"Well, I convinced Jack to bring Sean here for lunch today also. When Sean sees you with another man, he's going to totally flip."

"But I don't want that. We're in public."

"Don't worry. We're in public and Sean is a Detective. There's no way he'll make a big scene. We just want him to realize that if he doesn't man up, he'll lose you."

"Harper, I don't want to sound mean, but Jack was right. You're trouble and any plan you have is most likely going to blow up in my face."

She looked a little taken aback. "Well, I'm just going to pretend you didn't say that. You'll see. When Sean walks in here, the green eyed monster is going to come out."

"That's what I'm afraid of."

"Ooh! That's Jake now."

She waved her hand and I turned around to see a man that I could only describe as the hottest man I'd ever seen walking toward me. He had the looks of a GQ model, but the body of a demigod. I had to restrain myself from fanning my face and embarrassing myself. The man had inky black hair that was just long enough to run my fingers through. His unshaven face showed an angular jaw and a sharp nose that made him look like he had been sculpted by Michelangelo himself.

He had on a black suit with a grey shirt with the top two buttons undone and no tie. As he walked toward me, his swagger screamed that he was definitely a heartbreaker. When he reached the table, his smile about made me fall out of the chair and melt in a puddle on the floor.

"Harper, it's good to see you."

Harper stood and gave Jake a friendly hug. "It's good to see you too, Jake. This is my friend Lillian that I was telling you about."

"You were right. She's absolutely gorgeous."

Jake leaned in and brushed his lips over my outstretched hand. Tingles ran down my spine and I almost giggled in excitement.

"So, Sean should be walking in with Jack in the next half hour, so I'll leave you two to get to know one another." Harper turned to me with a smile. "Lillian, are you ready to put on a show for Sean?"

I was in a trance, staring at the beautiful specimen before me. "Ready for who?"

"Sean." Harper said insistently. "You know? The man you're trying to win back?"

"Oh, right. I'm sorry. I must have had a momentary..you know.." I cleared my throat as I tried to get out words. Yes, words. They seemed to be escaping me at the moment. "Anyway. What exactly am I supposed to do?"

"Flirt with Jake. Show him that you're ready to move on. It'll drive Sean wild," Harper said excitedly.

"You want me to flirt. With this man. Harper, you do see him, right? I can barely talk around him, let alone flirt with him."

Jake shot a sexy grin my way. There was no point hiding it. I had already made a fool of myself. "That's perfect. It'll drive him crazy that someone else has you tongue tied. I know if my woman was acting like that with another man, I would throw her over my shoulder and haul her out of the restaurant."

"This is such a bad idea."

"Okay, well I'm going to leave you two kids to get acquainted. I'll be at a table over there. Have fun!" She gave a flirty wave and headed for a table across the restaurant, leaving me alone with a man that made me almost as excited as Sean. If I had met him before Sean, it's very possible I would have wanted to date this man.

"Um..I'm not sure this is a good idea," I said nervously.

"Look, if this guy needs a wakeup call, this is definitely the way to do it. There's nothing that drives a man crazy like his woman with another man." He gave a charming smile and I found myself slightly more interested in continuing this rouse, if only to keep staring at his beautiful face.

"How do you know Harper?" I asked.

"I own the restaurant she used to work at."

"Oh. I just met her, so I didn't know she did anything other than write."

"And what is it you do?"

"I'm an English teacher at the high school."

"That sounds..like my worst nightmare."

I laughed at his honesty. "Well, it's not for everyone."

We continued to chat while I nervously played with my water glass. The waiter had brought over two glasses of wine that Harper had sent over. I was glad for something to ease my nerves.

I saw Sean approach the restaurant and my pulse skyrocketed just from his presence. His jaw was covered in at least two days' scruff. He had on a simple t-shirt that stretched his muscled arms and a pair of blue jeans. He looked much better since the last time I'd seen him and I momentarily wondered if maybe it was because I was no longer around.

I quickly averted my gaze and started playing nervously with the stem of my wine glass. Jake reached across the table and swiped his thumb over my hand as he squeezed it.

"Hey, relax. Just follow my lead. It's showtime."

I thought he would pull back, but instead he leaned across the table and held my hand tighter.

"You really are the most beautiful woman I've ever seen."

I blushed from his compliment and tried to reign in the smile that was breaking free, but there was no stopping it. Sean had been the only man to look at me the way Jake was.

"What the fuck is this?" Sean's booming voice cut through the air. Startled, I looked up to see Sean stalking toward me with murder in his eyes. Jack was following closely behind trying to hold back laughter. Did I mention this was not a good idea?

"Sean, I..I didn't know you'd be here." I tried to sound convincing, but it sounded rehearsed even to my ears. I rolled my eyes at my poor acting, but Sean didn't seem to notice. His eyes were focused on my fingers entwined with Jake's.

"Lillian, do you know this guy?"

"Umm.." I looked at Jake and tried to decipher what I was supposed to say. They told me to play along, but honestly, they should have given me a script. I had no clue how to play this. "This is Sean. He's my.." I glanced at Sean's angry face. "My ex-boyfriend.

Or..maybe my almost boyfriend that slept with another woman, so we never really had a chance for it to become more?"

I hadn't meant to say that last part, but I got the feeling it was the right thing to say because Sean's fists started clenching tighter and tighter.

"Sounds like a jackass to me. Good thing I met you. Now you don't have to waste your time with douchebags who can't see what's right in front of their face."

I wanted to roll my eyes again. That was the worst line I'd ever heard. Talk about being obvious.

"Lillian, I think we need to talk." Sean held his hand out toward me and I tried to pull my hand from Jake's, but he held tight and shook his head minutely.

"I don't think that's a good idea, Sean. We had time to talk, but you didn't want to."

"Lillian, I'm not going to ask you again. Get your ass up. We need to talk."

"Hey, asshole. I don't know what century you live in, but that's no way to talk to a lady," a woman at the next table said as she stood and glared at Sean.

"Stay out of this," Sean sneered.

"I don't think I will. You need to learn some manners. No wonder she left you."

My heart was pounding in my chest. This was escalating and would turn out so bad if I didn't put a stop to it. I started to stand and that's when I noticed Jake was too. He took a step in Sean's direction and got in his face.

"Look, friend. The lady doesn't want to talk to you, so walk away."

I looked at Jack for help, but he was no longer there. I glanced around and saw that he was now over with Harper and they appeared to be in some kind of argument. I looked back at Sean just as he gripped Jake by the collar of the shirt and pulled him right up to him.

"You ever try to get between me and my woman again, you won't like the consequences."

"Remove your hands from me. Now." Jake was seething and I stood there wringing my hands, thinking this was getting way out of control. I had no idea what Harper thought would happen, but I was pretty sure this wasn't it.

"Sean, I think you need to leave. You're causing a scene," I said, a little scared of what was going to happen.

"I'm not going without you," he growled as he stared down Jake.

"Too bad. Lillian, this has gone on long enough. I'm not letting you leave with this asshole. You really aren't a man if you need to order your woman around," he smirked at Sean.

Before I knew what was happening, Sean reared back and punched Jake across the jaw. Jake stumbled back a step, but then righted himself and ran forward, ramming himself into Sean's stomach. I cringed, knowing that had to have really hurt Sean. The two of them went flying across the table of the woman that had stood up for me. The little, old woman at the table started beating both men with her handbag.

Sean flipped Jake off him and rolled off the table holding his side. Jake got up quickly and threw a punch at Sean, who just barely avoided the hit. I had to do something. I was sure Sean would have a major setback if he kept this up. Jake was going after him and landed a few punches that I was sure Sean would have been able to avoid if he were one hundred percent. I glanced over to see Harper and Jack still fighting.

Not knowing what else to do, I picked up the bottle of ketchup on the table, popped the top and started squirting it at the men. They continued to fight, despite now being covered in the condiment. When I ran out of ketchup, I picked up the mustard, but this time I aimed for their faces.

"What the fuck?" Sean said as he swiped at his face. Jake took the opportunity to get one last punch in.

"What is wrong with you two? You're not acting like grown men, but children fighting over a toy!"

At that point, the manager made her way over with a stern expression. "This is a restaurant, not a gymnasium. Now, you need to leave before I call the police!"

Sean walked over to her and handed her his card. "Please send me the bill. I'll pay for the damages."

She pursed her lips, but took the card and nodded. He turned back to me and stared at me a moment, his eyes cold and unfeeling. Then he turned and stalked out of the restaurant, leaving me wondering what exactly Harper thought would happen. Sean had looked at me like I had betrayed him. Jake looked back at me and shrugged, then waved to Harper and headed for the door.

"I definitely did not expect that to happen," Harper said as she walked up behind me and took in the wreckage. Jack now stood behind her and looked pissed.

"I told you it was a bad idea. Obviously you don't understand from our time together how possessive men can be."

I rubbed my forehead and walked over to the table, grabbing my purse. "I'm going home. I want Sean back and I want him to apologize, but this was too much. I'm not the kind of person that plays with someone's emotions."

I stepped over the broken glass and headed for the door. I'd had enough for one day.

I WAS MENTALLY exhausted after my afternoon. I wanted to kill Harper for putting me in that situation this afternoon, but I was even more upset with myself for going along with it. I was not that person. I was honest with people and I didn't play games. Part of me had wanted to go to Sean after I left the restaurant, but I wasn't sure that was a good idea. I needed to apologize for my part in what happened at the restaurant, but I still needed Sean to come to me on his own and tell me that he wanted me back.

It was only five o'clock at night, but I was feeling tired and just wanted to be in my nightgown with a glass of wine. I had just poured myself a glass when I heard a knock on my door. I quickly grabbed a robe and headed for the front door.

I was shocked to see Sean standing there. He was leaning against the doorframe and looked a little worse for wear. I crossed my arms over my chest and did my best to look angry, even though I wanted to pull him into my house and give him a hug. I had missed Sean so much over the past two weeks and that was really hitting me hard right now.

"Can I come in?"

I thought about making a snarky comment, but good manners took over and I stepped back, allowing him to enter. He walked further into the living room and I motioned for him to sit down. I took a chance and sat next to him.

"It's a little early for bedtime, isn't it?"

"Today took it out of me. I just wanted to be comfortable."

"I'm sorry about earlier. I never should have reacted like that. After kicking you out and not calling for two weeks, I didn't really have any right to say whether or not you should be out with another guy."

"I wasn't."

"Lillian, you were sitting at a table with a man who was holding your hand."

"I was supposed to be having lunch with Harper, but she blind-sided me with a date to make you jealous."

"Huh." He rubbed a hand over his jaw and shook his head. "I guess I should have seen that coming when Jack dragged me out of the house and insisted we go to that restaurant."

"I should have stopped it the moment Harper suggested it."

"Why didn't you?" He asked curiously.

"I guess I wanted to know if it would work. I wanted to know if I was worth fighting for."

"How could you think your aren't?"

I shrugged. "We were pretty new when everything fell apart. Then, you kicked me out and didn't speak to me for two weeks."

"Still.."

"Sean, I don't have a lot of experience with men. I know that I leave a lot to be desired-"

Sean's hand flew to the back of my neck and he pulled me in closer. "Don't you ever talk that way about yourself. You are perfect. I like that you don't have a lot of experience with men. It gives me the chance to make you mine. I know that I've screwed up a lot, and I don't deserve yet another chance, but I really hope you'll give it to me because the man that wins your heart is going to be the luckiest bastard on the face of the earth."

"Sean.." My heart stuttered in my chest at his words. I never thought any man would make me feel like Sean had. It had been a rough road so far, but I thought if we could just get past all this, things could be really good.

"Please, the next time you need space, just talk to me. I don't understand a thing about men and I don't read body language that well. You're going to have to spell stuff out for me."

"I can do that. I'm sorry I didn't talk to you. I was stuck in my head, pissed that I couldn't do anything. The more you wanted to help, the more pissed I became that I couldn't help myself. I never should have taken it out on you. Believe me, the guys tore me a new asshole over the way I treated you. Can we start over?"

I smiled at his frankness. I wasn't used to people being quite so crass around me, but since I met his friends, I just learned to roll with the punches.

"I don't want to start over. I want to learn from our mistakes and move forward."

"As long as you realize there will probably be many more mistakes for me to learn from."

He pulled me forward, sealing his lips over mine in an earth shattering kiss. There was no gentle anymore. He had shown me that he would respect my wishes, but now he was showing me that he desired me. We made out on the couch the rest of the night. My lips were swollen by the time he left and my heart was in danger of being completely stolen by this man.

CHAPTER 26

SEAN

"Sir, I'm not sure I follow. What exactly do you want me to do?" The woman behind the counter at the spa looked at me in confusion.

"I want you to pretend that my girlfriend won a free spa day. It's for her birthday."

"We don't just hand out free spa days for someone's birthday. That's not the way this works."

I sighed in frustration. "I'm not asking you to give her a free spa day. I only want you to pretend you are. I'll buy a gift card and then you can pretend she won."

"I'm confused. Why don't you just give it to her as a birthday present?"

"Because her birthday was last week. It'll make her feel like she's won something wonderful. It's exciting when that kind of stuff happens."

"Won't you just look like an ass for forgetting her birthday?" she questioned.

"We weren't together last week." She pursed her lips at me. "We had a fight and broke up. Now we're back together and I want to make her feel extra special. So, I would like to buy a gift card from you for her spa day. Then, I'd like to send her something in the mail that specifies a day that she can come in for a free spa day because she's won a free spa day. Meanwhile, I'll be getting a big party together for her for when her spa day is done."

"That seems awfully complicated."

"Can you just do it for me?"

"Let me talk to my manager about this."

I growled in frustration. How difficult could this be? I wanted to surprise her and make her feel extra special for the day. The manager walked out a few minutes later and I explained what I wanted again. She smiled and started clicking on the keys.

"Okay, what day would you like to have her here?"

"How about next Saturday?"

"Of course. What package would you like?"

"Give me the ultimate package. I want her to be pampered the whole day."

"Alright. I'll just need a credit card and we'll finish getting everything set up."

"Perfect. Can I also have you write up a letter for her stating that she won a free spa day and the details of it?"

"Sure, I'll even mail it for you. This is so romantic. I would love it if someone went to all this trouble to make me feel special for one day."

I turned and glared at the other woman that had tried and failed to help me. She looked a little ashamed, but said nothing. When I finished, I headed back home to finish up my plans for the rest of her party.

―――――――

I was close to being cleared to get back to work, but I still had a few therapy appointments to go to and I had to pass the field test. My final doctor's appointment was in a week, so hopefully I could be back to work within two weeks.

I spent every minute of the last week with Lillian. We spent as much time as we could going on walks and exploring nearby parks. I could tell that I was still dragging a little, so I pushed her to go on longer hikes every day. She thought I was pushing it too hard, but if I didn't, there was no way I'd be ready for the physical and field test.

It was five days until her party and she hadn't said anything yet about going to the spa. I was getting a little worried that the lady had forgotten to send the card. I was on my way over to her house, so I'd have to do some snooping when I got there.

Originally, the plan had been to have the party at my place, but I changed my mind when she told me she had been wanting to paint her living room and kitchen. Her going to the spa would be the perfect way to get her out of the house. I called all our friends and roped them into coming over to help paint while she was at the spa. With all of us working, it would be done in no time. It took a lot of persuading, but I finally got her to pick out paint colors, and I would pick them up later this week.

When she opened the door, a bright smile filled her face. She pulled me inside, practically bouncing off the walls. "Guess what I got in the mail today?"

"I don't know. What?" Thank God I didn't have to snoop.

"I got a free spa day. Apparently I won some contest, but I don't remember entering."

Shit. I hadn't thought out how she won the contest. "Huh. Well, when's the spa day?"

"It's this Saturday. Good thing I don't have anything going, right? I mean, what kind of business gives you something for free, but then demands you use it on a certain day?"

She shook her head, but her smile remained. Inside I was grumbling that she was complaining over something that I put so much thought into, but then I had to kick myself because she didn't know I had done it. I was such an idiot. I should have just given her the gift card.

"Anyway, it's really exciting. I've never been to a spa before, so this'll be fun!"

I sighed in relief that she was excited about my present. Now I just hoped that everything else went off without a hitch.

———

I WALKED into the chief's office at the end of the week, hoping he would shed some light on the case. He had been unwilling to talk to me up to this point because he knew I would want to get involved. I was through with that shit, though. I needed answers. I had given my account of what happened, but when I asked what happened after- ward, all that was said was that Officer Stevens was in the hospital with some facial injuries, but he would recover. Nothing had been said about Carlos Ramirez or the other officer that had been at the scene.

I knocked and waited for the chief to let me in, but I already knew he was available. I had made sure before I came down.

"Chief."

"Donnelly. It's good to see you doing better. Sit down."

I took a seat across from him and watched as he watched me shrewdly, looking for any sign of continued injury.

"How are the ribs?"

"Good. My last doctors appointment is tomorrow. I should get the all clear. I've been feeling pretty good."

"Still taking pain pills?"

"Not since my third week home. I hated the way they made me feel."

He nodded. "Well, that's good. As soon as you get the all clear, you can take the field test again. I guess we'll see you back in here next week. That's if you're cleared with the psychologist, of course."

"Of course."

He went to stand but I stopped him. "Chief. I need answers." He sighed and sat back down. "What's going on with Ramirez?"

"We put out a statement that he was killed, then we had him transferred to a different hospital. He was in pretty bad shape. Just got released a few weeks ago. He's in protective custody now."

"What's the plan for him?"

"We still need him. We think he could still be useful to us. I think we could use him against Sawyer and Calloway."

"To set a trap."

The chief nodded. "What about the assailants? Are they all dead?"

"You killed one. The other officer on scene killed the other. The third got away and Ramirez couldn't identify him."

My thoughts immediately went to Lillian and a conversation we had had when we first met. Would she think of me as a killer now? Would she think I was going to hell because I had killed a man? My second kill. Most officers didn't have a need to pull their weapons in a small town like this. I had already discharged mine several times.

"Donnelly."

I hadn't heard the chief talking until he practically shouted at me. "Yeah, sorry. Lost in thought."

He eyed me warily. "I'll set up that appointment with the psychologist for you. I'll call you with the details."

He turned to his phone, dismissing me in the process. I left his office questioning for the first time if what I had done was wrong. I knew that it was what I had to do because it saved my life and the lives of others. More than that, it was my job. Still, Lillian's voice was in my head and I had to know what she thought.

I headed over to her house, not wanting to wait another minute before I talked to her. When I pulled up, she was just leaving her house.

"Sean. What are you doing here?"

"I need to talk to you. Can we go inside?"

"Sure. Is everything okay?"

"Yeah," I said distractedly as we walked inside. I began pacing her living room, trying to find the right words. I wasn't sure what I needed to hear from her and that was part of the problem.

"Sean, whatever it is, you can talk to me."

I stopped and turned to her. "I killed a man. The night that I was attacked, I killed a man."

"Okay," she said hesitantly.

"And you don't believe in killing others, even if the kill is righteous. This is the second man I've killed in the line of duty. There could be more before I retire, and I never really worried about it all that much. The first man deserved everything he got. The night I was attacked, I was defending myself and others. In my mind, there was absolutely nothing wrong with what I did."

She didn't say anything, but continued to stare at me curiously. I watched her, wanting to ask her, but not sure I would like the answer. Her beliefs were strong and so different from mine.

"What do you need to ask me, Sean?"

"You believe that killing is a sin and that you'll go to hell for those sins."

"If you don't repent."

"The whole point of asking for forgiveness is to atone for sins that you've committed and pray for the strength to not repeat those sins."

She nodded again.

"But I can't do that. I can't ask for forgiveness for something I may very well go out and do again the next day."

"I understand what you're saying. What I don't understand is what you're asking me."

I took a deep breath and ran my hand over my mouth. "I need to know if you think what I've done is wrong. What I may do in the future. I need to know if you stand by me and the decisions I make. Because I can't be out there doing my job and then questioning whether or not I'll lose you if I have to make a tough decision. It'll fuck with my head and likely get me killed. I need to know that you're behind me one hundred percent."

She stood and walked over to me, placing a hand on my chest. "What you do out there is dangerous, and I know that you have to make tough decisions. I know that you're not a murderer and it's not easy for you to take a life, but you do it without thought when necessary because you are a protector. My beliefs should never enter your thoughts when you're out there-"

"But they will," I interrupted.

"I don't want you to think about anything other than doing what is necessary to come home to me. I don't believe that you'll go to hell for killing someone that is trying to kill you. What I meant before was that I didn't think I would be able to because of what it would do to my soul. I think it would eat at me and I'm not sure asking for forgiveness would ever make me feel clean again."

"I don't want you to ever look at me like I'm a monster. I don't think I could handle that."

"Sean, I think you made peace with your decisions a long time ago. Don't let my beliefs influence what you believe is true. I will stand by you and support you whatever your decisions because I know you're a good man."

I took her in my arms and crushed her to me. I needed to hear that more than anything else. As long as I had her by my side, I could do anything.

It was the day of Lillian's party and I had gone to her house early with a bag of groceries. When she answered the door, she looked confused, but I told her I was planning a nice meal for when she got back. She was so thrilled that she didn't even question me further. After she left, I hauled in the rest of the groceries and the painting supplies, then called the guys over.

When Harper showed up, I gave Jack a stern look. "Why did you bring her? You know this doesn't bode well for us."

"Relax. We're painting. The girls can do the trim work."

"The girls? What the hell? I said for the guys to come." I gripped my head and looked at the ceiling, praying that I could find a way out of this. "Shit. This is going to be so bad."

"Hey. Calm down. It'll all be okay."

Two hours later, we were almost done with the living room. Cece, Sarah, and Maggie were taping the kitchen while Anna, Harper, and Alex worked on the trim in the living room. There were way too many of us trying to work around each other.

"Harper, how many times do I have to tell you to be careful? You keep dripping all over the place," Jack scolded.

"So what? That's what the plastic is for."

"I'm stepping in paint. Just be more careful," he said in irritation.

"Luke, what are you doing? You're getting paint on the top of the trim," Anna asked with her hands on her hips.

"You can't see it anyway. What does it matter?" Luke said.

"I'll know it's there and when Lillian goes to hang the curtains, she'll see it. It'll drive her nuts!" Anna responded.

"She's not gonna care. She'll be so grateful it's painted that she'll overlook it."

Anna glared at Luke with wide eyes. "Really? Have you ever met Lillian? Everything has a proper place with her and she's not going to like it. No woman would like it. She'll always know it's there and every time she looks at that window, she's going to notice that there's something not quite right about it."

"Fine, woman. I'll fix it."

I'd had enough of the constant bickering and needed to get out of there.

"I'm gonna go clean up these brushes so we can start on the kitchen."

I walked outside and over to the side of the house to the spigot. This wasn't what I had planned when I asked for help. There were too many of us and the women were all arguing with us over every single detail. There's nothing a man could ever do that would be right in a woman's eyes.

When I finished washing out the brushes, I walked back inside and grabbed the next color of paint. After I popped the lid, I brought it over to a clean pan.

"Wait! Don't step there!" Harper shouted.

I looked down to see a giant puddle of paint that my foot was hovering above. I took a step back, sighing in relief that I hadn't just stepped in that.

"Sorry. I was going to clean it up. I just got preoccupied."

I took a step to the right just as Drew backed up from where he was working. I took a step back to avoid colliding with him and stepped right in the puddle of paint. I tried to catch myself, but I was sliding backwards too quickly and couldn't hold myself up. The paint can flew up and out of my hands.

Paint fell over me as the can catapulted through the air. I watched in slow motion as it headed toward Lillian's couch.

"Oh, shit!" I shouted, just as the paint can landed on the middle cushion. Paint flew out of the can and splashed the back and seat cushions. I fell to my ass, splashing in the paint and no doubt ruining my clothes.

I glanced up and saw Harper and Anna covering their mouths in horror. The guys looked like they were trying to keep from laughing.

I sneered at Jack. "Trouble. I told you this was trouble."

I got up and glanced back at my ass that was now covered in yellow paint. My hands and most of my face also had paint on them, and now Lillian's couch too.

Taking a deep breath, I glared at Harper. "You're done for the day. No more touching paint. No more taping. In fact, I don't even want you in the house. You and I are going to the furniture store because now I have to buy her a new couch before she gets home in four hours."

"Um..you have to change first. You have paint all over you."

"Really? I hadn't noticed."

I thought Harper was going to cry for a second, but then she burst into a fit of giggles. Soon, every woman in the house was laughing at me covered in paint. I shook my head and went out to my truck where I always kept spare clothes. After showering, Harper and I headed for the furniture store.

After paying extra for delivery in two hours and carry away, Lillian had a new living room set, complete with a sofa, two armchairs, two side tables, and a coffee table. The delivery truck had just left and I still had to finish clean up in the kitchen and start the grill for the food. We hadn't decorated a thing.

"She'll be happy with the place being painted and new furniture. You don't have to decorate the place, too," Logan said.

"I wanted this to be perfect. This day is going to crap."

"It'll be fine. We'll finish cleaning up. Why don't you go get the grill started and the girls can start making the girly food."

I nodded and got to work getting the grill out and the outdoor furniture set out. Since it was still the beginning of summer, Lillian hadn't gotten any of her summer stuff out yet. I got it all wiped down and ready for her party. When I went back inside, the girls had hung my decorations I had bought and the place looked fantastic.

"Hurry! She's home early," Sarah said as she ran into the kitchen. We all hustled into the opening to the kitchen so she would see us as soon as she opened the door. I heard her walk up to the door and prayed that this was a good surprise and she wouldn't be pissed about the furniture.

She opened the door and before we could say a word, she said, "Who moved my furniture?" Then she looked at us and gasped in surprise.

"Happy belated birthday!" we shouted.

"Oh my gosh. It's just-"

"I know, babe. We gotcha!" I said excitedly.

"I was going to say, it's just that happy belated birthday isn't grammatically correct," Lillian said. Her dainty fingers pinched together in front of her as she bobbed her head side to side.

"Why not?" I asked.

"Well, my birthday isn't belated, the greeting is. So, really it should be a belated happy birthday to you," she said with a satisfied smile.

I looked at everyone staring at her with bewildered expressions. "Happy birthday," we all shouted.

Lillian's smiled at us all and then looked back at the room. "Oh my gosh. You painted the living room for me. It looks wonderful!" She walked around the room admiring it and glancing questioningly at the furniture.

"Um, why do I have new furniture?"

"Harper, you want to take this one?" I asked.

"Okay, don't be mad, but I spilled some paint-"

"On my couch?" she shrieked.

"He did it!" Harper pointed quickly at me.

"Only because I slipped in paint she spilled on the plastic. I swear it was an accident, Lil."

"The poor guy feels terrible about it, Lillian. Don't be too hard on him. He was covered in paint from head to toe," Cole said.

"Did you at least take pictures?" Lillian asked.

I smiled in relief that she wasn't upset. The rest of the party went well. We grilled out and spent the rest of the night hanging out outside. If you forgot about the paint incident, the day turned out pretty well.

CHAPTER 27

VIRA

I was almost packed. I had decided that I needed to get away from here. This was no longer home to me. I had lost Sean, and Cece wouldn't be far behind. She had a new life that just didn't fit in with mine anymore. It wasn't her fault. She was right. This was never her lifestyle. She'd always been the one that was more level headed and was really looking for someone to fill the void. She hadn't known it, but the moment she ran into Logan a year and a half ago, I'd seen it in her eyes. I knew she belonged with him. Maybe that's why I suggested revenge. Maybe if she pushed him away, he wouldn't take her from me.

I hated my job and had no family close by, so it was an easy decision to move on. I was thinking of moving to California where it was warmer and I could lounge on the beach in my off time. I had plenty of money saved up, so I could take my time finding a job.

A knock at the door had me putting down the last of my dishes and walking over to answer. I was expecting it to be Cece since she was really the only one speaking to me, but I was completely taken aback by the man standing at my door.

Richard Arrington III stood in front of me with a smirk on his face. This was the man my parents wanted me to marry all those years ago. I hadn't heard from them or him since I left, so why was he here now?

"Anna Belle, it's lovely to see you again."

"I don't go by that name anymore."

"I know. What kind of name is Vira anyway? A classy woman like you should never have chosen such a vulgar name." He looked me over with a look of disgust. "I see your taste in clothes and hairstyles has changed quite a bit also. Luckily, that can be easily fixed."

"I'm not changing a single thing about the way I look. I happen to like it."

"You're dressed like a slut."

"That's because I am a slut. I bet you could walk outside and meet at least ten men I've slept with."

"Regardless of your sexual history, I still need you to come with me. I've got a deal that I need to close and the only way that's going to happen is if I marry you. It would seem your parents have finally had enough of your games and would like you back home."

"Well, you can tell them to fuck off. The only way I'll be seeing them is if I'm standing at their graves, which probably wouldn't happen."

He pushed inside and wrapped his hand around my neck, thrusting me up against the wall. He was cutting off my air supply, making it impossible to think clearly.

"Listen here, you little bitch. I need this deal to go through and I'll go to any lengths to get it. If your parents want us to marry, I'll make it happen."

Spots were dancing in front of my eyes and I was starting to worry he wouldn't release me before I passed out . When air filled my lungs suddenly, I started coughing and gagging. My throat hurt from the pressure he had applied.

"Does the name Sarah Matthews ring any bells?"

I shook my head, not knowing or understanding where he was going with this.

"Of course, when she moved here, she would have been known as Sarah Anderson."

I looked at him in confusion. "What do you want with her?"

"She has some very rich, very dangerous people looking for her. The things they want to do to her.." He made a tsk noise. "Mobsters can be very brutal when someone destroys one of their own. Imagine the things they would do to her and her little babies if they ever got their hands on her."

I swallowed down the bile that was threatening to come up. No matter how much I wanted to get away from this psycho, there was no way I could let him hurt Sarah and her kids.

"I'll do whatever you want, but don't tell anyone what you know."

"That's a good girl. I see you're already packed, so I'll be back tomorrow morning to collect you. Good night, Anna Belle."

He brushed his hand over my cheek before opening the door and walking out. I ran to the bathroom and vomited what little was in my stomach. There was no way I could go with him and live my life with him. The things he had done to other women back when I was a teenager were horrendous. I couldn't imagine what had happened in the meantime. But if I left him, I would put Sarah in danger. I had no idea exactly what she was running from, but I couldn't be the one that hurt her.

I ran to the window and looked outside. When I didn't see anyone outside, I ran and got my purse and headed for the door. There was only one person I could think of that could help me right now.

I HAD BEEN POUNDING on the door for what felt like five minutes, but in actuality had only been twenty seconds. The door flung open and Sean appeared in front of me in jeans and a t-shirt. At least I hadn't pulled him out of bed.

"What?" he scowled. I didn't care. I pushed past him into his house, seeing Lillian walk out of the kitchen. I didn't care. Right now I had bigger problems than whether or not they were together.

"Why are you crying?" Lillian asked in concern. I hadn't realized I was. I reached up and touched my face, my fingers coming away wet. "Oh my God! What happened to your neck?"

Lillian was by my side in an instant examining my swollen neck. Moments later, Sean was beside me also.

"What the fuck happened? Who did this?"

"Sean, I need help. I know that I don't deserve it, but I need you to help me. He knows about her. I don't know how and I'm not even sure exactly what she's hiding, but he said he could make a phone call and she would be gone. He threatened her kids! You have to do something."

I was talking so fast that Sean couldn't have asked a question if he wanted. Tears were pouring down my cheeks again as I remembered what he had said. It felt so hopeless and I wasn't even sure if there was a way out of this.

"Vira, slow down. Who is he? And who does he know about?"

"Richard Arrington. My parents wanted me to marry him when I was younger. He's a horrible person. I ran away and he's never come for me, but now he wants me to go back with him so that he can make some deal happen with my parents. He brought up Sarah. He said that people were after-"

Sean silenced me with a hand.

"Don't say anymore. Just sit here with Lillian and keep your mouth shut. I have a phone call to make."

Sean walked away and I heard him say Sebastian's name and then there was some mumbling about Sarah, but I couldn't really understand any of it. The silence between Lillian and I wasn't uncomfortable. I didn't really care about anything that had happened at this point. I just wanted to get away from this guy and move away from here. Somewhere he couldn't find me again.

"Lillian. I have to go. I want you to stay here and set the alarm. I don't know how long I'll be," Sean said urgently.

"Okay. Is everything alright?"

"I don't know. I have some stuff to work out with Sebastian. Just promise me you won't go anywhere."

"I promise," she said. Sean leaned in and kissed her before turning to me.

"Come on. Sebastian needs to see you."

I nodded and followed him to the door. We drove in silence to Reed Security. When we got there, we had to identify ourselves at the gate. Then we were met in the garage by a man so devastatingly handsome, he immediately made my panties wet. He rode up in the elevator with us and showed us to a room that was filled with computer screens.

"Vira, what exactly did this man say to you?"

There were no pleasantries from Sebastian, which led me to believe that this was very serious and not just Richard trying to force my hand. I closed my eyes trying to remember.

"He said that he wanted me to go back with him and that we were going to get married. He has some deal that he needs to go through and he needs my parents. Us marrying was their condition. He said he would do anything to make it happen. Then he asked me if I knew a Sarah Matthews, but said I would know her as Sarah Anderson."

Sebastian exchanged a worried look with Sean. "What? I don't understand what's going on."

"Was there anything else?" Sebastian asked.

"Yes. He said something about very dangerous people looking for her and that mobsters didn't like when someone hurt one of their own. He asked if I could imagine all the things they could do to her and her kids."

"And how did you respond?" Sebastian questioned.

"I told him not to say a thing and that I would go with him. He's supposed to be coming back in the morning for me."

"Becky!"

A short, skinny woman with black glasses came into the room a few seconds later. "Yeah, Cap?"

"I need you to find out everything you can about.."

Sebastian's gaze cut to mine. "Richard Arrington III."

He nodded. "Everything you can find out. We need something we can use as leverage. Get Rob to help you on this. You have anyone on the team at your disposal. We have until sunrise to get something on him."

I started fidgeting because I was nervous. This all seemed very unreal. This was not supposed to be my life.

"Vira, you stay here tonight. We'll figure this out."

"You'd better figure this out, Sebastian. You know if she runs, my sister runs with her," Sean said angrily.

Sebastian nodded in understanding. "We'll take care of it. I promise."

"I've got to get back to Lillian." Sean turned to me with a look I couldn't decipher. "Thank you for coming to me."

Then he turned and left. I stood in the massive room surrounded by screens and a few people milling about, but I had never felt so alone.

The man that had met us in the garage came and sat down by me a few minutes later. He held out a bottle of water to me that I gratefully took.

"My name's Mark, but everyone calls me Sinner."

At any other time, I would have flirted with this man, but right now I just felt sad. My life was like a really bad soap opera.

"Vira."

"You don't have to worry. Sebastian's very good. Everyone here is."

"That's great, but none of this is for me. They're all worried about Sarah. Sean's worried about his sister. I'm just the person that brought the information."

He glanced down at my neck, his eyes boring into the fingerprints that were forming in bruises. He reached out and brushed his fingers lightly over the bruises.

"If they find something incriminating about this guy, you're free and clear."

I huffed. "I'm an afterthought. Sure, I'm free if they find something. If they don't, I go home with a monster that will probably kill me within five years."

"We won't let that happen."

I looked deep in his eyes and saw the sincerity there. I smiled slightly at him. "I think it's admirable that you think so, but the alternative is that Sarah and her kids are in danger. It might be one thing if it was just her, but he threatened her kids. I could never let that happen."

"Have faith, Vira. It's not always as bleak as it seems."

"I think God is the last person I should turn to for help right now."

"Don't turn to God. Turn to us. We won't let you down. I promise you that everyone here is just as concerned about what happens to you as Sarah and Cara. There's not a man here that would willingly let you go with a monster. Everyone here will defend you and protect you. That's just what we do."

He said it so easily that I was inclined to believe him. There was nothing I wanted more than to believe that someone cared enough to not allow me to fall into the hands of an evil person. He pulled me into his body, allowing me to be comforted by his warmth. It was nice to feel protected and for the moment I would take it, come what may.

"Boss! Boss! I've got it!" Becky came running into the room, waving around some papers. I had been sleeping on Sinner's shoulder, but was jolted awake when she ran in the room. I wiped the sleep from my eyes and listened intently to what she had to say.

Sebastian stormed over to her and snatched the papers from her hands. Looking it over, a grin split his face before he wrapped Becky in a big hug and twirled her around.

"Becky, you outdid yourself this time. Alright. Get this all put on backup drives and store it in the necessary locations. Cazzo! You're with me on this. Let's go."

"Wait! Where are you going?" I asked Sebastian.

"We're going to meet Arrington. We have something on him that will ensure he never comes looking for you again."

"I want to go with. I mean, I don't want to talk to him, but I need to see that he walks away."

"Fine. Sinner, you're on detail. Let's go. We don't have much time to get over there," Sebastian barked out.

Minutes later, we were down in the garage loading into vehicles. I was hoping that this would all be over in a matter of an hour or two, but my gut was telling me it wasn't that easy. Nothing had ever been that easy.

We waited outside my apartment building for about twenty minutes before Richard's town car pulled up. He stepped out and headed for the building entrance, but Sebastian and the man he called Cazzo got out and met him at the door. I cracked the window so I could hear the conversation.

"Richard Arrington III?" Sebastian asked, though he knew it was him.

"Yes. What can I do for you?"

"I have something you need to see." Sebastian handed over a manilla envelope which Richard took and opened. He scanned the pages and then visibly paled.

"Where did you get this?"

"I have my resources. Just know, there's more where that came from."

"What do you want from me?"

"You leave and never return. You don't speak to Vira ever again, try to come near her, or even go to the same town she's in. If she goes on vacation and you happen to be in the same place, you leave. You

forget that you ever heard the name Sarah Anderson or anyone asso-
ciated with her. If you ever so much as whisper her name or Vira's
this information goes to them, and I don't think you want that to
happen."

Richard shook his head.

"I have copies in secure locations, so don't think that you'll ever
get around this. Just remember, these people wouldn't be as nice as I
would and give you a bullet to the head."

I had never heard Sebastian like this before. His voice was lethal
and it made me very glad that he was on my side. Richard took the
envelope and quickly headed back to his town car. After he had gone,
Sebastian and Cazzo walked back to the SUV and got in. Sebastian
turned in his seat to talk to me.

"It's over. You don't have to worry about anything anymore. We'll
play it safe for the time being and have someone stay with you in case
Richard decides he's stupid."

I shook my head. "I'm not staying. I was going to move to
California."

He looked shocked by this. "Sean didn't say anything. Does he
know you're leaving?"

"No. I haven't told anyone."

"Not even Cece? You know she's going to be pissed at you."

"I'll give her a call. I just need to start over."

Sebastian nodded. "Sinner will stay with you and make sure you
get to California. Then he'll stay until he's sure you're safe."

"Thank you, Sebastian."

There was nothing more I felt I could say. He no doubt knew
about everything that had happened and wouldn't be on my side. It
was best to just move on. I stepped out of the SUV with Sinner
following behind me and we headed up to my apartment.

Hours later, I was just about finished with my packing when
there was a knock at the door. Sinner waved me into the bedroom and
walked to the door. After checking, he called out to me.

"Vira, you have a guest."

Cece was standing at the door with murder in her eyes.

"Bitch, what do you think you're doing?"

"I'm moving on."

"And you weren't going to tell me?"

"Cece, you have a new life here. I just don't fit in anywhere anymore."

"This is not the Vira I know. She was kickass and didn't take any crap from anyone."

"I'm still that person, just slightly worse for wear at the moment."

"Look, I understand if you want to find someplace else. I understand the need to run away from it all, but you talk to me. I understand exactly what you're going through."

"I know you do. I just didn't want any big goodbye's."

"No, you just assumed that I wouldn't care enough anymore. You think that because I'm married now with kids that I don't value our friendship anymore."

I didn't say anything because part of me really did feel that way.

"You don't get to just walk away. You're my best friend and no amount of mistakes could make me not want you in my life."

She pulled me in for a hug that lasted way too long. We both cried for a good fifteen minutes while Sinner stood around uncomfortably.

After many promises to call when I got settled and her promising to come visit, she finally left and I helped Sinner load up the boxes into the truck that Sebastian had sent over. A few of the guys from Reed Security came over to help load up the remaining boxes and the furniture. Sinner and I would be taking a road trip across the country and I was looking forward to the fresh start.

I looked around the apartment that I had called home for the past ten years. There were so many memories here that I hated to leave. Most of them revolved around Cece and Sean. There was no way I could stay here where so much of my heart was. I shut off the light and walked down the stairs for the last time. It was time to start over. Maybe I'd even get a different kick ass name to go with my new life.

CHAPTER 28

LILLIAN

Sean had been back to work for a few weeks now, which left my days pretty open. I spent a lot of time around the house reading and lounging on my new living room furniture. I had to thank Harper for causing the mess because my furniture was so comfortable.

I was feeling slightly bored now that Sean was no longer around to spend my days with, so I decided this morning to make lunch to take to the station later. When I walked in, several of the officers walked over and said hello. I had been to visit Sean several times at the police station and he had introduced me to some of his coworkers. I now knew that the men started salivating as soon as they smelled my cooking, so I made sure to bring enough food for the men that would be working during the day.

"Hey, Lillian. What did you bring us today?" Officer Wheeling, the officer that had been shot when we were on our wild car chase with Carlos Ramirez, asked.

"I brought Italian beef. I figured I needed to bring something to counteract the donuts."

"Here. Let me take that from you," Chief Jameson said as he

came running out of his office. He reached for the crock pot and practically yanked it out of my hands. One of the other officers grabbed the bag of hoagies I had picked up at the store. I did a head count and figured that if they didn't go overboard, I should have enough to feed everyone.

"There's a jar of spicy pickles for Officer Oster," I shouted to the man that had grabbed the bag.

"How many times do I have to tell you to call me Bull?" Officer Tate Oster walked up and gave me a big hug. "Thank you for thinking of me, sweetie."

"Well, I didn't want you to be left out."

"Sean, you've got one special lady here," Bull said as Sean walked toward me.

"Yeah, well don't try anything. She's all mine." Sean wrapped his arm around me and pulled me in for a scorching kiss. I blushed when the men all started whooping and hollering.

"Do you want to come over for dinner tonight?" I asked, trying to draw the attention away from him kissing me.

"I can't tonight. I have to get some hours in at the training facility."

"Oh." I smiled to hide my disappointment. I had gotten so used to spending time with Sean that it was hard when he had a case to work or had paperwork to finish up.

"If you want, you can come see if you can keep up with me."

"You want me to come train with you? Is that allowed?"

"Sure," the chief said as he walked up to us. You keep bringing us lunches like that and I'll let you go train with Donnelly as much as you want.

"Oh, I don't want any special favors."

"Nonsense. This isn't an official training session, so it's fine," the chief assured me with a smile.

"I didn't even know you had a training facility."

"Sebastian built one for his company and he rents it out to emergency services departments," Sean said.

"Oh. Okay. Well what time should I meet you?"

"I'll pick you up at five. Wear something to work out in."

"You got it, Detective," I said with a wink.

He pulled me into his arms and gave me another earth shattering kiss. "You can't keep calling me detective if you want me to continue to be a gentleman. I'll see you at five."

I left the station feeling dizzy after kissing Sean like that. He was definitely getting to me and I didn't know how much longer I could hold back the fact that I was falling in love with him.

"Okay, so what do you want to do? We can box, or there's the training course, or-"

"The training course!" I said, jumping up and down.

"Alright. Let me walk you through it and then we can test your skills." We walked over to the glass enclosure that overlooked the facility. "Okay, so we start with running the course to the climbing wall. Once you're over that, you have to crawl under the netting through the mush pit. When you get out of that, you have to climb the rope and touch the top. You don't get to move on until you've reached the top," he said with a smirk. I nodded for him to continue. "Once you get back down, you pick up that paintball gun and go through the shooting course.."

He continued to go through the details of the course, but I was stuck on the paintball gun. "Wait, what do you mean, shoot the paintball gun? I've never held a gun, let alone a paintball sized gun."

"It's a handgun. It doesn't hold as many rounds as a regular gun, so you have to be a good shot."

He continued to talk me through the course, but I was so excited to get started that I stopped listening.

"Okay, enough explaining. Let's go kick some donkey butt."

Sean just shook his head at me and smiled. "Okay, sparky. Let's go down and get started. I was already ready to go. I had worn black leggings, a sports bra, and a t-shirt. Sean had to go change and I was more than a little distracted when he came out in black gym shorts and a grey tank top. Oh dear Lord, save me. I wanted to lick his body. I shook the thoughts from my head and stretched as he walked over to me.

"You ready for this, Miss Daisy?"

"You know, if I didn't know better, I would think you were taunting me."

"Because Miss Daisy is a little old lady?"

I narrowed my eyes at him. "I'll show you. You're going to eat my dust."

Sean barked out a laugh and we headed for the starting line. Several other officers joined me and suddenly I was feeling like I was not going to come out of this on top. The bell rang and we all started off running. Determined to not end in last place, I pushed myself as hard as I could. When I got to the wall, all the other men were already climbing. I noticed that Sean was holding back some to keep pace with me. It was sweet that he wasn't trying to show off for me.

I started climbing and slipped several times as I tried to reach the top. The last time I slipped, I would have fallen, but Sean was there and grabbed my hand, pulling me the rest of the way up the wall.

"Come on, Miss Daisy. You're slowing me down."

"Ha! I'm going slower to make you look good for your friends!"

"Don't do me any favors, darlin'."

I pushed over the wall and slid down toward the mush pit. Sean was already on his belly crawling under the netting. I got down and started belly crawling, only realizing after I got in that the mush pit was actually a big pit of mud. My arms started cramping from slipping and sliding in the mud and I had to take a break. I laid down in the mush pit, my face getting covered in sludge, but I didn't care. I was already exhausted.

"Come on, Lil. You're falling behind."

I glanced up to see everyone had moved on. "I'm not even close to them. Just leave me here. I'll crawl out when I can feel my arms again."

"Not a chance darlin'. I never leave a man behind."

He pulled on my arm and I reluctantly started crawling behind him. We finally made it out from the netting and I stood huffing and puffing in front of the rope. I wiped off as much of the mud as I could with a towel that Sean produced from a table on the side.

"Come on. Everyone's waiting on you."

I noticed then that all the men were waiting at the next course for Sean and I to climb the ropes. I huffed and jumped up on the rope, wrapping my legs around the rope and pulling myself up. By the time I was halfway up, Sean was on his way back down. I looked down and noticed Officer Wheeling waiting at the bottom of my rope, probably in case I fell.

"You're falling behind again. Supposably, you can keep up with less than the ten men here training."

I turned and glared at him. Now he was just egging me on. "You know that's not the right way to say it, Sean."

"I don't know what you're talking about."

I huffed and growled as I pulled myself higher and higher. "You know..it's pronounced..supposedly. Argh!" I reached the top and took a moment to catch my breath. My arms were shaking, but now that I was at the top, I had to pull myself together so I didn't fall and break something.

"What the hell is she talking about?" I heard Officer Wheeling ask.

"I said supposably, but it's really supposedly. It's a common mistake that drives her crazy," Sean stated.

"Seriously?" Wheeling asked. "Supposedly. Supposably. I don't see the difference," he muttered to himself.

I jumped down from the rope and panted out a few breaths. "Not only did you say supposably, but you also misused less incorrectly." I said panting.

"How did I use less incorrectly?" I hadn't yet corrected him on this one, so I smiled as I caught my breath.

"Less is used when you're talking about things that aren't quantifiable. Since you could easily count the number of men in the room, you should have used fewer. Also, you said here training, but you should have said training here, but it's a common mistake."

"Have I entered some kind of alternate universe where correcting grammar is some kind of dirty foreplay?" Officer Wheeling asked.

"Can we get this moving? This isn't so much of a race anymore as an English lesson," one of the officer's bellowed.

The other officers picked up their paintball guns and started going through the course. I ran over with Sean and he quickly showed me how to use the weapon. In my excitement, I didn't really pay attention to what he said and just started pointing and shooting. When I heard the first yelp, I turned quickly, pulling the trigger as I did so. I ran through the course, half aiming at the targets and half hoping that I was pointing the gun where I should. I was having so much fun that I hardly noticed Sean waving to me. I waved back excitedly and continued through the course. The kickback from the gun was stronger than I expected and I found it was just easier to keep pulling the trigger instead of trying to aim again. When the bullets were all gone, I put my arms down and started walking back through the course.

Officer Wheeling was on the ground in the fetal position with his hand over his groin. I knelt down beside him and placed a hand on his shoulder.

"Are you okay?"

"You shot me in the nuts," he groaned. My hands flew to my mouth in horror. I looked up to see several other men favoring some part of their bodies. One man was holding his shoulder. Another was his butt cheek, but the one that got me was Bull. He was lying on the ground holding his head. I ran over to him and saw that he had a big paintball splatter on the side of his head.

"Holy rabbit ears! Did I do that to you?"

"You're lucky I have good reflexes. I moved just enough for it to be a glancing blow."

"I'm so sorry, Bull."

"You can make it up to me by bringing me brownies for the next week."

"I will. I'm so sorry."

"Lillian, I'm not sure what to do with you," Sean said. "You took out half the police department without even trying. I'm not sure if I should make you an honorary member or ban you from the police station forever."

Officer Wheeling hobbled over, still holding his groin. "Don't be insane, man. What's a little shot to the nuts in exchange for her food?" He groaned as he said that last part and I had to laugh that he thought my food was worth the pain I had caused him.

Sean walked me over to the locker rooms where the showers were and caged me in against the wall. My breath came out in little pants. This had become the new normal with me when I was around Sean. I constantly found myself wanting to touch him and kiss him, but I held back knowing that I couldn't give him false hope for more.

His lips brushed against mine in a soft kiss. He started spreading little kisses all along my jaw and down my neck. My eyes fluttered shut as I enjoyed the feel of his lips on my body. When I felt him move back, I opened my eyes to find him staring at me.

"I don't know how you did it, but you somehow got me and my brothers wrapped around your finger."

"My brothers and me." I bit my lip, vowing that I would try less to correct his grammar. He just chuckled and ran his thumb over my lip. "They just like that I bring them food," I laughed.

"No," he said seriously. "It's you. You're the most amazing woman I've ever met and I'm lucky that you stuck with me after I fucked up."

My heart softened into a puddle of mush. I didn't know how I ever thought Sean wasn't the man for me. He was tough as nails on the outside, but when you got to know him, you really saw how big his heart was.

"I'm the lucky one, Sean. You came into my life and showed me everything I was missing. I would probably be a cat lady by now if I hadn't met you."

He seemed to want to say something else, but then he took a step back. "Go take a shower. I'll be waiting for you out here."

CHAPTER 29

SEAN

I was so close to saying it. I wanted to so badly, but I just couldn't get the words out. I was staring into her beautiful eyes, wanting to tell her I loved her, but thoughts of Vira crept in. I had said I loved her and not only had it turned out to be untrue, but she hadn't said it back.

Lillian wasn't someone I could risk hurting like that. When I told her I loved her, I would know deep down in my soul that it was true. A part of me knew that she was the one I wanted for the rest of my life. I wanted to be the man that tasted her for the first time and gave her pleasure, but I needed to know for sure that my head was in the same place as my heart.

I took her home after we were showered and walked her to the door. I knew I couldn't stay tonight. I wanted her too badly and I couldn't risk pressuring her into something I knew she didn't want.

"I was just going to get a pizza or something. Does that sound good to you?"

"Actually, I need to get home. I have some stuff to take care of."

"Oh. For work?"

"Yeah."

I was a shitty liar. She could see all over my face that I wasn't being honest with her. A look of disappointment crossed her face and I couldn't take it. I leaned in, my arms on either side of her head against the door.

"I don't have work to do, but I want you so bad and I need to leave before I ask you to do something you don't want." I pushed my raging cock against her stomach to let her know how serious I was. "I just don't want you to think I don't want to be with you. I want to be with you too much, so I'm going to leave, but I'll be thinking about you tonight."

I gave her a deep kiss before I turned and walked away. I didn't miss the lust in her eyes and she took deep gulps of air. I got in my truck and headed home. I wasn't two minutes down the road when Lillian called.

"Miss me already, darlin'?"

"Sean, you need to come back now."

Her tone was fearful and I quickly pulled a U turn and slammed on the gas to get back to her. "I'll be there in a minute. Are you okay?"

"Yes. I'm fine, but someone sent another message for you."

I pulled into her driveway and barely slammed into park before I bolted for her front door. Fury raced through me when I saw her living room. All her furniture had been slashed. Every lamp was broken and there was a note for me written on the wall in what I hoped was red paint.

BACK OFF OR *next time it'll be her in pieces on the ground*

I GRABBED her hand and pulled her out of the house. We got in my truck and headed for the police station. I called the chief on my way and asked him to meet me at the station, then I asked dispatch to send a unit over to her house.

When we reached the police station, I hauled her out of the truck and inside. Several of the guys must have heard what happened because they started pouring into the station and demanding to know what was going on. I told them all they'd have to wait until I spoke with the chief. When he arrived, I asked Bull to take care of Lillian and I followed the chief to his office.

I glanced back at Lillian to see that she appeared to be okay. She hadn't said anything since I picked her up and she didn't appear flustered. I hoped that meant that she was holding it together well enough.

"Chief, we have to figure this shit out. Her house was trashed."

"I heard. I'm calling an emergency meeting tomorrow. We'll have Ramirez come down to the station and slip some false leads. Hopefully, we can catch Sawyer and Calloway in the act."

"I'm taking Lillian home with me. I can't risk leaving her on her own right now. This is the second threat they've made against her."

"I know. We'll get to the bottom of this. If we have to, we'll put someone on her."

I sighed in frustration, knowing Lillian was going to be pissed about the whole situation. "Alright. I'll see you in the morning."

I turned and walked out of his office only to stop dead in my tracks. Lillian was hanging out with all the guys and she was..laughing. I was so confused. Shouldn't she have been upset or angry? I walked closer and understood why everyone was laughing.

"I hadn't charged the car because I don't normally drive it quite so much. When Sean started driving, I had leaves flying off my eco tree on the dashboard. He turned to me and asked why I had a battery indicator on my dashboard, like it was the most absurd thing anyone had ever seen!"

"It is! No man drives a car that's powered by a battery," Bull said.

Wheeling turned to me with a grin. "So, Donnelly. You got outrun by a suspect because you were in a toy car?"

"I still caught the guy."

"Couldn't even get the windows to roll down," laughed Bull.

"I bet the Flintstones wouldn't have let the suspect get away."

The guys all laughed and Lillian did her best not to, but it was a losing battle.

"It wasn't my car!" I said in frustration. They all laughed harder because they were getting me worked up. I grabbed Lillian's hand and dragged her toward the door.

"Yabba dabba do!" I heard one of the guys yell.

"Wiiilmaaa!" Another shouted.

Lillian was laughing hysterically as I dragged her out of the station. When she didn't stop laughing, I hauled her up against me and kissed her until she was breathless. There was something about seeing her laugh with all my brothers that made me want her even more.

"Come on. Let's get home, Wilma."

I WALKED into the station the next morning after dropping Lillian off with Alex. I wasn't comfortable leaving her alone until this drug situation was taken care of. I was headed toward my desk when the TV in the corner flipped on and The Flintstones started to play. All the guys started to laugh and I found myself joining them.

"Meeting in twenty, boys. Donnelly, run over to the fire station. The chief has a file for us. Here, take my car." He tossed me the keys. "I put gas in it this morning."

The guys busted out laughing and I whipped the keys back at the chief, who caught them easily.

Ramirez came into the station under protection fifteen minutes later and we all went back to the conference room. The story Ramirez told was that he had contacted one of the men, Samuel Marks, in the organization that he trusted. There was a large shipment that was due in tomorrow. The plan was for Marks to change the shipment drop off and then Ramirez and Marks would cut and run with the product. Since everyone thought Ramirez was dead, no one would be looking for him at the location.

Sawyer and Calloway gave each other furtive glances throughout the whole meeting, which to me confirmed that they were going to try something. Most likely, they would try to arrive early and warn their associates that we would be moving in.

When the meeting was over, I finished out my work day with several more ribbings from the guys about driving an electric car. I headed over to Cole's house and picked up Lillian to take back home with me. We stopped off at The Pub and picked up dinner to go. I was just getting in the truck when Lillian peered out her window across the street.

"Sean, isn't that Officer Sawyer?"

I looked out the window to see Sawyer and Calloway in a heated argument in an alley. "Looks like our meeting earlier today really shook things up."

I watched as they continued for a few minutes. Sawyer grabbed Calloway around the collar and yelled in his face before shoving him further into the alley.

"I'm gonna go check it out. Stay here."

I got out of truck and ran across the street, sticking as close to the building as possible. They were almost to the end of the alley, so I picked up the pace until I was practically jogging.

Peeking around the corner, I saw them opening a door and slipping inside. I followed and grabbed the door before it could snick shut. Slipping inside, I slid along the wall into the shadows.

Ramirez was sitting in a chair with his hands tied behind his back. He looked like he'd already gotten quite the beating at the hands of Sawyer and Calloway.

"You'd better start talking and tell us what you know," Sawyer sneered.

I took out my phone, sent a quick text to Bull, and then hit record. I wasn't sure how much would be heard at this distance, but I needed this recorded if possible.

"I told you. It's exactly what I told the chief earlier."

"I don't buy it for a second. You know why?" Sawyer asked.

"We've all been left in the dark for months about the case. All the sudden, he brings you in and you're back from the dead and you have all this inside information."

"Nobody was allowed to talk about it, but I wanted this over. We needed to get the top guys in the organization to come out. This was the way to do it. Stealing a shipment from them would make them so mad they would come after me."

"No. I talk to them several times a week. There's no way Marks would turn on the bosses. He's loyal," Sawyer said emphatically.

"He's more loyal to me. I've known him since we were kids. There's nothing like the bond you form growing up on the streets together."

"If you do this, you put us all at risk and I can't afford to have that happen. That means you have to go before you blow the whole operation." Sawyer pulled his gun and pointed it at Ramirez's head. I was going to have to step out, but chances were that I would end up dead unless I could surprise them. I couldn't just shoot two fellow officers.

"It's already going down whether I'm dead or alive." I was surprised that Ramirez was holding out, but then I supposed if he told Sawyer the truth, he was as good as dead anyway.

I was about to step out when the door squeaked and then slammed shut. Standing inside the doorway was Lillian with a blush staining her cheeks.

"Oops. I think I'm in the wrong place." Sawyer swung his gun to Lillian. Her eyes widened and I could feel the fear rippling off of her. My only thought was getting over to her and stepping between Lillian and the gun that was now pointed at her.

"You're Sean's girl. Get your ass over here."

Lillian stood stock still. I stepped toward her, hoping she would play along with my new game plan. I needed to distract Sawyer and move his focus from Lillian.

"Lillian, what the hell are you doing? I told you to stay in the truck," I said as I stepped out with my gun aimed at Sawyer.

"I got worried when you didn't come back."

"So you followed me into a building in the back of an alley without anything to protect yourself with?"

"I grabbed your spare gun from under the seat."

She pulled out the gun from her purse. I rolled my eyes in frustration. Why she thought that she could help me was beyond me.

"Jesus, you gave your woman your backup piece?" Calloway asked.

"You wouldn't be worried if you'd seen her shoot," I grumbled. Sawyer was moving his gun back and forth between us, not sure where to point his weapon.

"I'm sorry. I swear, I didn't think I'd be walking into..this," she said, waving the gun around. I flinched back as she waved the weapon around the room, hoping she didn't accidentally shoot someone. I wanted to step in front of her, but I couldn't make any sudden movements with Sawyer still holding his gun on us.

"Sawyer, I think you need to put the gun down. She's got nothing to do with this."

"Really? So, you've been hiding out, listening to everything I've said and then your girlfriend walks in and you don't think she's involved in any way?"

"She doesn't know anything. How about she walks away and you and I deal with this?"

"Do you really think I'm that fucking stupid? If she leaves, she's going to call the chief." He shook his head in disgust. "There's only one way the two of you are leaving here, and that's in a body bag."

I saw his hand tighten on his gun and knew he was going to pull the trigger. I didn't think twice before putting a bullet in his shoulder. His gun fell to the ground as he gripped his shoulder. Calloway stood there with indecision on his face. He had never been the brains behind the operation. In fact, I would say at that moment that he wanted nothing more than to walk away and pretend he had never met Sawyer. Calloway had been a decent cop before Sawyer took him under his wing.

"Calloway, put the gun down."

He looked nervous and unsure about what he wanted to do. Nervous people with guns were dangerous and if he gave even the slightest indication he would pull the trigger, I would put him down.

The sound of the door opening made Lillian jump and swing her gun around toward Bull, who was now standing in the doorway taking in the scene. I kept my gaze trained on Calloway who was now sweating and looked nervous as hell.

"Sean, you know I like Lillian, but dude, you don't bring your girlfriend along to a shootout."

"I didn't bring her. She followed me," I bit out.

"Why would you give her a gun? You saw what she was like at the training center."

"I didn't give it to her. Why does everyone assume I would be stupid enough to give her a gun?"

"Hey!" Lillian said indignantly.

"Can we please just move on with this? It's bad enough that Lillian's here, but Sawyer's over there bleeding out and Calloway looks like he has a nervous trigger finger."

"How about you disarm the lady first. I think we'd all be a lot safer if she wasn't holding that," Bull suggested.

I stepped closer to Lillian and pulled the gun from her hand. "I think that's enough gun play for you for one day."

"Sorry. I really was just trying to help."

"I know, but I think we've established that you and guns don't work well together."

"Calloway, why don't you put down the gun? This isn't gonna turn out how you want," Bull said.

"Are you fucking kidding me? It's better if I just take you both out. If I leave Ramirez here, it's a drug deal gone bad. You two are pinned for the missing drugs and Sawyer and I are in the clear."

"One problem with that. Sawyer is now passed out and bleeding out next to you. How are you going to explain that?"

"Gunshots were reported and we came to intervene. Sawyer was shot in the process."

"Yeah, there are two of us and only one of you. There's no way you can take both of us out before one of us takes you out," I reasoned with him.

"I'll take my chances." Yet he didn't seem to really want to take a shot. His finger hadn't moved to the trigger yet. I took my chances that I would be able to reason with him.

"The problem is that there was never a deal between Ramirez and Marks. He never called him to set something up. That was all a trap for you and Sawyer. We knew you'd been stealing the drugs. We needed to push you into making a move and you did," I said with a satisfied smile.

"Fuck! I can still take you down with me," Calloway sneered.

"Or you could turn state's evidence. Turn yourself in and maybe you can get a deal. Help bring down a major drug dealer and his whole operation. They might even paint you as an undercover cop that dedicated himself to the job."

It was a load of bullshit, but I'd say anything right now to get this guy to put his weapon down.

"You know the first one to turn himself in is going to get the better deal, and I have Sawyer on record admitting to all his crimes." I dangled that last little bit over his head in the hopes that he would realize he'd been bested. We waited for a good two minutes for him to finally make up his mind and put his gun down.

Bull walked over and handcuffed Calloway and took his weapon and the one that was now laying on the ground next to Sawyer. I called everything in and requested an ambulance. When I turned to Lillian, she looked in awe of everything.

"You're really good at your job," she said.

"I'm even better when my hot girlfriend isn't with me, distracting me and making me worry that she's going to get shot."

"Or shoot someone."

"That's not very likely."

"Care to make a bet?"

"Lil, with my luck, you'd hit the target every time."

CHAPTER 30

LILLIAN

"I just can't believe how exciting that was. I mean, it was kind of scary and I'm sure now that I couldn't do it as a job, but it was such a high," I said with a sigh.

Sean was being quiet on the other side of the truck on the way back to his house. My house was still a disaster and I hadn't been cleared to go back yet. I glanced his way trying to read him, but he just stared out the windshield.

"Is something wrong?" I asked.

Silence. He just kept staring ahead. He didn't glance my way or show any signs that I was even talking. I looked out my window, trying to understand what had made him so upset. He seemed fine when we were at the crime scene. The chief had us go back to the station and he had to fill him in on what happened. He held my hand as we left, but then once we were on the road, he completely shut me out.

We pulled into his driveway and he slammed the gear shifter into park. I thought we would get out, but he continued to sit there and not say anything. I finally opened my door and headed for his house. I knew where he kept his spare key and I'd use it if he didn't follow me.

When I reached his front door, he still hadn't followed, so I let myself in and sat down in the living room. I waited ten minutes and then decided that I might as well get ready for bed. I went through my night time ritual and then got into a t-shirt and sweats that I was borrowing from him. I would have to go to my house tomorrow and get more clothes since we didn't do that today.

The front door opened and closed, so I walked downstairs in the hopes that he was ready to talk. He was in the kitchen pouring himself a glass of what looked like whiskey.

"May I have one?"

He got down another glass and poured me a small amount. I picked it up and sipped from it, hoping that he would start talking. He didn't.

"Are you going to talk to me or should I just go to bed?"

He didn't answer, so I set down the glass and headed for the stairs.

"You didn't fucking listen to me tonight."

I sighed in relief. We were finally getting somewhere. I turned to face him and prepared myself for him yelling at me.

"I told you to stay in the truck and you followed me anyway."

"I was worried about you."

"It doesn't matter. You had no business following me. You knew that Sawyer and Calloway were dangerous and you still followed."

I didn't have anything more to say to that, so I kept my mouth shut.

"Then you took my backup weapon with you and pulled it out when Sawyer was holding a gun on you." He laughed and shook his head. "It could have turned out so much different. Do you realize that he could have shot you when you pulled out the gun? That was beyond reckless. Then, you were waving it around like it was a toy. You could have shot someone. You would have lost your job, not to mention how it would have screwed with your head."

I chewed my lip as I thought over what he was saying. I had never done anything so stupid in my life, and I only had one excuse.

"I know it was stupid and I shouldn't have done it, but I did it because I was worried about you. I know I took it too far when I brought out the gun. It definitely wasn't one of my finer moments, but I was scared for you."

"I know." He stood in silence for a few minutes staring at the floor. "There are going to be many more times when I'm in dangerous situations and I can't have you following me, pulling a gun, and going all Lone Ranger on my suspects. This is my job and I take those risks willingly, but you..you're my girlfriend. I love you more than anything in my life and I can't ever see you with a gun pointed at your head again."

I was still reeling from what he just said, when he walked toward me and pulled me against him. His hand cupped the back of my neck and he brushed his lips to mine.

"I love you and I want you to be my wife. The whole time we were in that building, I kept thinking this woman is nuts, but I want her crazy and all for the rest of my life. There's no one like you or that I would rather have by my side, but for you to be by my side, that means that you support me, from afar, when I'm working."

I smiled and wrapped my arms tightly around him. "I love you, too. I'm sorry that I interfered, and I promise that from now on, I will sit at home and worry about you from afar."

"I would appreciate that."

He kissed me again, but this time the kiss became more intense to the point I could hardly breathe. My panties became wet as he ran his hands up and down the sides of my body. He had always respected my wishes and never tried to touch me any place that would make me uncomfortable, but now I found myself wanting to take this further. Maybe it was seeing how he could be gone at any minute with his job. Maybe it was that he told me he loved me and wanted me to be his wife. Maybe it was just that I was tired of fighting my attraction for him. Any way I looked at it, I just didn't care anymore. I wanted him and I was going to live like it was our last time together.

I pulled back from him and stared into his eyes. "Sean, I want you to make love to me."

He flinched back and shook his head. "No. No, I didn't say that so you would sleep with me. I just wanted you to know how I feel."

"I know, but I don't care anymore. I know you love me and I know you would never hurt me. I trust you with my heart and this is what I want. I don't need to wait to know that you're the one for me."

He reached down into his pocket and pulled out a simple gold band and held it out to me. "I've known for a while now that I loved you, but I didn't know how to tell you. I got this ring from my mom a few weeks back. It was my grandmother's wedding ring. I wanted it for you because it was so simple, exactly the way I feel about you."

I quirked an eyebrow at that, not sure I wanted to be referred to as simple.

"Just wait. Let me finish. I love you more than I ever thought I could love another person. I was scared to death when you entered that building tonight because the thought of you being taken away from me was too much. My love for you is deep and all consuming, but simple in that there is no wavering. I simply love you. There is no second guessing or wondering if I'm making the right choice. I know that you were meant to be mine, and I know you don't need any fancy display of love. You just need to know that I'm yours. That's what this ring is. No frills. Just a symbol of my unwavering love."

I smiled at his overwhelming explanation. He was right. It was simple, and I didn't need anything big and splashy from him. I needed to know that no matter what, I would have him.

"I love you, Sean."

He kissed me deeply and then picked up my left hand.

"What are you doing?"

"We will be married in the eyes of God before I make love to you. I know how much that means to you and I won't make you break something so sacred to you."

He held my hand and started to slide the ring onto my left ring finger.

"I, Sean, take you, Lillian, to be my wedded wife, and I promise before God to be your loving and faithful husband in plenty and want, in joy and in sorrow, in sickness and in health, as long as we both shall live."

A few tears slid down my face as he recited wedding vows so accurately. He must have looked them up and read them several times. This was crazy, but I didn't care. He was making sure that my faith remained intact because he respected my beliefs.

"I, Lillian, take you, Sean, to be my wedded husband, and I promise before God to be your loving and faithful wife in plenty and want, in joy and in sorrow, in sickness and in health, as long as we both shall live."

When he kissed me, it truly felt as if I was kissing my husband. It didn't matter if we were legally married. We had just pledged our lives together in front of God and that was all that mattered to me.

He lifted me up and carried me bridal style up the stairs to his bedroom that would now be ours. When he set me down, he ran his hands slowly down my arms, sending tingles down my spine. His hands went to the hem of my shirt and he slowly pulled it up. I lifted my arms, allowing him to pull it over my head. I thought he would continue to undress me, but instead, he walked me back to the bed and then pushed me gently to the mattress.

He caressed my cheek with the back of his hand and placed gentle kisses all over my face. I felt cherished. I felt loved. His kisses glided down my neck and across my collarbone. When he reached the swell of my breasts, he trailed hot kisses across to each nipple, nipping lightly through the fabric of my bra. I felt my nipples tighten in response and my pulse quickened with every touch.

He ran his fingertips lightly over my breasts. My breaths started coming in short pants as he caressed my body. I felt his fingertips run along the waistband of my pants, never dipping more than a fingertip inside. I was shaking with need, wanting him to put his hands on me and get on with it. As if he sensed my frustration, he looked into my eyes.

"Lil, I'm going to take my time with you and make this everything you ever wanted. This is your first time, but this is my first time with my wife and I'm going to treasure every second of it. By the time I'm done with you, there won't be a single piece of your body that I don't have ingrained in my memory."

I ran my hand over his cheek, feeling the stubble from the day against my palm. "I'm just nervous. I've never..I don't know what to expect."

"Have you ever touched yourself?"

I shook my head no.

"What do you feel when I kiss you?"

"I feel..tingles. I want more and I feel like if you stop, I'll explode. I get..wet." I blushed. This was so unlike me to talk about this, but he was my husband now and if I couldn't talk about it with him, then what was the point of this?

He ran his hand down my pant leg and up my inner thigh. When he reached the apex of my thighs, he ran his hand lightly over my mound. I moaned at the feeling and felt my panties dampen further. I was sure that he could feel it through my pants.

"You get wet for me. You get hot. I can feel how much your body wants me." He rubbed the heel of his palm over me, my pulse skyrocketing. "I'm going to make you come and when you do, you'll know it. You'll feel like you can't hold back the feeling that wants to break free, but at the same time, your body will be curling into itself to stop the intense pleasure."

He rubbed me harder through my pants as he described what it would be like. I could feel my body pushing higher and higher. "When I touch you with my fingers and spread your cream over your clit, you'll feel like you can't catch your breath. Those tingles that you feel when I kiss you will feel like thousands all over your body."

He removed his hand from my mound and ran his hand up my bare belly to my breasts. "Do you feel your nipples tightening? That's another way I'll give you pleasure. I'll pinch them and twirl them in my fingers or I could suck them into my mouth and run my tongue all over your beautiful breasts. You'll feel yourself soaking your panties from the sensations."

He moved his hand back down to my pants, hovering over the waistband. He bent over and placed a few kisses on my belly as he slowly pulled the sweats down, exposing my panties. With both hands, he pulled my pants down my legs, leaving me naked. I was shivering, but not from cold. I was nervous and excited. I wanted him to touch me, but was afraid I would disappoint him.

He kissed down one leg in slow, wet kisses and then back up my leg. He placed hot kisses on me through my panties and then kissed back down my other leg. My body convulsed from the desire that was building. When he reached my foot, he ran his hands back up my legs and latched on to my panties. As he pulled them down, he kissed my most sensitive area.

"Ahh!" The sensations were beyond anything I could have ever imagined. I writhed under his touch, but pushed my body closer to his hot mouth. He pulled back and finished removing my panties.

"Are you beginning to get the idea?" he asked.

I nodded excitedly, breathing heavily and needing to feel his tongue on me again. When his mouth was on me again, I let out an aching scream. I had never experienced anything so moving in all my life.

He continued to lap at me and it only took a few minutes for me to feel what he had described. My legs shook violently. My breathing was so rapid, I thought I might hyperventilate and pass out. When my orgasm hit, my back bowed off the bed and my legs squeezed shut, trying to dull the sensation that was so powerful, I thought I might not recover. He continued to lick me until my orgasm dulled to a low throb. Spasms wracked my body for minutes after the experience.

Sean crawled up next to me and wrapped his arms around me, pulling me in close to him. He ran a hand up and down my arm, trying to calm my body again.

"Wow. That was..I don't think I could accurately describe what that was." He chuckled behind me. "Why do I feel so tired? I didn't do anything."

"It's the rush. Close your eyes."

"I don't want to stop," I said sleepily.

"We've got all night. Believe me, I'm not through with you yet."

I WAS warm and cool at the same time. Sean's warmth was wrapped around my skin, but the kisses he was leaving on my body left me shivering with need. I moaned as his tongue left a wet trail up my neck where he was now kissing behind my ear. More shivers raced through me. Then I felt his hand skim down to my legs and his rough fingers massaged my button. It was exactly as he described it. When he pushed a finger inside me, I gasped at the new feeling. I could feel that he was getting close to my hymen because of how tight it felt.

I wasn't sure that I was ready for this now. I wanted it so badly, but I was nervous how badly it would hurt. I didn't want to stop him, though because I knew how much he wanted this.

"Relax, Lil. I'm gonna get you nice and wet before we go further. Just let your body relax. The more you tense up, the more it'll hurt. Just let your body feel the sensations." He kissed my neck again, sucking lightly and eliciting another moan from me. The more he kissed and sucked at my neck, the more my body melted from his touch.

I felt his finger slowly pump in and out of me as his thumb rubbed circles over my clit.

"That's right, sweetheart. Feel it. Just allow your body to take over."

I was breathing hard now from all the sensations and my eyes fluttered shut.

"Keep your eyes open, Lil. I want to watch you when you come."

A few more circles and I was coming once again from his touch. His eyes never left mine as I came hard. His mouth enveloped mine as I moaned my release. When my breathing calmed, he stood and pulled his shirt over his head, then undid his pants and kicked them off. My eyes were glued to his erection that was threatening to break free from his boxers. When he lowered them, my eyes bulged at what he had hidden from me.

"I've never seen..I mean, it's so much different than in a text book."

He gripped his erection and started stroking himself. I found my eyes glued to his actions. It was so erotic and so much more than I had ever thought I would see. I always pictured sex being with a well mannered man and the sex was never this exciting, but then again, I didn't really know all that was involved with sex. He stepped toward me and placed a knee on the bed.

"Lillian, you're going to have to stop staring at me like that or I'm gonna come in my hand, and that's not how I pictured coming with you for the first time."

I giggled a little because, frankly, this was the strangest conversation I'd ever had. I wasn't used to talking about sex so bluntly, but I had a feeling that once Sean and I got into a rhythm, I would be hearing something more scandalous.

He crawled over me, pushing me down as he did. When he was lying over me, he rested on his forearms and kissed me deeply. "You're not the only one that's nervous, Lil. I want this to be perfect for you. I've waited so long to feel you that I can't believe this is real. I've never wanted anyone the way I want you, need you." He bent down and kissed me again. "I love you so much."

"I love you, too, Sean. I'm ready."

He palmed his erection and I felt him guide it toward my opening. As he pushed in slowly, I could feel him stretching my body and I started to tense up. He stopped and looked down at me.

"Don't. Just relax." His hands roamed my body as he sat still inside me. He kissed my neck as his hands cupped and played with my breasts. Slowly, my body melted into his and I barely noticed when he started pushing inside me again. I was distracted by the other sensations so much that the pain of losing my virginity barely registered.

When he was fully seated inside me, he gave me a moment to adjust before he slowly moved in and out of me. I wrapped my legs around his back as he moved deeper and faster inside me. I pulled him closer, needing to feel as close to him as possible. His tongue tangled with mine as he pushed me closer and closer to orgasm. His mouth caught my screams and moments later I felt him still inside me as he grunted his release.

He placed gentle kisses all over my face. I had never felt so special or cherished in all my life. What he gave me exceeded my expectations and left me feeling more than ever that he was the only man that could have captured my heart and soul.

He got up and went to the bathroom, coming back moments later with a warm cloth. He washed me up and then put the washcloth back in the bathroom. When he cocooned me in his arms once again, I drifted to sleep in moments. The steady beat of his heart lulled me into a dreamless sleep.

CHAPTER 31

SEAN

I never thought I would be so lucky to have a woman like Lillian in my bed. From the moment I met her, I knew she was different, but I never would have guessed the impact she would have on my life. She challenged me to be a better man, not because she wanted to change me, but because I wanted to be the man she deserved.

When I had asked my mom for my grandma's ring, she smiled and got if for me. She knew that only the most special woman could entice me into matrimony. I told her all about Lillian and showed her pictures of us. I promised her before I left that I would bring Lillian by soon for her and Dad to meet.

Lillian stirred next to me and I tightened my arms around her, needing to stay in this cocoon for a little while longer. The sun was just rising and the first rays of light were shining through our bedroom window. Our bedroom. We'd have to work out all the details now, but one thing was clear. She was my wife now and we would be living together from now on. There was no way I was letting this woman get away now that I had tasted her.

"Good morning, husband," she said with a smile as she turned in my arms to face me.

"Good morning, wife."

I kissed her, relishing in the feel of her body against mine and had to restrain myself from rolling her over and pushing inside her.

"Are you sore this morning?"

"A little," she blushed.

"How about I make you a hot bath to soak in? I have a few things to take care of and then we can pick up where we left off last night."

"Don't you have to work today?"

"You know, I'm feeling a little under the weather this morning. I think I'm going to have to take a sick day."

We smiled at each other and I kissed her one last time before getting out of bed and filling the tub with water. While she was soaking, I called the chief to let him know I wouldn't be in today. He didn't believe for a minute that I was sick, but I didn't care. There was nothing that could drag me away from Lillian today.

I made her a big breakfast because I had plans for her today and she would need her energy. When it was all ready, I headed upstairs and called her from the tub. She put on one of my t-shirts and we snuggled under the covers as we ate.

"So, what are we going to do today?" she asked.

I looked at her and let my eyes drift down to her plump lips and then further to her breasts that were just barely covered by the blanket. A beautiful blush spread from her chest, up her neck, and then stained her cheeks red.

"I think you already know the answer to that."

"Can I ask you something?" She was fiddling with her fruit, so I figured this was something she wasn't comfortable asking.

"Of course."

"When we first met and you were trying to get me to sleep with you, you talked differently."

"Okay. How did I talk differently?"

"You were more crass..when you spoke about sex."

I nodded, unsure of where she was taking this.

"Why don't you speak like that to me now?"

I lifted her chin so she could meet my gaze. "Because back then you were a woman I wanted to fuck. Now you're my wife and what we did last night wasn't cheap or meaningless. I wanted you to have the best experience possible for our first time."

"Does that mean you'll never speak that way to me again?"

"Do you want me to?"

"I'm not sure."

"There are many ways to enjoy sex. What we did last night was..tame compared to some things we could do, but we'll just take it one day at a time. If you want me to talk dirty to you, just say the word. If you want me to tie you up and take you hard, I will." Her eyes widened and I could see her pulse jump under her skin. She liked the idea. "You have to tell me what you want and when you're ready for it. Until then, I'll continue to make love to you just as I did last night, and it'll be great every time because it's with you. All that other stuff doesn't matter."

"I think we should wait a little bit to try something different. What we did last night left me sore."

"Then we'll take it slow." I ran a hand down her soft cheek and leaned in for a kiss. "I just want to give you pleasure. All the rest will come with time."

Our kisses turned frantic until I shoved the breakfast trays off the bed in my haste to get closer to her. The dishes crashed to the floor, but I didn't care. I needed her more than I needed air. I took her gently again because I knew she was still sore, but it didn't matter to me. It felt like heaven to have her any way I could get her.

By the time afternoon rolled around, we finally decided to go downstairs and get some food. I cleaned up the mess I made with the breakfast trays and made us some sandwiches.

"So, wife, where do you want to live?"

"I just assumed I would move in here," she said around a bite of food.

"If that's what you want, or we can move to your place."

"Would you prefer to live there?"

"Honestly, this is where we said our vows and I'd like to stay here, but I want you to be happy. I want to leave it up to you."

"I think this is a good house. I don't have any sentimental attachment to my house, so I think this would be a good move. I should probably get some of my things or I'm going to be walking around in your t-shirts all day with no clothes to wear."

"I wouldn't be opposed to that, but I would have a problem with you answering the door with no pants on, so let's go grab as much stuff as we can this morning."

"Okay. Let me just throw my clothes on."

I followed her upstairs and it took a good hour for us to get dressed because we had a little trouble with getting our clothes to stay on. It seemed that we both preferred the other naked.

After running to her house and packing all the clothes and other essentials that we could, we headed back to my house, both smiling like fools. We were hauling her bags inside when Sebastian and Maggie pulled into my driveway.

"Uh, what's going on? Are you moving in, Lillian?" Sebastian asked with a laugh.

"Yep. She is. Lillian and I got married last night."

I dropped the bags I was carrying and wrapped an arm around Lillian's shoulder, pulling her close. Sebastian and Maggie stood there, mouths gaping for several seconds before they burst out laughing.

"No, seriously. Is this about the drugs?" Sebastian asked.

I looked at Lillian with a grin and she held out her ring finger, showing Sebastian and Maggie how serious we were. Maggie squealed and then ran over to Lillian, wrapping her in a hug.

"Oh my gosh! This is so exciting! Why didn't you call us?"

"Well, it just sort of happened. It's not official."

"What do you mean it's not official? How do you sort of get married?" Sebastian questioned.

"We said our vows last night, but obviously there was no minister or friends and family," Lillian said smiling at me.

"So, you're not really married?" Maggie asked with a raised brow.

"In every way that counts to us," I said, wishing they would just accept it and stop questioning us. Sebastian walked over to me and pulled me in for a guy hug. His hand squeezed my shoulder as he pulled away, making me realize how badly I had wanted the support of my friends.

"Well, this is ridiculous. We're all standing around here and we should be getting everyone together to celebrate. You guys go unpack and meet us all at The Pub in two hours." Sebastian started to walk away, but I stopped him.

"Hey, what did you stop by for?"

"Oh, I just wanted to let you know that Vira made it safely to California and everything's taken care of."

"Good. We'll see you soon."

Lillian and I walked inside and I hoped that we could side step that conversation, but I could tell Lillian was curious.

"When Vira stopped by, she was trying to get away from someone. He had sensitive information that we couldn't let get out. Vira decided that she was going to leave anyway, so when Sebastian got everything taken care of, one of his guys went out to California with her and made sure she was safe."

"Okay. Thank you for telling me."

"You're my wife now. I won't ever keep secrets from you."

I kissed her and then we went upstairs to unpack her stuff in our bedroom.

———

WE WALKED into The Pub and all our friend were already there, no doubt gossiping about what was going on with Lillian and I. When they saw us, everyone stopped and stared at us for a moment.

"Yes, we're really married. You can all stop gawking now."

Questions started coming at us rapid fire, so to ward off all the questions, I gave a loud whistle that made everyone stop.

"Lillian and I said our vows last night. It's not legal, but it's official to us. I'm sure we'll plan a wedding soon, but for now, we're married and that's all there is to it."

The girls all gathered around Lillian and I walked off toward the bar where the guys still stood. I ordered champagne for everyone and I toasted my beautiful bride.

"Lillian, from the moment I met you, I knew that you were different and would change my life if I was lucky enough to keep you in it. I admit that our first few encounters were not what I would call love at first sight-"

"If I recall, you wanted to jump from my car," she said.

"I think that's about right, but despite everything, you were the one I fell in love with. I'm a better man because I have the love of a good woman. I hope that in twenty years, you still challenge me the way you do now. If I'm lucky enough to be stuck in a slow speed car chase with you again, I'll thank God every day that he brought you to me."

The ladies awed and the guys grumbled about me making them look bad, but I only had eyes for Lillian. I stalked over to her and pulled her in my arms, kissing her silly. There was nothing that I wouldn't do to see that look in her eyes. I would pour my heart out in front of all my friends every day to have her look at me like I was her king.

"Now that I'm married to The Fuzz, I'll have to know my onions, otherwise I'll look like a complete numpty around his mates," Lillian laughed.

She had finished her second glass of champagne about thirty minutes ago and was working on her third. Not only was she speaking in a British accent, but so were all the other ladies. All of us guys just sat back and watched. A few had their phones out and were recording for blackmail later on.

"So what inspired this very sudden arrangement?" Ryan asked.

"She walked into the middle of one of my cases and almost got herself shot. It scared the piss out of me. All I could think was that she was going to die and I hadn't told her I loved her."

"Still, you tell her you love her. You don't marry her," Ryan said.

"I disagree. When you know, you know. Life's too short to waste time thinking about whether you should do something," Cole answered. We all knew that he was referring to when he almost lost Alex. He would have been destroyed if she had died.

"Am I the only sane one out of all of you?" Ryan asked in disbelief. "Jack, you practically had Harper moved in with you a month after you got together. Cole, you were trying to bully a woman with amnesia into moving in with you. Logan, Cece tortured you for months and then tried to destroy our business. Now, you know I like her, but you flew off to Vegas a month after you got back together. Drew, well, I guess you're fine. Sebastian too."

"Hey, what about me? Anna and I had a completely normal relationship," Luke interjected.

"Yeah, but you got her pregnant and ran off to Vegas," Ryan quipped.

"I've actually been thinking of asking Maggie to marry me," Sebastian said thoughtfully. "I just don't know how to do it. I mean, when she came back to me, she went all badass on me and wanted to blow people up. Maybe I need to take her on an adventure. It's where the best foreplay happens."

Ryan took another drink of his beer. "Like I said, you're all pussy whipped."

That didn't jive with what I knew about all these guys. We all loved our women fiercely and would do anything for them because of what they meant to us.

"Sorry man, I'm not pussy whipped. In fact, we didn't even have sex until after we got married."

"What?" Ryan turned to me in shock. "You mean to tell me that you married her after a few months and you'd never slept with her?"

"Nope. She didn't believe in sex before marriage and I respected that."

The guys all stood in stunned silence. Lillian's laughter broke the silence, causing me to look over at her. I'd never seen her so relaxed and happy. I walked over to her and pulled her into my arms.

"How's it going, baby?"

"Jolly good. I'm just having a chin wag with my mates. I'll be totally legless with a few more drinks. Maybe we can go to the loo and have a little slap and tickle," she grinned.

"I'm pretty sure you're already legless."

"Then let's go home and I can play with your twig and berries. Maybe you can get me up the duff," she said with a wink.

"If that means what I think it does, I don't think you're ready for that yet."

She slapped me and laughed. "You've lost the plot. It's not at all how it sounds."

I wrapped my arms around her, pulling her back to my front and whispered in her ear. "Then how about you tell all these nutters to piss off and we'll go home and have a little 'how's your father'?"

"Detective, have you been looking at my dirty British slang book?"

"Yes, and I may be off my pull. Let's go home and have a little Rumpy-Pumpy."

She looked into my eyes and smiled and then, no shit, we both turned and yelled, "We're off to Bedfordshire!"

CHAPTER 32

LILLIAN

I walked into the bedroom in a white negligee that had breast cut outs and the crotch was open. I would never have thought I would wear anything like this, but Sean brought out a sexual appetite in me that I didn't think I had. I found that when he talked dirty to me, it made me so wet that there really was no foreplay necessary.

"Damn. Woman, I just went from soft to rock hard in five seconds. Are you trying to give me a heart attack?" he asked.

"I've been thinking all day about you. Do you know what I thought about the most?"

"God, I hope it's something dirty," he said as he stroked his cock. I spread my legs and put a hand on my center, spreading my juices around my clit. His eyes narrowed in on my movements and he started stroking faster.

"I was thinking about riding your face."

He started to walk toward me, still stroking his rock hard cock. My breath stuttered in my chest at the sight. My nipples pebbled the closer he got and I could see his eyes watching the rise and fall of my chest.

"What else were you thinking?"

"I was.." My breathing increased and I swallowed hard. "I was thinking of trying those balls you got for me."

"Yeah?" He walked behind me and wrapped his arms around me. His cock dug into my ass, making me push back against him. One hand squeezed my tummy while the other came up to massage my breasts. His fingers twirled my nipples, pulling them tight before massaging them again. "Were you thinking of my cock inside you?"

His other hand trailed down to my wet folds and spread my juices all over. My head dropped back to his shoulder as shudders raced through my body.

"I want to play with you, but I just can't tonight. I need you so bad." His lips caressed my neck as his fingers slid inside me. He pulled me over to the bed and sat down on the edge, pulling me to sit on him. My breasts brushed against his bare chest before he lifted me and seated himself inside me in one thrust. He was so deep inside me, it was almost painful. I started moving up and down, impaling him deeper every time. His arms pulled me tight against him, caging me to his sweat slickened body. His tongue ran up my neck and then his mouth latched onto the skin beneath my jaw.

"Oh, Sean. Yes," I moaned. I rode him harder and harder, needing everything he gave me. Tears pricked my eyes from the intimacy of us being wrapped in each others arms.

CHAPTER 33

SEAN

Every time she moaned my name I grew harder inside her. It was always like this with Lillian. I couldn't keep my hands off her and when I was inside her, it felt like I would lose myself in her. Like I would starve if I didn't have her, I grabbed her ass and pumped myself harder and faster into her, chasing my orgasm.

When I felt my balls start to pull up, I reached between us and thumbed her clit.

"Give it to me, Lillian." She pulsed around me. "Grab my cock with your pussy." She moaned and I almost lost it inside her. I closed my eyes and willed my orgasm to hold off until she came with me. "Squeeze me tight. I want to feel your cream on my cock." Her pussy clenched so tight around me, I worried I would lose my dick inside her.

"Fuck. Goddamnit."

She continued to ride me, pushing through the waves of her orgasm. I thrust up into her one last time and spilled my seed inside her. We sat holding each other for what felt like an hour after as we both tried to catch our breath. She rested her head on my shoulder and I felt her soft pants against my skin. I ran my hands up and down her back, just needing to feel her and know she was real. After all this time, I still couldn't believe that she was mine.

When I finally pulled back, I looked into her beautiful eyes and kissed her on the tip of her nose.

"Soon I won't be able to sit on you like this anymore," she said with a sigh.

"Hey, you're the one that wanted it up the duff," I laughed.

ALSO BY GIULIA LAGOMARSINO

Thank you for reading Sean and Lillian's story, but it doesn't end here! Read more about your favorite characters in the next book Ryan!

Join my newsletter to get the most up-to-date information, along with new content in the Reed Security series.

https://giulialagomarsinoauthor.com/connect/

Join my Facebook reader group to find out more about my obsession with Dwayne Johnson!

https://www.facebook.com/groups/GiuliaLagomarsinobooks

Reading Order:

https://giulialagomarsinoauthor.com/reading-order/

To find the individual series, follow the links below:

For The Love Of A Good Woman series

Reed Security series

The Cortell Brothers

A Good Run Of Bad Luck

The Shifting Sands Beneath Us- Standalone

Owens Protective Services

Printed in Great Britain
by Amazon

85214525R00154